Scripted

Love

By the Author

Call to Me
Scripted Love

Scripted

Love

by Helena Harte

2021

This trade paperback original is published by Butterworth Books, Nottingham, England

Cataloging information
ISBN: 978-1-8380668-9-5
CREDITS
Editors: Jan Stone & Nicci Robinson
Cover Design: Nicci Robinson, Global Wordsmiths
Production Design: Global Wordsmiths

Butterworth Books is a different breed of publishing house. It's a home for Indies, for independent authors who take great pride in their work and produce top quality books for readers who deserve the best. Professional editing, professional cover design, professional proof reading, professional book production—you get the idea. As Individual as the Indie authors we're proud to work with, we're Butterworths and we're *different*.

Authors currently publishing with us:

E.V. Bancroft
Valden Bush
Michael Carter
Michelle Grubb
Helena Harte
Lee Haven
Karen Klyne
AJ Mason
Ally McGuire
James Merrick
Robyn Nyx
Simon Smalley

For more information visit www.butterworthbooks.co.uk

to, Matt

Writing your own script? Stay true to your lovely self :)

Helena Flante ♡

Acknowledgements

Once again, thank you to everyone at Global Wordsmiths involved in the production of this book. Thanks to Margaret Burris for her wonderful proof reading. And thank you to all you wonderful readers who read Call to Me and said lovely things about it. Your reviews mean the world to me.

Dedication

For everyone who believes in
happy ever after.
It does exist.

Chapter One

TERI MOVED CLOSER and tenderly ran her hand through Marianne's hair. "I promise to find you in the next life, and the life after that."

Marianne smiled. "I'll hold you to that. But for now, let's concentrate on living this one to the full…together."

Teri smiled gently and pressed her lips to Marianne's.

"CUT! That's a wrap."

Mac's yell parted the two actresses instantly. They gave each other a curt nod and headed in different directions.

Layla sighed and flipped over the last pages of the script. If she were the director, she would've had Teri and Marianne redo the scene from the top. Both of them lacked their usual passion. This was the culmination of the whole movie: where the two main characters declared their undying love for each other and the audience got their happy ever after. The words were on the page—she'd written them perfectly—but neither actress had caught the emotion.

She looked around as the crew began to drift away. This hadn't been quite what she'd expected. Surely the final day went with more of a bang. That's how she'd always imagined it. Talk about a letdown.

"You look like you've just been to your own funeral. What's the problem?"

Layla looked over toward Syd, who had a box of Dani's Deadly Divine Donuts in one hand and a tray of two iced coffees in the other. The perfect friend. "That." She waved in the direction of the final scene and the now almost desolate set. "That's my problem. So neither of them believes in forever love, I get that. I'm a card-carrying member of that club. But isn't that why they get paid millions of dollars? To act like they believe it in their bones?"

Syd handed Layla the cup with extra fresh cream topping. "I thought they were doing okay."

"Okay isn't good enough. *Okay* won't fool the audience. Watch the dailies. You'll see. Look into their eyes. There's nothing there. It was garbage."

"You're too damned picky, Adams." Mac, the director, patted Layla's shoulder. "And you give the audience way more credit than they deserve. The girls did just fine."

Layla clenched her jaw against Mac's use of *girls*. Both actresses were in their forties. They were hardly *girls*. "And you're happy with fine?" She wanted to reel the words back, but it was too late.

Mac raised her eyebrows. Layla had learned early on in this production that meant trouble, but it didn't keep her from poking the bear and taking the consequences. This was her novel and her screenplay, and she didn't want it going out into the world half-assed.

"Does it say director on the back of your chair? Pretty sure it doesn't. You write. They act. Let me direct."

Mac punctuated each of her last three statements with a rigid finger point, and Layla fought to stop the response bubbling at the tip of her tongue. She didn't have to battle for long because Mac turned away and stalked out off the set, grabbing a giant chocolate muffin as she did, thus reminding Layla about the box of sugary delights Syd had arrived with. She snagged a glazed cruller and chowed down for the kind of satisfaction that only comes with a bite so big, it's hard to move your mouth around.

"Wow." Syd scrunched her nose and tilted her head. "That was harsh."

Layla tugged her hair out of a ponytail and shook it out, trying to lose the tension of the day by releasing her hair. It didn't work immediately so she went with another giant mouthful of sugar. That should kick-start the process. "Not really. You've heard the way she talks to everybody. That was pretty mild." She'd had far worse treatment from Mac over the past two months, and though it could be argued that some of it was her own fault—she had a problem with someone else having the final say on most things, let alone her creative baby—the way Mac dealt with people wasn't quality management.

Bullying bothered her, and even when Mac's ire wasn't directed her way, Layla still intervened and shared the wrath. She'd always stood up for the little gal. She'd done it as a kid, and she wasn't about to stop now.

"Are you glad it's over?"

Syd's question pulled Layla from her thoughts, but she didn't answer right away. Was she glad she didn't have to put up with Mac anymore?

Sure. Was she happy that her novel-turned-movie had finished shooting? *That* was a more complicated question. "I guess in some ways, I am…" But there was a niggling doubt. A question of integrity. "Do you think I sold out? Let Hollywood do what it does just to make more money?"

Syd's raised right eyebrow was all the response she needed.

"'Just to make more money?' Do you have any idea how many wannabe scriptwriters, published authors, and budding writers out there would smack you upside the head for that dumb question?"

Layla held her hands up. "Don't hold back, will you? I mean, you know, you don't have to spare my feelings or anything."

"Ha. That's not what real friends do, sweet child." She put her hand on Layla's shoulder and squeezed gently. "But no, I don't think you sold out. You got to write the screenplay on your own book, and that's pretty special. Think of all those writers who've had their babies torn from their inky hands, only to have their limbs pulled off and big fat surgical implants stuck on their chests."

Syd was right. There were plenty of books out there whose movie form was a mere shadow of its literary glory. So many stories whose fundamental premise or ending had been altered beyond recognition. "I guess so."

"You wrote a happy ending, and you got your happy ending in the movie. It's not like you wrote *Romeo and Juliet* only for them to have them ride off in the sunset together. Not so bad, huh?"

"You're essentially saying that I should stop moping around because there are thousands of people who'd kill to be in my heels, and I didn't have to compromise either. You're right. I know you're right. I just hoped for more from Teri and Marianne."

Syd laughed and shook her head. "I have a question, if you please?"

Layla narrowed her eyes. Syd never asked permission to question her, she just said whatever was on her mind. Which probably explained why she'd never quite made it to the big league and always played cast characters instead of the leads. She didn't play nice with the boys. "Why do I have a feeling I might regret saying yes?"

Syd grinned. "Can I ask or not?"

"Sure."

"How do you know what look either of them should've had in their eyes when you don't even believe in true love and happy ever afters?"

3

That was fair enough. "Research. You don't have to *believe* in something to know how it's supposed to be." She sucked on her straw and took a long hit of coffee. "I've written murder scenes, but I didn't have to believe in someone's right to kill someone, did I?" She smiled, probably rather smugly at her defense. But she was right, wasn't she? It was a writer's job to grasp the world and retell it through their own lens of understanding, and they didn't need to experience everything to write about it.

"You're comparing murder to love? That's a stretch, even for you."

Layla popped the last bite of her sweet treat into her mouth and washed it down with a slug of iced coffee. "Come on, let's go to Betsy's. Didn't you say it was mud wrestling night?" All this talk of forever love had made her a little antsy, and there were few better ways of getting back on kilter than watching semi-naked hot women grappling with each other.

"And now you're going from true love to gratuitous ogling. Nice."

Layla laughed and shoved Syd lightly. "So I'm going alone?"

"Hell no. Someone has to keep you from jumping in with them."

Layla grabbed her leather messenger bag from the back of her chair, patted it to make sure her trusty MacBook was tucked up inside, and took a final look around the set. Getting published had been her dream, but having her book turned into a movie had seemed beyond her grasp. Now that she'd had a taste of it, however bitter some of it had been, she was ready for more.

***

"I thought you were in the mood to celebrate?" Syd asked.

Layla held her wine glass aloft. "I am. See?"

"Then why are you playing hard to get? We've been here an hour and there have been four particularly eligible women who've tried to help you revel in your recent success, but you've given all of them the cold shoulder. What gives?"

Honestly, she didn't know. "I'm feeling picky." The idea of women mud wrestling had appealed when Syd had sent her the invite before she'd started filming that day, but in reality, it was a little too tacky. She enjoyed her fair share of voyeurism as much as the next red-blooded lesbian, but there were limits, and apparently, women frolicking in slimy brown liquid was hers.

"What *are* you in the mood for?"

"I'm not sure." Nor was she sure she could be bothered even if someone did "tickle her fancy" as Syd was fond of saying since she'd been an extra on a British period piece and picked up some of their Britishisms.

"Femme? Butch? Gender-free? Threesome?"

"Funny girl. I haven't celebrated with a threesome since my late teens. I'm a one person at a time woman, you know that."

Syd swirled her wine glass as if the conversation had just taken a seriously boring turn. "I know, I know, you're a serial monogamist."

Layla sipped her wine. Syd had never understood her lack of desire to taste the rainbow. Even in college, while Syd had enjoyed a different person most weeknights and multiple consorts on weekends, Layla had been happy to stick with one woman. "You say that like it's a bad thing. Working in Hollywood doesn't mean I'm going to change my modus operandi and become a player."

"But it would be *so* easy to—"

"Abuse my position as a writer and tell would-be actresses that I can get them a part in my latest movie if they sleep with me?" She raised an eyebrow. "I don't think so, Syd. That sleazy scene gave Hollywood a bad name."

"Hey, if the cap fits, they've earned it."

"Things are changing. Execs can't get away with the shit they've been pulling for decades. Not anymore, thank God. And as an actress yourself, you really shouldn't be encouraging anyone to do that."

"Okay, okay. I was just kidding."

"Some things aren't to be kidded about, Syd."

Syd held up her hands and lowered her eyes. "I'm sorry, you're right."

She looked suitably chastised: apology accepted. Layla returned to a more pleasant topic. "Anyway, I think the four women you're talking about were busy cruising you, not me."

Syd gave her a light shove. "Why do you do that? You're hot property, lady. Any one of the women lovers in here would be lucky to get their hands on you."

"I love you for saying that, even though it's one of the designated responsibilities in the friendship contract and if you didn't, I'd have to fire you, but this is LA. Look around. This place is wall to wall hotties as defined by the Hollywood standard. And before you say it, I'm not down on myself—in plenty of other states, I know I'd be considered 'hot property,' but not here. I like my donuts and wine too much for this city to consider me sexy." Layla waved her hand up and down the five-foot ten-inch frame of her college buddy. "You, however, *are* all that…in any state and any country."

Syd harrumphed and pouted and still managed to look incredibly alluring. "If that's the case, then why do I keep getting passed over for the big roles?"

"Because the big boys still don't like sassy, smart women who don't play their game by their rules." Things were changing, sure, but the machine was slow to be reinvented. Powerhouse women like Ellen and Oprah, women who only needed a first name to receive worldwide recognition, were still the exception rather than the rule. And their successes were hard-won against very different prejudicial beasts.

"I have two degrees and an IQ of over a hundred and fifty. I'm not dumbing that down to further my career."

Layla put her glass down and drew Syd into a quick hug. "And that's just one of the reasons why I love you. But there are more female directors than ever before; your big break might be around the corner."

"Not if Mac is anything to go by. She was as chauvinist as a male director."

Layla couldn't deny that. Mac had shown herself to be irritatingly integrated into the boys' club. "I think she's taken the old adage, 'If you can't beat 'em, join 'em,' a little too seriously, but hopefully she's not the yardstick by which we should judge everyone else. My next project is with one of the most morally righteous women alive, if I'm to believe the gossip." Layla had only been in Hollywood a few months, but she'd heard all about Rix Reardon and how she was *the* hot director to work with. The prospect of teaming up with her for Layla's secret agent books as a limited series was exciting and terrifying in equal measure. And her agent had told her that Reardon was trying to secure the rights on a lot of her other books too.

"That's such a brilliant project for you. I hear she's an amazing director. Shame the lead for that went to Rachel Harari before casting had even begun. I would've killed for that role."

"I love you, Syd, you know that, but your arms are like twigs. How could the audience be expected to believe that you could hold your own in a fight with a guy?" Her spy was the antithesis of almost every woman in every TV show or movie before it, and Layla had been amazed that the network wasn't insisting on casting a size zero as her heroine.

"Winning a fight isn't about the size of the dog. It's the size of the fight in the dog."

Layla laughed. "You're calling yourself a dog?"

"Fine." Syd scrunched her nose. "Bad analogy, but you understand what I mean. Look at Wonder Woman. I'm about the same build as her." She stood and put her hands on her hips as if to prove her point.

"You are, but she doesn't count. She has superpowers and she's a god. She doesn't need muscles; her strength is implied." Not that Layla would be averse to that particular actress demonstrating her power between the sheets. "Would you have been prepared to put on twenty pounds?"

"Is that what Rach is doing?" Syd retook her seat and pressed the buzzer for more drinks. "She's so cool. Did you see her in *Pity*?"

"Of course." It was a silly question. Every self-respecting lesbian had seen all of her films, and Layla couldn't wait to see her in action on set. "With the make-up and two stone of extra weight, she managed to go from beauty queen to plain Jane and then some."

Syd nodded. "It's little wonder she got an Oscar for that."

"The first Oscar for Best Actress to an out lesbian. See, things are changing—and no, Jodie Foster doesn't count because she was in the closet when she won both of hers."

"There's hope for me yet."

Syd's words were jovial, but the façade didn't fool Layla. They'd known each other far too long to have any hope of hiding behind falsities or masks. While the merry-go-round was relatively new for Layla, Syd had been in town for over three years. She'd landed a TV show early in her career, but things had never quite worked out for her after that promising start. Though she'd figured out what it would take to work the system, Syd wasn't prepared to sacrifice her integrity or keep her mouth shut. It was a damning indictment of an organization unwilling to embrace the creative potential of powerful women…and it pissed Layla off. Her best friend's lack of commercial success had been a sizeable factor in Layla's decision to up sticks and join Syd in La La Land, more for support than any naïve notion that they could change things together. After her writing career took off, her interest lay in commercial success and behind the camera was a slightly less complicated and intimidating prospect. Layla had no aspirations to change a broken institution; she was happy merely to profit from it while her work was in favor. And if she could provide encouragement and back-up to her best friend at the same time, it was a win-win.

Layla raised her glass. "Come on. No maudlin sentiments for us. We are strong, intelligent, and independent women with lots to celebrate." She waited for Syd to clink their glasses together. "Let's get good and buzzed and focus on all the good stuff going on in our lives." She took a long drink of her wine and as she placed her glass back on the table, she caught the gaze of a woman with long dark hair. She glanced away but when she returned her attention to the bar, the woman was still looking directly at her. Layla pointed to Syd and raised her eyebrows, half expecting the woman to nod, just like when they were in college and all the cute women approached *her* to get an introduction to Syd. The woman shook her head, pointed at Layla, and mouthed, "You."

"Invite her over," Syd said, obviously having caught the exchange. "Your last two relationships have been butches, haven't they? Your quota is probably due some lipstick and lace."

Layla shot Syd a disapproving look. "You're so box and label-oriented."

"I can't help it. It helps me make sense of this crazy world."

Layla shook her head at Syd's tongue-in-cheek irreverence. "Okay, I'll get her over here, but if she's a single-serving, she's all yours." Layla beckoned the woman over. It'd been a while since her relationship with Frankie ended. Four months, relocating two thousand miles away, and a couple of one-night stands had gotten her over that. She was ready to start looking for someone to share the journey with again, at least for a little while. Writing happy ever after was her livelihood, but in life Layla had always been okay with happy for now.

Chapter Two

"I'm sorry, Rix, that's all I can say. She got a better offer."

Rix plucked her black gel exercise ball from its stand and began to squeeze it repeatedly. "She signed a contract, Will. Don't they mean anything anymore?" She concentrated on the steady motion of grip and release and watched the muscles in her forearm respond. If she could keep some of her focus on that, perhaps she could also keep some of her cool in this conversation.

Will sighed and held his hands aloft. "She had a clause written in to release her in the event of a movie offer."

Rix rubbed her fingers across her forehead. Agents were strange and wild beasts, one moment predatory and the next, obsequious and subservient. She inwardly cursed their necessary evil. "Short-sighted. This isn't the old days when TV was the poor cousin of the silver screen. Actors can earn more on a series than on the average movie, especially when there are multiple seasons and they're a main character. She had the lead role, Will. This might be a limited series, but I think it's got legs. I'm sure it'll do well, and the network will want more."

"And I'm sure you're right. She'll be the one cursing her decision when you turn this into an epic twelve-season, award-winning show."

She rose and pushed her chair back so hard that it hit the rear wall of her office. "I wanted her for this role, Will. Only her. She was one of the main reasons I took this project on." That wasn't true at all, and Rachel would know that, but it never hurt to appeal to an actor via their agent's ego. She glanced out her window and could see the woman they were discussing on a giant billboard across the street. Rachel Harari was her directing equivalent of Moby Dick. Rix was desperate to work with her, and Rachel had said the same about Rix. What had changed?

"You know that I can only see your belt buckle and your fancy vest from this angle, don't you?"

Goddamn video conferencing. She needed one of those swirly, tripod things that followed her around when she was in motion. She'd never been one to stay still when she was talking, let alone when she was agitated. She scribbled a note for her assistant, Jack, to source one and dropped back into her chair. "What movie is it? Who's directing?" Though it made no difference, Rix still wanted to know, if only to torture herself more.

"Some romantic comedy book adaptation. It doesn't matter; it's done."

"I want to talk to her." Rix replaced the black ball on its little stand and steepled her fingers. If she could get back in the room with Rachel, they could hash this out. Rix could convince her why it was so important that she took this role and what it meant to people, to the community. She could make her remember why she joined the project in the first place, and that it was her involvement that really got it off the ground.

Will tugged on his ear, the way he always did when he was stressed. "There's no point, Rix, you have to let this one go. Your powers of persuasion are legendary, I acknowledge that, but the movie she's gone for is a mainstream rom-com. You can't blame her for taking it."

Rix uncoupled her fingers and picked at the calluses on her left hand. The chainsaw carving she'd been working on all weekend was coming along, but her skin was suffering because of it. She should wear protective gloves, but they created an emotional barrier between her and the wood, so she took the consequences. She pumped some lotion into her palm and rubbed it in, trying unsuccessfully to ignore the lack of jewelry on her left ring finger. *One day.*

"Rix? Has the connection dropped? You're frozen."

She shook off the distracting thoughts. "Yeah, sorry about that. We can talk to people on rockets to the moon, but we can't get a clear reception within a mile in the city. What's that about?" She didn't wait for his response. "And yes, I can blame her. Not everything about this business should be driven by the number of zeroes on a check."

"Maybe it shouldn't be, but for the most part and for most people, it is."

"Make it happen, Will. I want to speak to her today."

Actors like Rachel had a responsibility to their community. Until being any kind of different didn't matter in Hollywood, Rix believed successful individuals should think about the power they held as role models and put that before a big payday.

Will agreed to do as she asked, and she ended the Zoom. She flexed her hands and spotted a number of cuts and scrapes she hadn't registered before, making them look like she'd had a fight with a wall. Perhaps her fugly hands were the reason she was still single. That and the fact that the only women who seemed to be interested in her were actresses who thought she could give them their big break. God, how she wished they'd have more respect for themselves.

She pressed the intercom on her desk. "Jack, clear the rest of my day, please. I'm waiting on a video call with Rachel Harari."

"Sure thing, Ms. Reardon."

"And would you bring me a root beer?"

"I'll be right in."

Rix picked up her iPad and flicked to her schedule. In a few days, they started auditions for the rest of the cast and she'd finally get to meet Layla Adams, the author who seemed to have reached inside Rix's brain and pulled out each and every element of her dream woman and the idyllic life she envisioned she'd one day experience. It didn't matter whether Layla wrote contemporary romance, adventure, or sci-fi, she made the pure love between the romantic leads so realistic and tangible that it rose from the pages and wrapped the reader up in a sweet embrace. As soon as Rix had realized her vision of owning her own production company, getting the rights on as many of Layla's books as she could afford had been her one of her goals. Inevitably, due to competition, she'd missed out on a few and there were still a number in bidding wars, but the project she was about to begin was based on the characters and plot lines from a series of three books she adored, and she couldn't wait to bring it to life for a whole new audience. The LGBTQ community needed a strong lesbian lead character as a role model, and Rix would be proud to make it happen.

Jack knocked and waited for her to give him permission to enter. He placed the ice-cold soda on a coaster. "Is there anything else you need?"

Rix looked up when he didn't turn and leave. He stood at her desk with his face tilted toward the window. "That's some impressive facial hair coming in, Jack."

Jack had been Melissa when she'd first hired an assistant, and Rix had been honored when he came to her to help him achieve his true self. The low interest loan for surgery and a guaranteed job for the rest of his life hadn't just been a selfless act though. Rix had been through a few people in her quest to find the elusive and rare beast that was the perfect assistant:

someone who knew before she did when she needed them and when they should make themselves scarce. In two short months, Jack proved himself to be just the person Rix had been searching for. She made a point of always trying to recruit from their community and finding Jack had been a most convenient happenstance.

He grinned and stroked his chin. "I was wondering if you were ever going to notice."

"Ah, you know what I'm like. If you don't slap me in the face with it, I don't see it." Until she was behind the camera. Then she saw everything, every finite detail and action and nuance, and anything outside that rectangle of high-definition pixels disappeared. "It suits you. Are you aiming for full bear?"

"Definitely not. Just the five o'clock shadow for me. I'm going for the Zac Ephron look."

"Perfect choice."

"Thanks, Ms. Reardon." He turned to leave but hovered at the door. "You're looking particularly sharp in that vest. I don't think I've ever seen you in the same one; can I ask how many you've got?"

She winked. "You can ask."

He laughed and, taking her answer as his signal to leave, closed the door behind him.

Rix took a sip of her soda and leaned back in her chair with a copy of the first book in Layla's series. She'd read it of course, three times, but with casting coming up, she wanted to refresh the characters in her mind. Rachel had been the only actress she could see as Lane, but she wanted to be more open for the remaining players.

She was halfway through chapter three when Will messaged with a Zoom link to meet with Rachel. After a quick check of her camera-readiness, she connected and tapped in the passcode. "Hi, Rachel, thanks for agreeing to chat with me."

"Of course, Rix," she said. "I'm happy to, especially after what's happened."

Her thick Brooklyn accent always surprised Rix. Rachel had an impressive range of accents, but her natural one had hardly ever been employed in her vast catalog of movies.

"Did Will tell you that's what I wanted to talk to you about?" Rix always preferred to get straight to business. Small talk held little interest for her, and she rarely had the time for it even if she did want to catch up on the gossip, which she didn't.

"He did." She fiddled with something off screen and didn't hold Rix's gaze. "And I'm sorry I wasn't able to tell you in person about the movie. I chickened out. I know how much this project means to you, and I really wanted to do it, Rix, but this movie has a twenty-million-dollar payday attached to it, and I've got to take the romantic leads while I'm still young enough for the studios. You know how this business works."

Rix knew precisely how Hollywood worked, and while she loved being a part of it, creating stories that moved people, she was eternally grateful her calling had been to peer into the viewfinder of a camera rather than its lens. There simply wasn't an age limit or beauty standard attached to the production side of movies and TV, but even she'd had to do her fair share of mainstream movies and TV to be in her current, more privileged position. It was a sad state of affairs, however, that a talented actress like Rachel knew she had to make the best of her career while it lasted, because there weren't the stories for older women like there were for men in their sixties and beyond.

"Let's talk about scheduling," Rix said, not interested in entering a philosophical discussion about the prejudicial patriarchy and hierarchy of their chosen profession. She would do her best to change it from the inside as long as she could keep making film.

Rachel frowned. "Rix, I took this meeting because I wanted to apologize to you face-to-face and make sure that it didn't affect our future working relationship. I want to work with you on something, I really do, but the timing on this project isn't right for me. And I'm sorry for that, I am. But I can't talk about scheduling as if there's something we can do about—"

"But there *is* something we can do about it. It's my production company, and I set the schedule. Hear me out?"

Rachel's face softened slightly. "Okay, I'm listening."

"When are you due to start rehearsals?"

"Mid-January."

"Any pre-shoot preparation, body-shape or appearance wise?"

"I have to be a size zero to two, no bigger, and definitely only yoga muscle." Rachel rolled her eyes. "And my hair has to be at least an inch below my shoulders."

Rix sympathized, knowing Rachel preferred a powerful frame, but

Hollywood actresses rarely got to keep the body size they favored or were born with. It was a problem for her too since Lane Roberts, the character she desperately wanted Rachel to play, was formidable in both size and attitude. In email exchanges with Layla, she'd already promised that Rachel would remold herself into the author's vision of her spy and she hated to go back on her word. Surely Layla would understand and be okay with that concession if they managed to keep Rachel onboard.

"You were going to put on twenty pounds of muscle to become Lane; what are you going to have to lose for the movie?"

"Ten pounds from my regular film weight, but I'm already twelve extra pounds of muscle up preparing for your role."

A thirty-pound difference was a helluva change even for an actress who had defined her career with dramatic physical transformations. Rix picked up her stress ball and started working it again. Maybe she'd underestimated the hurdles to making this happen. But Rachel was already twelve pounds up; maybe that'd be enough. "How quickly can you do that?"

"Three weeks with my trainer. Why?"

Rix didn't doubt it for a moment. Tilly Stevens was one of the premier personal trainers in Tinsel town, and her super successful combination of workouts and meal regimes kept her in constant demand. Rix often threatened herself with a Tilly program but had no follow through. She was far too fond of muffins, pizza, and beer to put herself through the agony.

"Because it's October, and we're already in pre-production. You've got twelve pounds of muscle, and we could work with that instead of twenty. If I crack the whip and everything goes smoothly, we could be in principal photography by the beginning of November. You could shoot with us until Christmas, and we'd focus on your main scenes, and that would give you time to lose the weight you need for your romcom. Then you come back to us once you've finished shooting, and I know you're a method actor, but we could use a muscle suit for your final scenes."

Rachel leaned closer to the screen. "What about my hair?"

"That isn't a problem; we can use a skull cap and a wig." Rix mirrored Rachel's movement, feeling like she might have her on the hook. If she could just reel her in... This was exactly the reason why she preferred physical meetings. Turning someone or something down was far too easy when you could just click *end* instead of having to walk away.

"You want me for this role that bad that you'd do all of that to make it happen," Rachel asked softly.

Gotcha. "I would—and happily." Rix grinned and leaned back in her chair. "We've wanted to work together for years now, and this is a brilliant vehicle for us to do that. If a little scheduling problem is all that stands in the way of that, I'm ready to do anything I can to get over those bumps." And Rix wasn't just blowing smoke; she believed in Rachel as an actor, she loved this project, and she wanted desperately to bring them all together. The end product would be worth any pain to get there.

"Okay. Let's do it." Rachel looked serious and peered closer to the screen. "Thank you, Rix, for making this happen. I didn't want to let you down but…"

All became clear, and Rachel didn't need to say anything else. Rix saw it all in her eyes. Agent pressure. External expectation. Management demands. "Do I get to tell Will you're back on board or would you like that pleasure?"

Rachel laughed. "As much as I'd love for you to save me from that conversation, he's my agent, and I should talk to him. I'd lost sight of the bigger picture, partially because he was willfully obscuring it. I'll pull him back in line."

"Perfect." Rix hated the thought of someone as talented as Rachel letting her management team call all the shots. Sure, they professed to always have her best interests in mind, but their own agendas were inextricably linked to hers, which could sometimes mean they were inclined to pander to those objectives instead of Rachel's. She was stronger than many other actors, who simply went along with what was expected of them.

"Before I go kick Will's ass, what does the schedule look like right now?"

"Fluid. I'll get Jack on it as soon as we're done, and I'll have it over to you before the end of the day. I assume you're still interested in being involved in casting?"

"Absolutely."

Rix gave her stress ball a final squeeze in triumph and popped it back on her desk, where it should stay for a while now that she had her first-choice talent back. "The sides have already gone out to talent agencies and specific actors. I'm meeting with the author on Thursday at eleven, and we begin looking at the invited auditions after lunch—there are only a few of them—then open auditions start on Friday and run through the weekend to Tuesday."

"I'll be there for lunch. I can't wait to get started, Rix."

It was clear Rachel's sentiment was genuine, an all too rare quality in this business: yet another reason to cherish the opportunity to work together. "Me too. I'll make sure they have plenty of protein-rich options."

They said their good-byes, and Rix called for Jack so they could work on the new truncated schedule. She gulped the rest of her soda down and looked out her window again at the giant Rachel reproduction atop the opposite one-story building. Rix had her Moby Dick, and she was sure that she would captain this particular chapter to a far happier ending than Ahab's.

Chapter Three

SYD HAD TOLD her not to be nervous. Told her to go into the meeting as if she owned the joint and belonged there. Like she had meetings of this import daily and thrice on Thursdays. Syd had done such a great job of pumping Layla up that she pulled it off right up to the point where the security guard asked for her name, ticked her off, and directed her to the parking lot. But by the time she'd gotten past security, parked her ForTwo Smart car, and made her way to the studio's production office, the bravado had all but worn off. Every fiber of her body screamed for her to stop kidding herself, turn around, and drive away before everybody realized she shouldn't be there and kicked her out on her ass.

By some spidey-sense miracle, her cell buzzed in her handbag, and she exhaled when she saw Syd's face grinning at her on the screen contact photo.

"You've got this, superstar."

Layla forced a smile that didn't manage to get beyond her tight lips. "Yep."

"Layla…"

Syd drew out her name the way she did when she was calling her on her bullshit.

Layla looked back in the direction of the lot and saw her ride looking like a Lego toy between a fancy Audi and an even fancier Bentley. "I parked my car in a spot where the top of my door came to the top of a mudflap on the car beside me."

Syd's throaty laugh reverberated in her ear. "Don't get all size-ist on me now that you're a hotshot screenwriter. Small is beautiful."

"I don't remember you ever saying that about my car whenever you have to fold your Amazon-like frame into the passenger seat. You only fit in it when I have the top down."

"Which is every day because you live in a lovely, sunny city. But that's true, I do feel like a pooch with my head popping out of a sunroof."

Layla laughed. Syd always managed to make her feel better, no matter the seriousness of the situation. "I'm a best-selling novelist. I can do this, and I'm being silly doubting myself. Fear is the enemy of success, and I want success above all things."

"You sound like a self-help audio book."

"Thanks…I think. And thanks for calling."

"Hey, no problem. Hollywood can shake even the strongest of confidences."

Syd spoke like she definitely knew of that which she preached, and Layla's heart ached for her. The starry lights and fame had always been Syd's dream, and yet it had been Layla who'd become the overnight success. And she owed a lot of that to Syd's constant nagging. "I'm beginning to understand that, buddy."

"Quit hanging around the outside of the building. Get in there and show them how lucky there are to have you on their team."

Layla looked to the sky. "Do you have a drone camera watching me?"

"Nope. I just know you inside out, just like you always say about knowing your characters."

"Fine." Layla turned back to the door of the production office and steeled herself. "And I'll work on being less predictable."

"Nah, don't do that. You're the only steady ship on this sea. I need you to stay exactly as you are."

Syd hung up and Layla slipped her phone back in her bag. The building door opened, and a skinny young man stood in the entrance looking at her.

"Layla Day?"

"That's me," she said brightly, thinking about how grateful she was to have a friend like Syd.

He tapped his watch. "Ms. Reardon is waiting for you."

"Oh god, am I late?" She checked the time to find she still had a couple of minutes before the meeting was due to begin.

"Ms. Reardon likes to start meetings on time, so it's best to get here at least ten minutes before." He looked at her and seemed to soften a little. "It's probably my fault. I should've told you that when I emailed the details."

Crap. He probably had. Layla wasn't one for reading the finer details of long emails, obviously a shortcoming she needed to address. "You're Jack?" Remembering his name had to win her some points.

"That's right. I'm Ms. Reardon's assistant." He waved her in, and she entered the building. "Please, follow me."

After the elevator to the second floor, he led her along a maze of corridors, and she wondered how he'd known she'd been standing at the entrance. Unless Rix Reardon was a bit of a ball buster and had ordered him to find her since she hadn't kept to their agreed schedule. She cursed herself for not paying more attention to the email. After the unpleasant working relationship she'd shared with Mac, she'd really wanted to get a better start with Ms. Reardon. They hadn't yet met and already, she'd committed a faux pas. It didn't bode well. She'd have to be on a major charm offensive from the get-go.

Jack showed her into a small casual space that instantly soothed some of her anxiety. The teal and tan walls coupled with similarly colored couches provided a welcoming feel, and her nerves began to fade when she settled into one of them and it all but molded around her body like a friendly hug.

"Would you like something to drink?" Jack asked.

What she wanted was an iced latte, but that request seemed presumptuous and diva-like. "I'd love a sparkling water."

"No, you wouldn't." He narrowed his eyes as if studying her and trying to divine her inner drink desires. "We have a coffee bar on the third floor. Maybe you'd like an iced latte?"

Damn, he was good, and she appreciated the lack of expectation that she might like it non-fat. "That'd be great, thanks."

He pointed to the assortment of muffins and other baked pastries on a low coffee table. "Please help yourself to a pastry or two. I'll let Ms. Reardon know you're here. She'll be along—"

"Right about now."

Jack looked startled for a millisecond before he regained his composure and held the door open. He gestured to Layla. "Ms. Reardon, this is—"

"Layla Day. Thanks, Jack. Would you grab me—"

"A fruit punch Crystal Light, ice cold. Coming right up, chief."

Jack left, and Ms. Reardon strode into the room and offered her hand. Layla got up from the sofa and shook her hand firmly, before retaking her seat.

When Ms. Reardon pulled away, she cradled her hand. "That's some handshake you've got there."

She had to be kidding. Ms. Reardon's hand had felt rough and strong, and while Layla had a firm shake, she wasn't exactly a bone breaker.

Ms. Reardon held up her hands. "I'm kidding. Relax."

Layla smiled, a little off kilter. She wasn't usually so slow. Why couldn't she say something, anything? Her silence was getting weird, but her words wouldn't come. It wasn't like Ms. Reardon was some huge movie star Layla had a crush on, though there was definitely a rugged, powerful appeal that wouldn't be denied.

Ms. Reardon flopped down onto the couch beside Layla and put her feet on the table. "Let's start again. I'm Rix Reardon, and I'm a big fan of your work."

She was a fan? That was unexpected. Though Ms. Reardon had purchased the rights to some of her books, Layla thought that might be driven by the current climate's leaning toward putting LGBTQ characters front and center. Layla was vaguely tempted to ask what her favorite read was but remembered Syd's warning words about flattery and its transience. "Wow, thanks, Ms. Rear—"

"Please, call me Rix. It's important to me that we're comfortable working together, and that can only happen if we're on an even footing." She put her feet down briefly to snag the pastries plate. "I'm assuming it'll be okay for me to call you Layla."

The way she framed it sounded rhetorical and almost bullish, but her approach held a certain straightforward charm, and she certainly seemed more friendly and potentially collaborative than Mac had been. But Layla still hadn't uttered anything coherent. "Yeah, that's fine. Great, actually."

Rix offered Layla the plate after she'd taken a particularly juicy looking Danish.

"No, thank you." She tapped her stomach. "Got to watch the weight in this town." She didn't, not really, since her job was all behind the scenes, and she felt silly for saying it, but her usual confidence had rather strangely gone AWOL, and it was better to say something silly rather than nothing at all. Maybe.

Rix replaced the plate on the table and reclined back in her sofa. "You're missing out. These beauties are from the Bakehouse in WeHo, best place in the city for baked goods. I guarantee you'll change your mind by the end of week one." She tapped her own stomach. "Being my side of the camera means I don't have to worry about carbs. Double standards, I know, but I like to enjoy life."

Layla smiled. And enjoying life looked good on Rix, which now struck her as a strange name for a director. Nowhere near as pretentious as McD, Mac's nickname, but she couldn't help but wonder where she'd gotten it from. Curiosity got the better of her. "Is Rix a nickname from school?" she asked just as Jack returned with their drinks on a tray balanced on one hand.

"Jack, just in time to answer a question." Rix gestured for Layla to ask again.

He swept his hair across his forehead and rolled his eyes when she repeated her question. "That's unfair. No one knows the answer to that." Jack placed Layla's coffee and Rix's neon-bright flavored water on the table. "It's one of the great mysteries of the universe."

"And so shall it remain," Rix said in an exaggerated, and terrible, English accent.

Layla did love a challenge. "Is there a long-standing prize for anyone who discovers the answer?"

"God, no." Rix waved her Danish in the air and flaked almonds rained down on her jeans. She collected each one and dropped them in a wastepaper basket beside her chair. "It's a secret for a very good reason, and I usually say that it's a weird moniker I picked up at college, so most people don't even know it's a mystery. Jack's just being melodramatic."

"Which you actively encourage." He turned to the door. "I'll let you know when catering brings lunch," he said and left.

"I like a good secret," Layla said, finding that she'd begun to relax now that they were talking about something not related to the project. And discovering that Rix appeared to be nothing like Mac was a joy. She hadn't realized how anxious she'd let herself get about that possibility.

Rix narrowed her eyes. "Am I going to regret answering your question truthfully? Which, incidentally, I only did because I thought it might be the only way to get you to speak to me. It's funny how people can be so different in email conversations than in person."

Rix's wide and genuine smile showed Layla she was teasing, and her body sank into the soft sofa a little more as the fears she didn't know she'd adopted began to melt away. "I'm still getting used to all the face time people expect in Hollywood."

"Oh, that's right. You've only been in town six months. Is it such a big change from being an author?"

"It's a *huge* change. Writing is a solitary pursuit. I'd spend days, and sometimes weeks, holed up in my apartment and not see anyone but delivery people."

"No family?"

"My family is still in Washington. I get to them on the holidays and whenever else I can but writing two books a year means there's not much time for anything else." She was rambling *and* sharing a lot of personal information, which wasn't her thing at all, but there was something about Rix that made it easy for her to open up. She couldn't decide if that was a good or bad thing.

"But you haven't been living in Washington?"

"No, I stayed in Denver after college, because I loved the area so much." Layla grabbed her coffee and took a sip. This was beginning to feel more like an interview or a date than a production meeting. Rix was way more informal than Mac had ever been. "Is this how you like to do things?" she asked, emboldened by their exchange thus far.

Rix sighed and leaned forward. "I heard you had a bad time on your first movie."

Crap. She didn't need that. What had Mac said? If Layla developed a reputation for being combative and difficult, her career as a scriptwriter would be short-lived. It wasn't like she could change though. She'd only challenged Mac when she thought her behavior could be seen as insensitive at best and as bullying at worst. If that was what Hollywood was about, she'd like to tell them to shove it…but she wanted to succeed here. And as long as she didn't lose sight of who she was, everything would be okay. "A bad time?" If Rix was fishing, Layla wasn't taking the bait. She wanted Rix's trust and respect, and she didn't think she'd earn that by telling tales on a sister director.

Rix took a bite of her pastry, and the icing sugar dusted her nose. She wiped it off but not before Layla half considered doing it. Which would be totally weird and unprofessional. They were about to be colleagues. They weren't old friends. Rix's informal manner had her far too relaxed. Surely she could work out some middle ground.

"Mac can be hard to take," Rix said after she'd swallowed. "She didn't used to be like that. We went to film school together straight after college, and she was a nice person back then. But a little success has gone a long way to making her a big asshole."

Layla tried and failed to suppress a smile at Rix's assessment, though she couldn't imagine Mac ever having been a "nice person." And did that make the two directors the same age? She would've put Mac at five to eight years older than Rix, easy. Layla studied her a little closer and spotted deep laugh lines around her eyes. Maybe she wasn't as good as she thought she was at guessing ages. "It's safe to say we clashed on occasion."

Rix laughed. "So I heard, but the way it's being told is that you ripped into each other every day."

It didn't seem like a good thing that she'd already gotten people gossiping about her, though Rix didn't appear fazed by it. Could it be that she was impressed? "We disagreed quite strongly on how to treat people. Have I already got a bad reputation?" She had to ask even if she wasn't going to like the answer.

Rix shook her head. "Far from it. Generally, people are impressed that you stood up to her. Most people don't. Even seasoned actors cow to her unreasonable behavior. The cast and crew might not have said it, but you were quite the hero to them."

She liked the sound of that. Good gossip was a relief.

"But don't expect to get a call to work on another Mac Miller picture." Rix winked then leaned over and gave Layla's shoulder a gentle tap. "And I have a heads-up now, so I'll know not to scream and shout at the grips and runners whenever you're around."

She looked serious for a moment before she broke into a wide grin, and Layla got the impression that Rix was the kind of person who never really had the need to raise her voice to get what she wanted. She suspected that anybody who worked for her would make things happen because she was so damn likeable. Layla was certainly leaning into that camp heavily already and they hadn't spent an hour together yet.

"Anyway, let's forget about that and concentrate on this series. I'm really excited to be working with you, and I'm eager to have you involved in casting." Rix placed her unfinished Danish on a plate beside her and rubbed at the palm of her hand. "But first, I've got a little bad news. But it's good news when you hear the full story."

"O-kay," Layla said, a little unnerved.

When Rix had finished relaying a tale about the lead actress pulling out of her contract to pursue a mainstream movie, Layla empathized.

Mainstream was where the big successes were. Mainstream was ultimately where Layla wanted to be. It wasn't like this series was a steppingstone, but she did feel like she had to earn her stripes with independent projects before a big production company would give her a chance. She wasn't about to voice that however, because Rix's passion for her work was so enthusiastic, it was almost overwhelming. And they'd developed a rapport Layla she didn't want to spoil by siding with Rachel Harari.

But Rix had promised the lead actress would be a realistic portrayal of Lane, like she'd come alive from her books. Disappointment settled heavy in her mind. Would this be the first of many compromises on her book babies? Maybe she was kidding herself that she'd have control over the content of adaptations. Her agent had promised it to her, and her contract gave it to her in black and white, but Rachel Harari's action showed that contracts could be bent and broken. She needed to figure out how far she was prepared to bend her own artistic integrity in the pursuit of success.

"I can't tell you that I'm okay with that," she said after a moment of silence. "I feel like we're going to work well together, but I won't lie to you." God, what was she doing? Her second job in Hollywood and she was trying to call the shots. This wasn't the path to commercial success. Syd had already spent the last two years beating that stick and proven it wasn't a viable approach if you were striving for the top of the tree.

"And I don't expect you to be okay with it, but it's that or a different actress. Rachel will bring Lane to life in a way that I'm one hundred percent convinced that you'll be happy with. And she was my only choice for that character. I really can't see anyone else in Lane's boots."

Layla nibbled at the skin on the inside of her lip in an effort to stay silent. She needed to think about what she was about to say rather than simply blurting out her first response. She was a big fan of Rachel's too, and she'd been blown away when her agent told her she'd signed up to play Lane, but there were other actresses out there who could do it. Syd could do it if she were willing to put the muscle on her Valkyrie frame, but it was very clear from Rix's tone that there was no room for movement on this particular casting decision. Rix wasn't exactly bringing the hammer down, but her friendly informality had been replaced by a steely determination that warned Layla not to test her. Was that how it was going to be for the next few days? Would her opinion only count if it seconded Rix's choice? She wasn't the same kind of director as Mac, no, but she obviously had limits to her collaborative decision making.

Layla sipped at her to-die-for latte and mentally retracted her horns. She had to learn her place in this new world. It wasn't like sitting in her writing studio at home, where she made all the decisions on who lived, who loved, and who died. She couldn't be the alpha because she wasn't running the show, literally or metaphorically, and if she did want this to be a long-term career and if she did want to make it in mainstream TV and movies, she had to earn it.

"Are we good?" Rix asked gently.

The silence must have stretched longer than was comfortable. And the question addressed several different levels: the here and now, and the future of the project. Layla had sold the rights to this series of books. It would be better for her to be involved as much as she was allowed rather than let her ego dictate that she step down and have nothing at all to do with it. Who knows what other compromises would be made if she wasn't there to stick up for her characters? Her books were going to be made into a TV series with or without her. And like Syd had told her, hundreds of writers would maim their own mothers to be in Layla's position. *Suck it up, buttercup.*

"We're good," Layla said. "Let's talk about how you want me involved in the rest of casting."

Chapter Four

RIX PULLED INTO the restaurant parking area on autopilot and had to slam on the brakes when the yellow-coated valet stepped in front of her Jeep Wrangler. She'd been way too busy thinking about the events of the day and had zoned out for a second. *Not* the best thing to do when driving four and a half thousand pounds of killing machine. After she'd gotten out of the car and thanked him with twenty dollars, she saw his greasy handprint on the Jeep's hood where he'd made a futile attempt to stop its progress. She looked back at him and saw wide-eyed fear settling a little as his chest heaved against the buttons of his jacket. She took another twenty from her billfold, went back around the car, and offered it to him. "Sorry about that, Jesse."

"Not at all, Ms. Reardon. It was my fault for getting in the road too soon." He took the money and smiled. "Thank you. I'll take good care of her for you."

"You're okay?"

Jesse had been working this restaurant for half a year now, and he always had a smile for everyone, regardless of how much or little they tipped, and she'd noted he remembered everyone's name. She valued that kind of even temper and attention to detail, and she'd been considering offering him a position at her production company. Crippling him *hadn't* been part of her plan.

"Of course. I'm peachy." He pocketed the notes and pulled a bamboo cloth from his jacket. He moved around her and buffed his handprint. "Have a lovely night, Ms. Reardon."

"Thanks, Jesse, I will." The front door opened as she approached, and the smell of perfectly cooked steak welcomed her. The maître-d greeted her and showed her to her regular table where Mac was already waiting and halfway down a bottle of red. Rix had last seen Mac when she'd just secured the rights to the Lane Roberts book series and as Mac was about to begin work on her movie with Layla Adams. Rix had shared her excitement at the prospect of working with Layla whereas Mac had seen the author's involvement as more of a hinderance.

"Hey, buddy, how's it hanging?"

"Pretty damn good." Rix sat beside her sister director, picked up the wine bottle, and poured herself a glass.

"Did you see the hot new waitress on your way in?" Mac asked.

Rix rolled her eyes at her friend's juvenile question. Somehow, as they'd grown up together, Mac's development had been stunted in her early-twenties, and she remained a weird mix of butch and man-child. It had worked for her through her thirties, but as they approached their mid-forties, Rix found it more and more irksome. If they didn't work in the same field, Rix was sure they would no longer communicate. "Do you ever think you'll stop being such a horn dog and settle down?"

Mac half-sneered and waved her hand at Rix dismissively. "That's not working out so well for you, is it?"

Rix took a long drink of wine. "Is there something wrong with wanting to find someone to share my life with?"

"No small talk for us tonight, then. Straight into the deep stuff. Okay. I'll answer your question with another question. Is there something wrong with wanting to find lots of people to enjoy *my* life with?"

Horses for courses, as her mom often said. "Maybe, maybe not." She shouldn't judge, but Mac's behavior was so cliché, it rubbed Rix the wrong way. It wasn't so much the constant search for new bed companions, it was the way she went about it. It lacked respect and class, and Mac hadn't changed her approach for two decades. Rix could swear that Mac thought she was some sort of divine gift to women, and she couldn't understand why they kept swarming back to her no matter how badly she treated them.

She pulled the front of her vest down and straightened her tie. It was going to be a long night if they started the evening this way. She reminded herself that they were once inseparable best friends, and Mac had always been there at the end of each and every one of Rix's break ups. "We're built different, that's all."

"I'm telling you, bud, you should relax and stop worrying about finding the right woman. Enjoy the women right now instead." Mac chinked her glass to Rix's and toasted alone.

"That's not me. It never has been, and it never will be."

"Are you ready to order, Ms. Daley? Ms. Reardon?"

The waitress came into Rix's sight, and Mac wiggled her eyebrows and grinned widely. Clearly this was the woman she'd mentioned earlier. She was beautiful, Rix couldn't deny that, especially if you liked that obvious, socially lauded beauty, which Rix appreciated but wasn't overawed by. And like most waitresses in town, she'd probably come to Hollywood to pursue her dream of acting, making Rix ever grateful that she'd only ever wanted to be on one side of the camera.

Rix ordered her usual cut medium rare with steamed broccoli—for now, her only concession to her doctor's instructions that she should probably lay off the red meat and eat healthier—and another bottle of the red Mac had chosen. Mac took her time with her own choice, getting the waitress to relay the specials and asking her what she'd recommend. The waitress giggled and bit her lip in all the right places, making Rix wonder if maybe she should take a lesson or two from her frisky friend. But she was looking for a soul mate, and she didn't think someone half her age fit that category.

When the waitress had gone and Mac had taken great pleasure in watching her leave, she tapped Rix on the arm. "Don't you get tired of getting your heart broken?"

"I'm not sure it's ever really been broken, not really."

Mac frowned. "You always seem pretty heartbroken when you come around to my place with your tail between your legs after the latest lady has left you wanting."

"But my heart hasn't been broken by them." More often than not, Rix was the one to end things, not because there was something wrong but because everything wasn't right.

"I don't get it. You've had a string of women, and they've all been pretty perfect."

Mac didn't get it. How could she when she was all about the women in front of her? "Not perfect for me."

"Maybe your standards are too high. Do you even know what you're looking for?"

That was one of the better questions Mac had asked in the near-constant interrogation of her love life, and Rix didn't have a ready answer because she didn't know herself. "I'll know when I find her."

"But there's a list she has to tick, isn't there? It's not like you're giving every woman an equal chance."

"Is that what you're doing?"

Mac laughed. "I'm equal opportunities, bud."

Rix drummed her fingers on the table. "I have to call bullshit on that, Mac. You size a woman up to your perceived measurements of perfection as soon as you meet them. You've got a mental tape measure, and if they don't fit your idea of an ideal woman, you don't give them a second look."

"I can't help that I appreciate symmetry. Beauty to me is 38-22-38."

"Pah. You've been indoctrinated by—"

"Nope." Mac raised her hand. "No politics tonight. Let's talk about something else, or you'll wonder why you're my best friend at all."

"I wonder that more than you know."

Mac averted her eyes for a moment longer than Rix expected. Had she hit a nerve and pierced Mac's armor? Rix thought Mac had long been desensitized to the effects of others' thoughts. Before she could consider whether or not to say she was joking, the waitress returned with their food, and Mac's demeanor brightened again, especially when the waitress slipped a card beneath Mac's fingers before she left again.

"Christ, your life is like an episode of *The L Word* on constant repeat," Rix said after Mac showed her the card with Lily and a cell number on it, complete with a kiss and call me.

Mac didn't respond and pocketed the card. "Didn't you start casting for your next project today?"

Rix sliced into the cooked-to-perfection slab of beef and took a bite before answering. She closed her eyes and chewed slowly. After her last doctor's appointment, she didn't know how long she might be able to keep eating red meat, so she was enjoying every steak as though it might really be her last one. She washed it down with a sip of wine and exhaled as pleasure rippled from her mouth to her stomach and brain.

"Earth to Rix? If you enjoyed your women like you enjoy your steak, you might not be so lonely."

Mac's words came with a verbal sting that felt a little like payback for Rix's jibe at their friendship. She ignored it and happily switched to recalling her earlier meeting with Layla, Rachel, and her casting director, Jude, though it was thoughts of Layla that had almost seen her roll over Jesse in the valet area. "Yeah, we did, and it went well. We might not even bother with callbacks for some of the parts. Jude did a great job of calls to certain actors. I expect we'll be finished a day early at the rate we're going."

"Did you end up letting Layla Adams in on casting or not? I remember you saying you were considering it. I thought it'd be a mistake then, and now that I've worked with her, I know it would be."

"What makes you say that?" Rix asked, knowing the answer but wanting to hear it from Mac's point of view. She'd had the gossip version courtesy of Jack's connections to the production team, but it'd be interesting to hear Mac's take on the situation and if she admitted to being the ogre everyone had been calling her.

"She's got ideas above her station." Mac stabbed a chunk of her steak and shoved it into her mouth. "We got the final scene down, and the girls did a great job but was Ms. Adams happy? No, she was not. She was mouthing off to her best buddy that the dailies would show what a poor job they'd done." She speared another piece of meat and waved it toward Rix. "Marianne and Teri, we're talking about here. How many movies have they done between them? And Ms. Adams comes on her first movie set and tries to tell them how to act."

Rix raised her eyebrows. Rachel wouldn't be happy about any intervention from a script writer—original author or not—and neither would Rix. Layla had come across as invested in their project, and Rix suspected she had high standards and a particular vision when it came to pivotal scenes for her characters. She'd created them after all, but she'd have to learn that TV and movies were an ensemble creation, and there was no room for her to be precious about her books, let alone try to do the jobs of others. Rix would find ways of handling Layla if she had to. But that wasn't the sum of what she'd heard from Jack's gossip mill. "Was that it? How did the rest of the filming go?"

Mac harrumphed and filled her face with another forkful of food. Clearly there was plenty more to tell.

She swallowed, emptied her glass, and refilled it. "Suffice it to say she was pretty opinionated and tough to take."

Rix considered how Layla had presented herself that morning, and for the remainder of the day throughout casting. She'd been far from meek, but she hadn't been domineering or inflexible either. And, watching her pace outside the building on the phone, she'd appeared more than a little nervous. Rix certainly hadn't found her "tough to take" at all. On the contrary, Rix had thoroughly enjoyed her company. "She didn't suffer your bullshit lightly?"

Mac put her cutlery down and jutted her chin. "What do you mean by that?

"Your approach isn't for everybody." Rix had tried to have this conversation a few times before, and it had never gone well. She'd left it alone for a while now, but for some reason, she felt rather protective over Layla and maybe Mac was finally ready to hear some criticism. According to Jack's gossip, Layla could handle herself and didn't need Rix's interference, but it was too late. Her natural desire to protect had kicked in.

"I'm the one with two Oscars on my mantelpiece," Mac said. "I think they're evidence enough that my 'approach' works just fine."

Rix clenched her jaw. Mac always went to the trophy comparison when cornered. Rix wasn't denying she made great films; it was the way she treated everybody on set that was the obvious problem. "The end product doesn't always justify the way you get there, Mac." Rix pulled from her college memories; Mac hadn't always been this way, and Rix could only think that the pressure to perform after her first Oscar had forced the change.

Mac nodded slowly. "I know what this is about. You've got the hots for Layla Adams, and she's laid on some sob story you couldn't resist, and you're coming to her rescue like a good butch should. Is that about the size of it?"

"That's—"

"I should've seen this one coming. She's just your type, all femme and curves, and lipstick and heels. All ice and steel. But I'm not worried. You'll soon measure her against your impossible scales of perfection, and she'll fall plenty short on most of them. Then you'll see I was right all along."

"What do *you* mean by that?" Rix rested her knife on the plate and gripped the stem of her wine glass so hard that her trimmed fingernails dug into her palm.

"C'mon, bud, you know what I'm talking about. It's why you're still single." Mac held up her hands. "Look, we don't see each other enough to spend this time quarreling." She picked up her glass and clinked it to Rix's. "Let's celebrate the start of your new show and toast its inevitable success."

Rix relaxed the hold on her glass and smiled. Despite her growing bad reputation, Mac's support for Rix had never wavered, professionally or personally, and that was something to be grateful for. Rix could count on Mac, always, and that was a rare thing in Hollywood where so-called friendships and allegiances changed according to TV ratings and box office numbers. Mac was wrong though; she didn't have the hots for Layla. Rix admired her body of work, first and foremost. She wouldn't deny that Layla was attractive—she'd have to be dead not to see that—but theirs was a professional relationship, and Rix had no intention of ever being one of those studio executives who took advantage of their position for meaningless sex. That was something she'd never been interested in anyway. She wanted a connection: something deep, and honest, and forever: just like the characters in Layla's books found.

Chapter Five

LAYLA TAPPED THE neck of her light beer. "We can't stay out late. We both have a big day tomorrow."

"And we won't, but we're celebrating." Syd gently nudged Layla's shoulder. "Tell me everything. I hear Rix Reardon is super smooth and sophisticated. Is she hot? Do you think she's sexy? Is she going to be easier to work with than Mac Mitchell?"

"Whoa, slow down." Heat prickled Layla's neck at Syd's line of questioning. She didn't want to think about Rix that way. Just because she was a dapper butch, one of Layla's favorite kinds of lesbian, it didn't mean she would let her professionalism suffer. "The initial meeting went well until I found out that Rachel Harari wasn't going to be bulking up as initially promised."

Syd frowned. "That doesn't sound like Rachel. What happened?"

Layla relayed the story, including her reaction and, as she did, realized she'd been more than a little petulant.

"You know Rix was right, don't you?" Syd popped a few wasabi beans from the small dish on their table. "You have to earn your stripes, babe. You can't show up to your first production meeting and tell the director how it's going to be."

"I know, I know. And when I was challenging her, I couldn't believe what was coming out of my mouth. But she'd made me feel so at ease that I didn't want to lie to her. She said she wanted us to be comfortable working together and for me, that means honesty even if it's painful. And I came around to her way of thinking anyway. It wasn't like she was 'my way or the highway,' but she *was* all alpha, and it did make me a little gooey, I'll admit."

Syd raised her eyebrows in that annoyingly knowing way she'd been doing since college. "Mac was alpha, and you didn't like that at all. How was this different?"

"Rix didn't do it in the same way. She wasn't overbearing or aggressive." Layla liked her. And the way she'd meticulously collected the toppings from her pastry rather than flick them all over the floor spoke of a healthy respect for other people. She liked her quite a lot and had a feeling she was going to enjoy working with her immensely. Rix wasn't like Mac at all, and that was a damn good thing.

"Gooey, huh?"

And there went Syd's eyebrows again. Layla took a long pull on her bottle, more to give her time to gather her thoughts than for the taste of the beer. "Not that kind of gooey." And she had every intention of keeping it that way. "You've warned me about getting involved with co-workers and how it's unhealthy; why are you changing your tune now?"

"Wait up. One thing at a time—how many kinds of gooey are there, and which one did you go?"

Layla waved her away and picked at the edge of the plastic label on her bottle for a moment before catching herself. She didn't want to break her nail or chip her polish. Rix obviously had no such worries; her hands had been surprisingly rough, like she was a manual laborer rather than a director. She should stop that right now. Thinking about Rix's hands was definitely not the avenue she wished to travel. "You know what I mean. A commanding respect kind of gooey." Layla flicked a stray few hairs from her eyes, slightly frustrated with her vocabulary and repeated use of "gooey."

Syd gave her a crooked smile and her expression made it clear that she didn't want to believe Layla's explanation.

"I don't recall ever saying that getting involved with co-workers was unhealthy; I simply said it made things complicated." Syd stretched out her hands. "I need a manicure. How about you?"

"Huh, a subtle change of topic." Layla allowed it and inspected her nails. If she didn't talk about Rix, then she wouldn't think about Rix. Right? "I'll make an appointment. Do you have work next week?"

Syd scrunched her nose. "I've got a couple of auditions but nothing solid. Aren't you working?"

Syd sounded a little forlorn, but she usually told Layla if she had something on her mind she needed to discuss, which was rare since she was always so upbeat and positive. Maybe she was imagining it. "Rix thinks the casting will be complete by Monday, and the writing team aren't scheduled to meet up until the end of the week. She's bringing everything forward to get as much filming in as possible before Rachel has to break for her other movie. It's going to get hectic soon but next week is relatively open for now." Layla reached across the table and lightly squeezed Syd's forearm. "Are you okay?"

Syd laid her hand over Layla's. "What do you mean?"

"I don't know… You feel a little low." Layla couldn't give her more than that. She just had a sense that not all was right in Syd's world.

Syd tapped Layla's hand and retreated, picked up her beer, and took a quick swig. "Nah, it's nothing. Come on, we're supposed to be having fun. I don't want to bring you down."

"There is something wrong then?" Layla squeezed Syd's arm again, glad that she'd picked up on it. Syd was always so in tune with Layla and her feelings, but it was an uncommon occurrence that Syd needed a deep and meaningful talk. "I can't enjoy myself if I know you're unhappy. Spill. Telling me about it might help."

Syd blew out a long breath and rolled her eyes. "And I suppose you're not going to let it go?"

Layla shook her head. "No, ma'am."

"Hey, less of the ma'am, I'm—"

"Old enough to be called ma'am." She let go of Syd's arm and sipped her beer, allowing Syd the time to talk.

Syd shifted her beer around the table in lazy circles. "I guess I'm seriously considering what my future holds. I was doing okay in New York; I was making an okay living, and I was doing what I loved…"

The pause Syd left extended long enough that Layla figured she was required to interject. She'd traveled to see every one of Syd's plays in her eight-year stint off-Broadway and had enjoyed all of them—some more than others, and some had made her laugh because they were tragedies in more than the Shakespearean sense. But it was exactly like Syd had just said; despite the quality, it was clear to anyone who watched that she loved treading the boards and performing *and* she was good at it. Her co-stars, the playwrights, and directors were often the problem, but Syd was a quality actress. "Are you thinking about going back to New York?"

"No. I like it here. The sunshine's good for my soul, and I hated the New York winters."

Layla tried to keep her sigh of relief from escaping her lips. She'd moved from Colorado to LA to be closer to Syd, and it was Syd who had convinced her to get a Hollywood agent when she'd been happy holed up in her little apartment, tapping away on her keyboard and sending manuscripts to her British publisher in Westminster. Guidance from her editor had been far easier to cope with than direction from Mac Mitchell. She chided herself; she wasn't sticking around just because of Syd. The move had lit a fire and set her ambition burning for the pursuit of mainstream success. But she would be lonely if Syd decided to leave. "If you're not tempted to return to the East Coast, are you thinking of London? Do they even have a Broadway?"

Syd laughed hard. "They have the West End, and some say it's the pinnacle of theater, darling."

Layla grinned at Syd's perfect hoity toity English accent. "And you want to desert us for the Brits?" Christ, New York would be a trek, but Layla didn't even have a passport to get over to Europe. She kicked herself again for making this about her.

"No, I'm not doing that either. I guess I'm just wondering if acting makes me happy anymore."

Layla hadn't expected that. Syd's positivity about her career choice had never faltered before, at least not to Layla's knowledge. "You're not doubting your talent, are you? Because you shouldn't be—"

Syd clasped Layla's hands and shook her head. "You know me better than that, babe. I know my self-worth, my strengths, *and* my weaknesses. I'm more than good enough to earn a living out here, but I'm not sure that I want to—ooh, hello."

Layla followed Syd's gaze to the focus of her sudden magpie-like attention switch. She recognized Rix's assistant, Jack, with a bunch of other people she'd seen at Rix's office throughout the day, including a cute girl she'd pegged as family. She offered a hesitant wave when Jack looked across and saw her. Both he and the cutie politely returned the greeting and smiled before the group moved toward the bar.

"You know them?" Syd asked.

"Not really. Jack is Rix's number one, and he talked to me a little bit, mostly to chastise me for being late for the meeting." She never did apologize for being late to Rix, and her charm offensive fell by the wayside as soon as the conversation about Rachel began. "And the pretty girl is one of the agent's assistants. I had a quick conversation with her in the restroom. Her name is Ella, but I only saw the others in passing."

"They're all pretty, don't you think?"

"You do say there's something attractive in almost every person." Layla didn't see life the same way. She wished she did, but she knew her type—she had several—and she stuck to them almost rigidly.

"Tell me more about Jack."

Ah, now Layla saw the reason for her friend's instant turn of attention. Jack was handsome, for a guy, which she could appreciate but couldn't go for. Layla was all about the women and always had been. "Sorry to disappoint you, but I can't tell you much. He seems nice, but I didn't spend much time with him. He didn't really leave Rix's side all day once we started the casting meetings, but he didn't make much of an effort to talk to me, other than in polite conversation."

"Do you think he might be gay?"

Layla scoffed. "Why would I think that? Just because he didn't hit on me?" She emptied her beer and looked around for a waitress, but it looked like there might not be any table service. When she turned back to the table, Syd's eyes were wide and her lips were pursed the way she did when she was expecting more information. "I have no idea whether he's gay or not. My radar is tuned specifically for women. I'm afraid it's not quite as universal as yours. Anyway, isn't he a little young for you?"

"I want to kiss him, not marry him, and don't be such an ageist. Will he come over and say hi?"

"I doubt it, and he definitely won't if you carry on looking at him like you want to devour him." She'd only just finished her sentence when Jack turned from the bar and came over to their table with two of the beers they'd been drinking and one of his own. Ella followed behind him and made brief eye contact with Layla.

Jack placed the bottles on the table and smiled, accentuating the sweet little dimples in his cheeks that Layla hadn't noticed despite spending most of the day in his company.

"I thought you might be celebrating tonight," he said. "Did you have a good day?"

Layla wasn't sure what she was expecting him to say, but that wasn't it. Though she hadn't thought he'd come over at all, let alone bring beers and a possible love interest. "It was interesting."

He arched his brow and tilted his head slightly. "Interesting? That's a muted response. I would've thought it was a great day compared to your movie with Mac."

Layla put her head in her hands. "Is there anyone who *doesn't* know all about what happened on that set?"

Syd rubbed her back. "Oh, honey, I told you how the rumor mill worked here. Everybody knows everything about everyone."

Jack laughed. "I don't know that it's quite like that, but you're not far off."

Layla lifted her head, realizing she hadn't introduced them. Syd's light kick to her shin had the same effect. "Jack, meet Syd. Syd, this is Jack." She looked beyond him to Ella, who looked like she was thinking she might've made a mistake by accompanying Jack. "Sorry, Ella. I'm new, and I have no idea about anything. Forgive me?"

Ella gave her a small smile and shifted around Jack to stand beside Layla. "Don't worry. We all felt like that when we started. You'll soon get used to it and find your rhythm."

Layla sipped at the beer Jack had brought. "I hope so. I'm not the most patient of people."

Syd exaggerated a near-choke on her drink. "You think?"

Layla swiped at her, but Syd evaded her with a feint to the right that resulted in her being pressed against Jack's chest. Jack caught her and grinned, and his cute little dimples caught Layla's attention again. She preferred chin dimples; all the best superheroes had chin dimples. Come to think of it, Rix had one too.

Syd seemed to make no attempt to move, and Layla tutted at her blatant flirting. Finally, Syd pushed herself away, and Layla heard her murmur of appreciation at the apparent firmness of Jack's pecs. His cheeks flushed, and he straightened his shirt. Uncharitably, Layla thought that Syd would ruin him and vaguely wished he hadn't come over to join them. He had no idea what he might be getting himself into, and he seemed so naïve and sweet: two things she wouldn't have called him after their earlier meeting. The feel of Ella's hand on the small of her back had her recalling that wish. Ella may not have come over alone, and that would've been an opportunity lost.

But shouldn't she be establishing boundaries to maintain her professionalism? Ella didn't work for Rix, so Layla figured that made it okay. And if she was going to be working fifteen hours a day on set, this might be her last chance to meet someone interesting for a while. It was about time she started looking again. New city, new woman. She'd given her last relationship time enough to fade.

"So, Layla," Jack said after he'd pulled up a chair and sat beside Syd, "explain 'interesting' to me."

Boundaries with Jack, however, *were* essential. His loyalties lay with Rix, and she suspected he would share any and all tidbits of info with his boss. She shook her head. "I don't think it's a good idea for me to say anything on the grounds you might use it against me." She was only half-joking, but she received another kick from Syd, though it wasn't quite as gentle as the first.

Jack clasped his hands to his chest. "You think I'm a spy?"

"I've got a feeling you might be the nexus of the gossip line running straight to Rix, yes."

Jack laughed. "I have no idea what nexus means, but I like it. I want it to be my new surname to go with my new first name: Jack Nexus."

Ella placed her hand on his upper arm. "It's a movie star name, for sure."

"What did your parents name you that was so bad you changed it?" Syd grasped Jack's other arm and ran her fingers along his bicep. "Did they name you after Grandpappy Walter? Or something wild and hippy like Atlas? You've got the body to carry that one."

Jack placed his hand over Syd's and met her gaze. "Melissa."

Syd dropped her eyes and shook her head. "Would you mind just helping me take my foot out of my mouth, please?"

Jack grinned. "Absolutely." He pretended to help Syd pull something from her mouth and winked at Syd before he turned back to Layla. "I promise I'm no spy. And I can assure you, Rix would never grill me about tonight even if I told her I'd had drinks with you."

Layla narrowed her eyes. "Mm, but you would say that, wouldn't you? No good spy ever fessed up to being a spy, did they?"

Jack shrugged. "I suppose not. I won't push if you don't want to talk about it…" he said in a way that seemed to mean he probably would.

Layla sighed over-dramatically. She had a good feeling about him, and she almost always listened to her intuition. It wasn't like she had anything bad to say about Rix anyway. "Okay, on the assumption that you're not a treacherous snoop, what I mean by interesting is that it wasn't what I expected it to be."

"What were you expecting?" Ella asked.

She was tracing light circles at the base of Layla's spine, making it hard to concentrate on words. "That's just it. I'm not sure what I was expecting."

"Were you hoping for more control?" Jack asked softly.

Yes, that was exactly it. "Maybe… I don't know why." Layla motioned toward her friend. "Syd told me what to expect. And I know I'm extremely lucky to even be invited to work on the show and that hardly happens unless you're some huge author like Gaiman." She clasped her hands together and put them in her lap, overcome with self-judgment and self-recriminations. She was being peevish when she should simply be grateful.

"Of course you feel like that." Jack reached over the table, took her hands, and squeezed lightly. "You're God when you write a book, aren't you? You get to decide everything: whether your characters live or die; whether or not they enjoy life; even what they eat and drink. But the movies and TV aren't like that. It's a family—that's what Rix says. She always goes all out to make sure people feel valued and included, but that doesn't mean people always get what they want. Just like you didn't when you were a kid with your own family."

Layla pulled one of her hands from Jack's grasp and rubbed her forehead. "How *old* are you? You're like some Buddhist guru."

Jack's dimples deepened when he smiled. "How old do you think I am?"

"Nope, I hate guessing games." Layla took a long pull from her beer. "Syd, you like guessing games. How old is Jack?"

Syd wiggled her eyebrows and winked at him. "Old enough."

"Cop out." Layla swatted at her and again, she fell against Jack's chest, though she stayed a little longer this time, just in case her intentions weren't crystal clear. Jack would have to be pretty oblivious not to realize.

He put his arm around Syd and pulled her closer. "Aw, leave your friend alone. She seems fragile."

Layla all but snorted. "You'll soon find out that's not the case if you stick around for more than one drink."

Jack tilted his head to make eye contact with Syd. "I'd like to, if that's okay with you."

Syd looked across to Layla, her expression clearly seeking her approval. Layla could tell Jack's mix of bravado and sweetness was catnip, and she'd never been one to curtail Syd's ardor. And she'd brightened considerably since Jack and Ella joined them, though Layla would file away their conversation as "to be continued."

"We'd really like for both of you to stay if your friends don't mind." Layla gestured to the group Jack and Ella had come in with. "Or we could get a bigger table, and they could join us too."

"That'd be great," Ella said and stood. "I think Teddi knows the manager; I bet they can get a booth on the mezzanine."

While Ella made arrangements and Syd set about getting to know Jack, Layla allowed herself a moment to think about what he'd said about Rix and family. He'd been spot on about the control issue, making her wonder if he was a writer too. He'd softened and sounded almost wistful when he spoke about Rix. It was obvious that she was more than a mentor to him; perhaps she was more his family. Layla had a feeling Rix simply made people feel that way: wanted, cherished, valued. Hearing Jack talk about her made Layla more determined to set aside her unreasonable desire for full control over her word babies and trust Rix to take the helm, as was her right as the director. Ten years ago, she'd never imagined her words would live outside her own computer, let alone on e-books and paper worldwide. To have the worlds she'd created brought to life by professional actors to be broadcast across the country was a dream, and one she didn't want to jeopardize by not learning her role in her new environment. She wanted this. Every time Syd pushed Layla out of her comfort zone, it was into something she didn't realize she'd wanted. It had been the same when Syd had submitted one of her novels to a publisher and it had been accepted; Layla hadn't wanted it, but once she was involved in the process, it had been all-consuming, and all she desired was to be successful, to be the best.

And now it was the same again. She wanted to be the best scriptwriter in Hollywood, not just for LGBTQ content, but for everyone. She wanted her own version of the Skywalker Ranch, the product of decades of tapping into the zeitgeist and coming up with gold. She wouldn't get it if she butted heads with respected directors like Rix Reardon.

Gentle pressure at the base of her back and warm breath on her neck made her jump out of her thoughts.

Ella leaned in closer. "Teddi got us a private space upstairs." She offered her arm. "Come with?"

"I'd love to." Layla picked up her beer with one hand and put her other arm through Ella's. Syd was already out of her seat, her hand in Jack's. In her stilettos, she was easily six inches taller than him, but Syd was partial to having her lover look up to her so the difference in height would suit her enormously.

Layla smiled. The night had taken an interesting turn, and she was looking forward to getting to know Ella better. They joined Jack's group in a plush, semi-circular VIP-type area just as a waiter brought two bottles of wine and a tray of glasses.

After the waiter had poured some into every glass and handed them to each of the group, Ella stood. "We're celebrating tonight. We can't afford Dom Perignon, but we've all chipped in for the house bubbly." Ella raised her glass and looked directly at Layla. "Here's to Layla Adams, newly-minted Hollywood screenwriter and esteemed author, and to new friendships and more." She winked and downed her drink in one go to raucous cheers from the group.

Layla took a sip from her own glass, trying to swallow down the rising ball of surprise emotion in her throat. It'd been three months since she'd moved in with Syd, and she'd been so busy with Mac's movie that she'd barely socialized. With Syd at auditions and on jobs most of the time, she'd begun to feel rather lonely. One day in Rix's employ and suddenly she was surrounded by ten people who looked genuinely happy to be in her company, one of whom seemed to have her sights set on something more than friendship. Layla returned Ella's lustful look with interest. It was about time she started having some serious fun, and Ella appeared to be just the kind of person to do that with.

Chapter Six

RIX LOOKED IN the mirror as she adjusted her tank top, thinking that she should've gone with something a little looser. She'd made the same mistake the last time she'd done this team building day, and every time she'd reached up when belaying or climbing, her tank top had reached up with her. A knock sounded on the bathroom door.

"Ms. Reardon?"

"Come in, Jack."

He held a Nike bag up, as if for inspection. "I remember six months ago," he said.

Rix took the bag and pulled out a roomy, sleeveless T-shirt. "I am ever grateful that you came to work for me, Jack."

He cast his eyes to the floor briefly. "Not as grateful as I am. They've moved the buses to the front of the building for you. Almost everyone is ready and waiting."

"Who's not here yet?" she asked, perhaps a little too quickly and with far too much interest. She hoped Jack wouldn't notice, though even if he did, she knew he wouldn't comment.

He tapped on his iPad, glued as usual to his left hand. "Rachel, Annabelle, and Layla...but I've had no apologies, and it's still early."

She nodded and he left. She glanced at her watch; Jack was right, of course. The invitation had been for nine, and it was only half past eight. Unless Jack had briefed them about her penchant for punctuality, she couldn't really expect anyone to be there until the clock actually struck nine. She'd worked with the rest of the cast and crew on other projects, hence why they were already gathered downstairs, but the three Jack mentioned were new to this event. She stared at her reflection and laughed at herself. While she absolutely wanted to spend this time with Annabelle and Rachel, it was Layla she was most excited to get to know. "It's just because I like her books."

She changed into the top Jack had brought her—it fit perfectly, of course—and ran her fingers through her short hair. Layla's adventure books always featured a butch and if there was only one hero, it was the butch character. But her romances employed the rainbow gamut of leads, so it was impossible to tell which coupling Layla preferred, if indeed she had a preference at all. Rix blew out a breath, slightly irritated about the discussion she was having with herself. It didn't matter what kind of partner Layla Adams was interested in, because they were about to be colleagues and the only interest Rix should have was professional. Layla's personal life was of no concern or consequence to Rix, as long as it didn't distract her from her work. And judging from her seriousness in their first meeting, Rix had a feeling that Layla would never let her personal life interfere with her job.

She went back into her office, pulled on a lightweight training top and tucked her sunglasses in the neck of her tee. "Jack?"

With the speed of a phantom, he stood in the doorway. "Yes, Ms. Reardon?"

"Do you know who's managing the center today?"

"George."

"I thought he was on vacation?"

"He was, but he came back early so he could be there today."

"Because of this, I'll bet." Rix shook her head. "Maybe next time, we should just turn up unannounced. I told him we'd be all right without him there."

Jack offered a small smile. "Your cast and crew days are their biggest events of the year, and you're their most generous donor; he'd never miss one." Jack tilted his head slightly. "You *know* that."

Rix shrugged. "But that poor guy never seems to get the time for a real vacation. His husband was bending my ear about it at the last gala dinner."

"You hold these events three to four times a year, Ms. Reardon. That leaves a lot of other days for vacations if he really wanted one. George loves what he does, and everybody loves George for what he does—including me."

Knowing Jack's background and his own time at the center, she couldn't argue with his assessment, and she adored George for his commitment. "Okay." She picked up her phone, slipped it into her shorts pocket, and zipped it closed. "Let's go."

When they got downstairs and out into the parking lot, the four buses were in a neat line, and Rix scanned the windows for Layla. She hoped Jack would've put her on the lead bus with Rix, but she hadn't made a specific request, and she always insisted on him mixing everyone up rather than keeping all the different departments in their own comfortable cliques. The music was already pumping, and some of the crew were dancing in the aisles. She took in a deep breath of hot LA air and sighed contentedly. This ritual she'd established to kick off every new project had become so legendary that Jack managed a long waiting list of production staff apparently desperate to work with them and experience the family atmosphere Rix liked to cultivate on set.

She was sure Layla would appreciate it after working with Mac. *Everyone* would appreciate it. No need to focus on the cute author she wouldn't admit she had a little crush on. Maybe more accurately, it was Layla's way with words she valued. And Rix could handle it anyway, just like she handled every other vague attraction she'd had to people she worked with. And she'd worked with some truly beautiful women, in mind and body. It was a rare occasion that she'd succumbed to the interest that usually faded once they stopped working together. Unlike the actors she'd worked with who seemed to fall in love, marry, and divorce their co-stars within a year.

"Everybody's here and ready when you are, Ms. Reardon."

"Excellent." Rix boarded the lead bus and made her way down to the backseat, always the coveted spot no matter how old people were, hand-slapping and high-fiving as many of her team as she could. She settled in beside some of the art and visual crew while Jack and his ever-present iPad remained at the front.

She'd scanned for Layla on the way to her seat to no avail and spent no more time searching for her once she was at the back. Instead, she focused wholly on the people around her. She despised people who were always looking over or around whoever they were talking to for someone more influential or worthy or useful, and that happened a lot in Hollywood, with so many people desperate to find a leg up in the business.

The two-mile journey took less than ten minutes, and Rix happily waved everyone else off the bus before she alighted.

George greeted her with open arms and a wide grin. "Well, if it isn't my favorite director."

She hugged him tightly then held him at arms' length. "You look great, but I think you'd look better if you were relaxing on a beach somewhere instead of babysitting us today."

He took her hands from his shoulders and squeezed them. "I've never missed one of these, and I don't intend to start now." He motioned for a group of five young people to come with him, hooked his arm through hers, and led her into the building.

"Jack told me you'd flown home from vacation to be here. I can see Jim hiring an assassin for me, and soon."

"Don't be crazy. Jim knew what he was getting himself into when he proposed. It was even in my vows that I was already married to this place."

Rix chuckled. "I remember, but everyone kind of thought you were joking."

George stopped and gestured around the spectacular glass atrium of the main reception area. "Look at this place," he said and motioned toward the tropical garden in the center of the giant space. "This is paradise. I don't need to vacation."

Rix huffed, quite certain that she couldn't marry someone quite so exclusively dedicated to their work but creating and maintaining a vital haven like this needed that singular drive. "I think Jim would disagree. You've got to squeeze out the sponge sometime, George."

He rolled his eyes and pulled her along. "When you love your work like I love my work, there is no sponge. Are we starting with some climbing and abseiling? You're going to love the new wall—it's made of glass colored in every flag of the community. It's fifty feet wide and three hundred and three feet tall, making it the largest climbing wall in the world."

"Sounds hardcore." Rix enjoyed bouldering, but she wasn't sure she was up to that kind of elevation.

He squeezed her arm as they walked. "Don't worry. There are elevators to the top so you can abseil down without all the hard work."

"I was thinking of other people who might not have climbed before. I'm up for the challenge." She said the words with as much bravado as she could muster, knowing that she'd have to do it.

George grinned. "I knew you would be. You can make the first climb and show them all how it's done." They rounded the corner, and George came to a halt. "Here it is."

Rix looked up…and up, and up still further and gulped so hard it almost hurt her throat. The vibrant colors, the pink, burgundy, and purple, all of them, shone like harlequin gems against a sky so blue, it almost looked like a hologram.

"Wow."

Rix turned at the sound of Layla's voice and smiled. "Hey. Glad you could make it." She lost her words for a moment while she swept her gaze over Layla's outfit of white chino shorts, cute white sneakers, and a flowy, maroon tank top. Her curly hair was caught up in a ponytail revealing an entirely kissable neck, which Rix somehow hadn't noticed at their meeting.

"Did I not dress right? Jack said casual and sporty." She tugged at her top and wrinkled her nose. "This is as sporty as I get."

"No. Sorry, yes, you look great. I mean, it's perfect." Rix looked to the sky. *Somebody help me.* "George, this is Layla Adams, the author of the books we're making into a TV show."

"What heathen-like creature do you take me for, Rix?" George waved his hand toward Rix dismissively then did a little bow toward Layla, took her hand, and kissed her knuckles. "Ms. Adams, it's truly a pleasure to meet you. Your characterization of young people and adults across the whole LGBTQIA spectrum is incredible. We have every one of your books in our library here. Is there any chance I could press you to sign them?"

Layla looked genuinely nonplussed by George's show of rather dramatic appreciation and didn't respond immediately. Rix felt honor-bound to step into the silence. "You have to excuse George, Layla. He missed his calling on the stage."

George swatted Rix's shoulder and Layla laughed. Rix hoped her interjection had relaxed her somewhat.

"I'd love to, thank you for asking." Layla gestured around the building. "This place is amazing. I can't believe all the facilities you've got here. It's like a mini city."

"I can give you the full tour if you'd like. We've just opened a block of affordable accommodation for young people, and we've broken ground for an extension to build assisted living for older LGBTQIA people."

"That would be wonderful." Layla glanced at Rix. "You don't mind, do you?"

Rix shook her head. "The guided tour is part of the day's activities, so I definitely don't mind." She looked back up at the climbing wall, conscious she could barely see its peak and not overly eager to tackle it just yet. "I'll be part of the first group too. I've only seen the plans for the assisted living quarters. It'll be nice to see the actual space and get a feel for what you're creating."

George linked arms with them both. "Since your hard work at the last gala practically paid for the whole venture, I think that's a perfect idea."

"I've organized the first fifty people to come with you on that," Jack said.

Rix hadn't noticed that Jack had joined them. When she turned toward him, the fifty people he was talking about were right behind him, and Rix hadn't noticed their arrival either. That was rude. This day was for everyone, and she was getting carried away with entertaining Layla. Maybe she shouldn't be going with the first group, but it would look weird if she pulled out now.

George tugged her arm. "Someone else can do the first climb. You'll just have to beat their time. Macey, will you and the team take care of the first group of climbers, please?"

Rix looked toward the small group of instructors George spoke to, dressed in leggings, shorts, T-shirts, and tank tops that matched the rainbow climbing wall. Jack was already moving toward them and motioning to another group from their company to follow him to the wall. He had this, of course, meaning Rix could concentrate on fostering the family environment she wanted. Rix turned back to her own group of fifty plus Layla and waved. "Okay, let's go exploring."

George instructed his five youngsters and they dispersed among Rix's group. "Follow me," he said in a sing-song voice and led the way, narrating as he went, with his youngsters parroting his commentary to each of their small groups.

As they progressed around the enormous complex of buildings, Rix pulled away from George to navigate through each of the five small groups of her crew. She'd always been good with names, but it was a point of pride for her to make sure she memorized those of everyone in her team, her extended family. It took a village to make a film and especially a TV series, and each person played a vital part. Of course, the cast were the glamorous element, and big-ticket positions like the producer and editor garnered the most kudos, but Rix valued the make-up artists and the runners just as much.

And as she made her rounds, she pushed thoughts of Layla to the back of her mind, where they belonged, so she could fully concentrate on the people she was talking to.

George eventually made it to the library, his final stop before the climbing wall, and Rix returned to the front of her group. She clapped along with everyone else when he showed them the shelves bulging with LGBTQ fiction from queer authors all around the world, and the noise grew considerably when he pointed out Layla's contribution, numbering eighteen. She looked genuinely touched and slightly embarrassed by the attention. If her career really took off in Hollywood, would she be able to handle the accompanying pressure? This town broke far more people than it made. Rix was overcome with the urge to protect her from the darker side of the business. Okay, maybe not protect—Layla had shown that she could take care of herself and others under Mac's reign. Maybe she could offer to mentor her instead. Rix would certainly have appreciated a guide when she started out. She sighed and tried to analyze her motives. Who was she actually thinking such an arrangement would benefit? Was she, a grown-ass woman in her mid-forties, fan-girling on Layla, and she was looking for any excuse to spend extra time with her? Or was it her words and books that Rix found so appealing? Anyone who was able to write such wonderfully romantic stories, of soul mates, of people destined to be together, were bound to hold a certain appeal to Rix, given that she was in search of her own heart's destiny.

Layla ticked a lot of Rix's boxes. Yes, she had a list, a criterion of sorts—didn't everyone? —but her ongoing pursuit of the perfect woman had thus far come up short. That was what Mac's dig had been about at their dinner the other night. But what was so wrong about not settling for anything less than she thought she deserved, anyone less than she craved? The perfect relationship and the perfect woman weren't the same as perfection. That wasn't what she was looking for, and she wasn't naïve enough to think that it existed. Perfect was just as much a social construct of subjectivity as was normal. Rix was simply looking for someone who was perfect *for her*.

But that likely shouldn't be one of her newest colleagues, particularly since they'd met once, and Layla had shown zero interest in her beyond the project. Rix was being unusually directed by her hormones and perhaps even a silly romantic notion or two, but she was sure it would fade once filming began and being around Layla was her new reality rather than a novelty.

"We have a movie and TV library too, Rix." George pulled a silver marker from the inner pocket of his paisley jacket. "Plenty for you to sign there, if you wouldn't mind?"

She smiled, happy to be distracted from her errant thoughts, and took the pen. "Lead the way." She glanced toward Layla, who was leaning over a table scribbling her signature on each book in a hefty pile. Layla looked up and smiled, a hint of her shyness clear. Rix winked, and Layla returned her attention to her novels. This TV series had been a long time coming, and she couldn't wait to get started. Having Layla on set would make it a huge success, she could feel it.

Chapter Seven

LAYLA HAD BEEN dreading this but knew she'd have to deal with it at some point. Jack's open expression, as if waiting for news of a lottery win, tugged at the thread of sad inevitability deep inside. It had only taken a few dates before Layla knew it wouldn't work. Ella expected roses and red wine, rainbows and unicorns, epic wooing and paradise. The same thing happened every time she got involved with someone who was just a little *too* attached to her books, women who took her passionate prose a little too literally and expected her every sentence to be swoon worthy. And boy, was she a pillow queen of the highest order. *You write it so well, I thought you'd like to practice what you preach.* Layla had no idea which of her books that Ella had digested, but she'd somehow gotten the idea that Layla liked to give and not receive. She'd encountered the problem before; her lovers had equated the sex she wrote about to be exactly like the sex she wanted. They didn't make the same connection in her thrillers, where she wrote about murder, and drug dealers, and human traffickers. It was a very specific and inextricable link they made to Layla's preferences in the bedroom.

"Didn't she tell you? We weren't on the same page, Jack." God, did that really just come out of her mouth? So cliché. But true. And as far as she was concerned, she'd conveyed that message to Ella. So why did Jack seem to be under the impression that they were still dating?

"I don't understand. Ella suggested we have a double date this weekend at Conundrum, the new fusion restaurant in WeHo. Syd said she was up for it if you were."

Crap. She hadn't seen much of Syd over the weekend and hadn't told her that she'd passed on Ella. And Syd was uncharacteristically nervous about her fledgling relationship with Jack, like this one might have the potential to go somewhere, and she'd mentioned double dates as a possibility. Layla didn't want to let her friend down but nor did she want to spend much more time with Ella. Talk about a rock and a soft place.

"Any chance one of you could be a second on my belay?"

"Absolutely." Layla responded a tad too quickly, but she'd do anything to get away from a conversation that might stray deeper into territory she didn't wish to explore, at least not with Jack. "Sorry, Jack, can we talk about this later?" She needed to speak with Syd, and she would as soon as she got home tonight. What was belaying anyway?

"Great."

Rix took hold of her upper arm and guided her away from Jack. The firm confidence with which she maneuvered Layla around caused her to clench a little. Maybe if Ella had taken some tips from Rix, she might have stuck around a little longer.

"This is Gerri. He's a grip."

Rix motioned to a guy in tight Lycra shorts with legs skinner than Layla's arms. She didn't know what Rix needed her for yet, but she'd bet it had something to do with her lack of confidence in this guy's strength. All the grips she'd met on Mac's movie had been well-built people. Gerri didn't look like he could lug around lighting equipment all day.

"I'm taking a rope up to the top." Rix took Layla's hand and placed a multi-colored rope in her palm.

Layla raised her eyebrows and then looked up the wall to which Rix had gestured. She didn't know much about climbing—scratch that, she didn't know anything about climbing—but whatever Rix was proposing looked way too dangerous for Layla to be even partly responsible for her life. "I don't think so."

Rix frowned. "You don't think I can do it?"

Layla suppressed a smile at Rix's wounded ego expression, a surefire indication of a sweet and macho butch, if ever there was one. "I don't think *I* can do it." She held out the rope, but Rix didn't take it.

"That's partly what this day is all about, Layla. Facing your fears and doing it anyway."

Layla tutted. "That's a lovely sentiment for a fridge magnet, but it's not applicable or healthy when you're talking about the difference between life and death."

Rix laughed. "And the other part of what this day is about is building trust and family."

Layla shook her head and held her ground. "I wouldn't trust any of my family to hold the rope either. And that's not just a retort; I really wouldn't trust any of them with my life at the end of a rope. With a cigarette or beer always in one hand, they'd be little use." When she saw Rix's expression grow serious, Layla smiled. "Don't worry, I'm kidding. I don't have a dark history of neglect." Well, not neglect so much as disinterest.

Rix took a step closer and put her hands around the one Layla was holding the rope with. "Gerri will do most of the work."

Rix tugged on a funny shaped chunk of metal dangling from a totally unflattering harness-type thing around his waist and junk, making her thankful there were no kids present.

"This little doohickey does most of the work. You and Gerri will just be counterweights if I fall."

Layla let out a gasp and shook her head more firmly, dismissing her interest in Rix's rough hands holding onto her. "I'm not going to be responsible for any harm to my boss before I've even started working for her."

Rix's lips quirked in an amused smile. "Is that what you're going to call me around the studio: Boss?"

Layla bit her lip and tried to keep her expression neutral. Was Rix flirting with her? If she was, Layla liked it *and* the idea of calling her Boss. She liked that a lot. Is that what you *want* me to call you, Layla was tempted to say but didn't. Gerri's unsubtle throat-clearing drew Layla's attention back to Rix's warm hands wrapped around hers and the flimsy bit of fancy, dual-colored string in her hand that was supposed to hold Rix's solid bulk, a bulk she wouldn't mind pressing her against a wall as they kissed. *Stop.*

"You're just a safety net," Gerri said. "Chances are, Rix won't need us at all until she's abseiling down."

She sighed. It was fast becoming clear that neither of them were going to let her out of this crazy obligation. She trusted Rix's judgment. If she was willing to put her life in the hands of Gerri, who looked more like a gaunt ghost each time she glanced at him, who was Layla to argue? She looked down again at the rope and Rix's hands. "Are you sure?"

Rix squeezed one last time before she released Layla. "I'm sure."

She winked again, just like she had at the library. She'd had to look away quickly then because of its unexpected effect on her, and again, she shook off the ensuing mini swoon. Rix's confidence was undeniably attractive. "And there are first aiders close by?"

Rix grinned. "Relax and have faith."

"And of course, you climb walls like this all the time, and this whole ordeal will be over in no time?"

"Are you saying that I *don't* look like I climbs walls like this all the time?"

This was only the second time they'd met and already, Layla was beginning to recognize and enjoy Rix's various tones and her playful nature. She may be older than Layla, but she certainly hadn't relinquished her inner child. But Layla had no benchmark to measure Rix's frame against. What were climbers supposed to look like? Strong and capable. Tick, and tick. Large and dexterous hands. Soft sigh and double tick. "I'm merely asking how long this trial of terror is likely to last."

"Let's set you up in a harness and an ATC," Rix said.

She dug around in a large plastic box beside them, pulled out a spidery-strappy thing, and held it up to Layla's body.

"This should fit." Rix sank to the floor and straightened the contraption out. "Step into these hoops."

Layla took a deep breath, hoping that it sounded like she might be bored rather than a little turned on at the sight of a strong woman kneeling at her feet. But they were responsible, mature women. As far as Layla knew Rix wasn't involved with anyone, and there was no ring on Rix's finger, and this was harmless flirtation. The day was supposed to be lots of fun—it said so in the email—and Layla was merely getting into the required spirit.

She placed her feet in the circles, and Rix lifted the harness upward, stopping at her knees.

"You might want to take it from here?"

The uncertainty in Rix's voice and the shy averting of her eyes emboldened Layla. "Not particularly. I've never put one of these things on before. Seems to me that an expert like yourself should do it, especially when your life depends on its safe positioning." Layla glanced at the climbing harness Rix already had on and imagined a very different kind of harness. Heat crept up her back, and her body flushed with giddy excitement. It'd been a while since she'd felt this brazen.

Rix arched an eyebrow and a knowing look shot across her eyes. She stood, coming face to face with Layla, her lips a couple of inches away from Layla's forehead as she stared into Layla's eyes. She held her gaze as she gently pulled the harness up and onto Layla's waist.

She tugged at the strap until it was snug and inched two fingers between Layla's tank top and the harness. "That's tight enough."

"Feels like it," Layla said. "Do the thigh hoops need to be—"

"Patience. I'm getting there."

Rix broke their eye contact and fastened the thigh straps firmly, once again slipping two fingers between the harness and Layla's clothing. Her confident, firm touch sent shivers all over Layla's body, and she was forced to remind herself where they were and who they were with: over three hundred people she'd be working with over the next few months. They were *not* in Layla's bedroom about to explore the delights of a different kind of strapping. Was Rix a traditional lover or was she open to experimentation?

Rix scooted away to another box, this one full of the things Gerri had attached to his harness. She stood to her full height once more and snapped a clip onto the thick loop at the front of her harness, deftly threaded the rope through the thing Layla assumed was the ATC and joined that to the clip. Once on, Rix gave it a tug that Layla wasn't expecting, pulling her off balance. She lurched forward and had to thrust her hands against Rix's chest to prevent herself falling.

She looked up at Rix, whose playful expression was clear. Layla straightened herself without comment and busied herself tucking her tank top in, filing away the sensations that coursed through her when she pressed against Rix's body. She flicked the rope attached to her and huffed. "Now what?"

"It's easier to show you, if you don't mind me coming behind you and getting close?"

No. She didn't mind that one iota. "If it's easier." She heard a low groan from Gerri and ignored him. This was the most carefree fun she'd had in quite a while, and she'd let it run its course, thank you very much, Gerri.

"It is."

Rix came around the back of her, put her arms on either side of Layla's waist, and took hold of both ends of the rope. She pulled some of the slack in from the side attached to Gerri at the same time as her other hand pulled it on her right side. Then she crossed her left hand over onto the rope and worked her right hand to lock it off at the ATC.

"Get it?" Rix asked.

Of course she got it. "Perhaps one more time, please?"

"Sure." Rix's light laugh caressed Layla's neck. "Gerri."

Rix released her right hand, and Gerri pulled the rope through so there was slack on Layla's left side again. She repeated the action, slower this time, and talked it through. Layla was more than slightly disappointed that Rix didn't press her body up close, but there were a few people watching now and maybe she too was conscious of where they were rather than where Layla wished they were.

Was she really developing a crush on her boss on their second meeting, or was she just having some harmless fun?

"Happy?"

"I'll be happy when you're back on the ground," Layla said. "I'd like it noted that I'm participating under duress."

Rix came around to face her again and smirked. "Duly noted." She walked to the other end of the rope and fed it through her own harness, swiftly tying some complicated-looking knot before turning back to Layla. "But when I come back down, you're going up."

She turned away and had scaled ten feet of the wall before Layla could muster an answer. Not many people left her speechless, but she hadn't met many people like Rix Reardon either.

Chapter Eight

WHEN RIX ENTERED the writing room at nine a.m., everyone else was already present and seated. Thanks to the bonding day at the LGBTQ center, they looked to be chatting amicably with each other, which made her smile. A happy crew made for a much easier shoot. She took the head of the table, seated between her producer, Joanie, and Layla. Rix had asked Jack to put Layla beside her so she could get her immediate, unfiltered reaction to the table-read. Rix didn't pretend that she could read energies, but she could read people, and Layla had so far proven pretty open and easy to interpret. Layla would be a poor poker player, for sure, but Rix liked that about her. Too often, Rix had to rely on her intuition rather than take what was being said at face value. Layla was refreshing, and in more ways than her honesty. Rix had loved the banter they'd had at the event day, particularly at the bottom of the climbing wall. Banter didn't quite do their exchange justice. She couldn't deny that she'd been flirtatious, and Layla had come back at her with some playful flirtation of her own. Had they not been there with the professional audience, Rix couldn't be sure that she would've stopped herself from attempting a kiss. They'd been close enough, and it would've been so easy to have dipped her head and pressed her lips to Layla's.

She was equal parts relieved and regretful that she hadn't made a move. Romantic entanglements in a professional setting could make for accusations of favoritism, and Rix worked hard to ensure everyone felt equal on her sets. But that didn't make her attraction settle down any. The what ifs had kept her awake that night, and the sleep she did get was filled with dreams of her and Layla together in various states of undress.

Wanting Layla's reaction to the read through wasn't the only reason she'd asked Jack to arrange the seating this way; Rix wanted another extended opportunity to talk to her and get to know her further. They wouldn't be filming the series forever, and if there was a spark from Layla's side, Rix wanted to act on it once this project was over.

There probably wasn't, of course. Rix had no idea what kind of women Layla liked, or what she was looking for, or even if she was looking at all. There was almost a decade between them, and age might be an issue. To Rix, who was blessed to look younger than her years, it was just a number, but she'd been on plenty of first dates that proved it was far more than that for some people.

Rix pulled out her chair and put her script folder on the table. "Good morning, everyone." The chatter ceased, and everyone turned their attention to her. "Some of you already know how important this project is to me." She looked to Layla, who looked a little nervous, though she still smiled. "I bought the rights for this particular series of books from this talented wordsmith quite a few years ago, but the networks weren't ready for such a capable, kick-ass, almost exclusively female cast of protagonists, and I couldn't get the project funded or cast." A few cast members who were of the community nodded. They would've come up against similar prejudice most of their careers, which was why many of them had stayed in the closet so long.

"But things are changing, albeit slowly, and I'm sure the world is now hungry for a serialization of *Section Spy*." Rix motioned to the star of the show. "I was joined early on in the production of this concept by the amazingly talented Rachel Harari, and her involvement really kickstarted the funding flow." She pressed her hands together. "So thank you, Rachel, for seeing the potential in this set of stories." She glanced at Jack, who raised a questioning eyebrow, no doubt because he hadn't forgiven Rachel for almost pulling out on them, but there was no need for anybody else to know of that particular debacle. The energy was high, and Rix wanted to keep it that way.

"I started this production company to make the kind of programming I would have loved access to as a kid, and in my twenties and thirties. I want people from our community on TV and cinema screens, showing new generations that we can be everything and anything we want to be." She looked down to pick up her script folder, but as she did, she thought she caught a couple of eye rolls from Des and Burns at the corner of the table. She clenched her jaw to resist the temptation to call them out on it. Perhaps she'd just imagined it, but had she misjudged them? Nobody was supposed to be here for the paycheck alone, and this wasn't just a TV series. "Anyone who knows me knows that I feel strongly about this subject, so I'll end by asking you all to put one hundred percent into the next couple of months."

She sat to choruses of "You've got it, boss," and "Amen to that," amongst others and cast a quick glance at Des and Burns. They looked animated enough, but now she couldn't shake the possibility that it might be for show.

Layla touched her arm gently. "I hope I can live up to your expectations."

She pulled her attention from the two actors and focused on Layla, whom Rix knew was committed to the cause. "You shouldn't doubt yourself." She tapped on the leather folder holding Layla's script. "I love your screenplay. It's not often an author can switch to writing for the big screen, but you've done it effortlessly." She placed her hand over Layla's and squeezed. "You've got nothing to worry about, I promise." Rix removed her hand and pulled herself away from staring too long into Layla's soft gaze. It was a few beats before Layla moved her hand from Rix's forearm, but her imprint remained like a delicately heated kiss from the sun. *Focus.* "Okay, let's start at page one, scene one with Rach and Zeb."

***

"I'm learning very quickly not to doubt you, Rix. With or without the extra muscle, Rachel is a perfect Lane." Layla eased herself into one of Rix's low lounge chairs.

Rix pushed her chair back and came around her desk to join Layla. She collected two glasses and a bottle of whiskey from her table bar, placed them on the table alongside the chairs, and settled into the one opposite Layla. She wouldn't usually be taken by such obvious flattery, but Layla sounded sincere and given that she'd had concerns about Rachel's ability to make the portrayal realistic without the added bulk, the vindication settled with more veracity. "I'm glad to hear it." She didn't point out that she'd been in this business a lot longer than Layla, and that it would be a poor show on her part if she wasn't able to make those calls. "Drink?" Rix laughed softly when Layla checked her watch. "Do you have somewhere else to be or are you worried it's too early for the hard liquor?"

Layla crossed her legs and smiled. "I'm not sure I should answer that for fear of judgment."

Rix arched her eyebrow. It seemed their flirting had resumed now they were away from the rest of the team. "Because you're a barfly or a prohibitionist? Seems like you might be the one judging me."

Layla laughed, and the melodic sound resonated in Rix's every cell like a heartbeat of happiness. Hers was a laugh that could draw a smile from the crabbiest of old codgers.

"I still can't answer. Do you *want* me to be pro liquor or not? I can't get a sense of where your opinion lies on this issue."

Rix unscrewed the bottle and poured two fingers' worth into each glass. "Really? You don't know where I might lie on this particular issue?" She picked up both glasses and offered one to Layla. Her fingers brushed over Rix's as she took it, and Rix didn't relinquish her grip immediately, relishing the contact.

Layla looked up into Rix's eyes and sighed. "Can I have it or not?"

Was she talking about the alcohol or something else? Things had escalated pretty fast from a little harmless flirting if she was. Rix was torn between continuing to play along or pulling back. She could see no harm in putting their cards on the table this early. She'd always hated playing games, and she much preferred to know where she stood. If Layla didn't return her interest, Rix could work on controlling her attraction and move Layla firmly into the friend category—a group already fit to burst, but that was a different issue entirely, and one she didn't care to think about right now. But if the attraction was two way, they could figure out the next steps before things got too complicated.

Or perhaps she was just getting carried away.

Rix released the glass. "How did you get into writing books?" She leaned back into the chair. *Chicken.*

Layla smiled as if she knew that wasn't the real question on Rix's mind. "I'd always written stories, starting from when I was a kid. I used it as escapism, I'm told, though I didn't know it at the time."

Something, some pain, flitted across Layla's eyes so quickly that Rix would've missed it had she not been staring so intently. She glanced away, wanting to ask what Layla needed to escape from but knowing it was too early to delve into such personal issues, unless she volunteered the information. With that look and the throwaway comments she'd made about her family at the LGBTQ center, there was obviously a lot more to Layla's background than she'd shared publicly. Rix wanted Layla to confide and trust in her.

"There's that look again," Layla said before taking a sip of her whiskey.

"What look?"

"The same one you got at your event when you forced me to be a possible accomplice in your manslaughter—or should that be personslaughter?"

She'd seen that? But Rix had a great poker face. "What do you mean?"

Layla shook her head. "You think you've got a great poker face, don't you?"

How was Layla in her head? "I wipe the floor with my buddies most game nights."

Layla pressed her lips together, suggesting she was suppressing a grin. "Buddies or employees?"

"You're suggesting my *buddies* let me win?" That could never be the case. These were people who'd happily bluff their cute old grannies out of their 401K to win a hand. Sure, they'd give it back at the end of the night, but they were poor winners and sore losers.

Layla shrugged. "No?"

"No."

"You should invite me to one of your games. I'd like to play with you for money." Layla giggled. "That came out wrong. I was doing so well."

Rix smirked at her sexy word slippage. "Doing so well?"

"At keeping the conversation in safe territory." Layla took another drink, her expression rather coy.

Rix was beginning to think there was nothing safe about their conversation, or with being in the room together, alone. But she was getting some indication of Layla's feelings, which was what she wanted and why she'd invited her for a post-read through debrief. "Is that something you do with everyone? Have safe and unsafe topics of conversation?"

"Don't you?"

She had a point. There were things she did and didn't talk about with all sorts of friends and colleagues. Except for her family; she could talk about almost anything with her family. "Maybe. What are the unsafe conversations you're trying to avoid with me?"

Layla swirled the remainder of her whiskey. "Maybe it's not so much about what I want to say as what I want to do."

Rix's heart thudded against her chest, her mind whirling with thoughts of what that might include. She moved to the edge of her chair and put her glass back on the table. "Why might the things you want to do be unsafe?" Layla emptied her drink and placed the glass beside Rix's. She looked at Rix, the intensity in her eyes matching the pounding beneath Rix's ribs.

"I'm trying to build a new career here, and I can't afford any missteps. Syd says this town is particularly unforgiving and quick to judge." She edged forward on her seat until their knees almost touched.

If there was a last opportunity to pull back, it looked like this was it. But Rix's curiosity had the better of her, and there was no way she was doing anything other than encouraging Layla to share her thoughts, especially when they all but promised to be aligned with Rix's wishes. "Seems like you should let me know what you're worried about in case I can alleviate your fears." Rix placed her hands on her thighs, her fingers practically itching to slip beneath the calf-length hem of Layla's skirt and caress her skin.

"I had a fractious relationship with the director on my first movie, and it seems like everyone knows about it." Layla smoothed her skirt then matched Rix's pose, their fingertips so close, "which implies that there are no secrets in this industry. And what I want to do with you, my current director, would be more fodder for the gossip factory."

Layla's sigh whispered through Rix's hair, and her responding exhalation took with it her resolve. "Can I kiss you?"

"Please."

Rix stood, taking Layla's hands and pulling her upright. She put her hand around Layla's waist and rested it on the small of her back, drawing her close so that Layla's breasts pressed against Rix's chest. Layla traced her finger along the edge of Rix's vest then slipped her finger between the buttons of her shirt. Rix wrapped her other hand around Layla's neck and kissed her. Softly. Always softly at first, the initial contact with a woman's mouth was so deliciously intimate. Rix's sigh echoed Layla's as her body surged with desire. She kissed her harder, and Layla relaxed in her arms. She held her tighter, and Layla moaned against her lips. Rix's core throbbed when Layla slid her tongue between Rix's lips, and she squeezed Rix's ass.

"Ms. Reardon?"

Jack's voice intruded from the hallway, startling her. She thought everyone had left the building. She reluctantly released Layla and stepped away. "I'm sorry," she said and walked to her office door and opened it.

"What is it, Jack?"

"I was checking to see if you needed anything before I left for the day?"

Rix pulled the door close to her when Jack's gaze went beyond her and into the office. She regretted the move instantly, knowing it gave the wrong impression, or rather, the correct impression. Glossing over the initial cover-up, she turned back into the office. "Would you like something to eat, Layla?" Now she regretted that question, because it gave Layla a potential exit before they'd had the chance to talk about what had just happened.

"I'm not hungry, thanks," she said.

Rix turned to Jack, eager to get him to leave in case Layla chose to flee. "Could you order a mixed platter?"

"No red meat and no batter?"

Rix blew out a frustrated breath. Damn that doctor and her dietary instructions. More fool her for passing the information onto Jack so that he could order appropriately. "Fine," she said, knowing her petulance came through loud and clear. "Then go home. It's late, and it'll be another big day tomorrow."

"Of course."

If he had any less than professional thoughts about Layla being with her, he was controlled enough not to show it. She was the show writer; it made sense for her to be having extra meetings with Rix. She stopped herself. Jack had never shown himself to be anything other than discreet, and she had no reason to start doubting him now. He wouldn't question her, whatever the situation. "Thanks, Jack. And good job today."

He stood a little straighter as he tapped away on a delivery app. "Thanks, Ms. Reardon. The food will be with you in thirty minutes."

She nodded and closed the door. Layla had retaken her seat and poured them both top-ups. Rix touched her lips, still tingling from the knockout kiss she'd just shared.

"Are you on a special purge?" Layla asked.

"Doctor's orders, I'm afraid." Rix waved the issue away. "But I don't want to talk about it, if you don't mind." Because she didn't know if Layla would shy away if she knew Rix had some health issues.

"Okay," Layla said. "You said you were sorry."

Rix rushed back to her chair and dropped into it. "Not for kissing you, if that was your question. I was sorry that we were interrupted."

Layla wiped her brow. "Phew. But it was probably for the best."

"You didn't take the opportunity to leave."

"I don't want to leave. But if Jack hadn't called, I'm afraid we might already be on your couch devouring each other."

"And that would be a bad thing?" Of course it would. She'd never been one to rush into sleeping with someone…but a heavy make-out session wasn't only the realm of young people and had always been one of her favorite things. It set the tone for what the relationship might hold.

"We should talk." Layla picked up her glass and took a long drink.

"Nothing good ever starts with *those* three words." And how could they follow a kiss like that? Rix reminded herself that she'd wanted this: a direction or an ending for her feelings toward Layla. And if they weren't to be romantic, she wanted to establish a solid friendship that would mean they could work well together now and in the future, especially given how many of Layla's books she had the rights to.

"I like you, Rix. And that was a helluva kiss—"

"But you're worried what people will think if we let that *spectacular* kiss be the start of something while we're working together."

"Exactly."

"Even though people get together on movie sets all the time?" Rix held back the details of actors and crew getting married, thinking it might sound like she was coming on too strong. That, and a lot ended in divorce.

"I understand that it happens—it can be hard to keep your hands off someone you're attracted to—but I don't want to be part of the rumor mill. I'm not comfortable with the notoriety I've developed after working with Mac, and a lot of that is sort of positive." Layla sighed deeply. "Do you understand what I'm saying?"

"I do. But I don't have to like it." Rix ran her finger around the rim of her glass, anything to keep her from reaching for Layla's hand. "Where does that leave us?" Because it sounded like some kind of purgatory.

"Let's get to know each other without getting physical. We're not teenagers; we can control ourselves, right?"

Rix nodded, though the heat level of that short kiss inferred otherwise. "And we're allowed to spend time off set together as friends?"

"Yeah."

It made sense. Rix didn't want to rush Layla into something she wasn't comfortable exploring, and new to the business as she was, she had to set her own boundaries. But waiting for more of Layla's lips on hers sounded more like torture than fun friend time. "This feels like it could be the plot of one of your romance novels."

Layla frowned. "This is real life, and it's my career."

Rix held up her hands, taken aback by the frosty switch in Layla's tone. "I'm sorry, I shouldn't have joked. I'm happy to take it at your pace."

"Good."

"In the spirit of getting to know each other, what look were you talking about?"

Layla gave a short laugh. "Is that bothering you?"

Grateful that Layla appeared to have relaxed, Rix nodded. "Honestly, I'm a poker king."

Layla sipped her whiskey then pushed back in her chair and crossed her legs. Rix tried, unsuccessfully, to keep from stealing a glance at Layla's thighs before she pulled her skirt back over her knees. What was she supposed to remember about *not* being a horny teenager?

Layla pointed her finger at Rix. "It wasn't a look like that one, that's for sure."

"That was hard not to react to. Sue me for being human."

"You're going to have to do better than that while we're filming."

"If I'm that obvious, you should probably stay behind me on the set. If I can't see you, I can't give anything away with my really bad poker face."

Layla shook her head and smiled. "I'm sure your poker face is just fine for your friends because you concentrate on keeping your feelings in check when you're playing. But you're pretty easy to read in general conversation."

Rix guessed she'd probably always been that way rather than Layla having some supernatural witch-like power to divine her inner thoughts.

"You should know that I think it's a good thing," Layla said. "I don't like games or hiding feelings. I'm a say what you're thinking kind of gal, and I like the people I'm involved with to be the same." She let out a short laugh that held no humor. "Which is probably why I'm still single."

"Because a lot of people think showing emotion is showing weakness?"

"Exactly."

"You won't have that problem with me. I'm all about talking it out." Rix was aware Layla still hadn't actually told her what look she was referring to at the climbing wall but didn't know whether to push or not. "Me wearing my emotions close to the skin should work for you then."

"Mostly. But pity can be harder to take."

Again, she smiled but the way she said her words seemed far lighter than their meaning. Layla clearly used humor to mask her pain. "And that's what you saw in my look before?" Now it made sense. At the climbing wall, Layla had mentioned something that hinted at childhood neglect. Who wouldn't react to that?

"Yeah. Look, I didn't have the perfect upbringing, but I've had some therapy and for the most part, I'm okay. There are plenty of people who had it a lot worse than me, but for better or worse, I'm not a family person. I don't see them at holidays, I don't call my mom when things are tough, and they're never my first port of call if I run into any trouble. And that's not going to change."

"You say that like you're expecting me to try to change you."

"That's what people do. They like to hang with people with the same outlook, the same moral code and beliefs. They want to be with people who value the same things. But I don't value my family. I'm sorry if that sounds harsh."

"This got deep and heavy fast." Rix tamped down the urge to draw Layla into her arms to comfort her. She wasn't sure if Layla even wanted or needed comforting; she was pretty matter-of-fact about her situation. "I'm not about changing anyone. You have to be who you have to be, and I'm not about to make judgments on your relationship with your family. That is very much your decision and definitely no place for me to interfere." She thought of her own relationship with her family; it wasn't always smooth, there were plenty of problems between her and her brother, and she could recount more days than she cared to remember when the roof came off the house with her parents arguing. But beneath it all, there was love. And it didn't sound like Layla had experienced a whole lot of that.

Layla twisted her fingers in her curls. "I'm sorry. And we were having so much fun. Should I leave?"

"No. Deep and heavy is good—I mean, in conversation." She put her hand over her eyes and shook her head when Layla arched her eyebrow and gave her a sexy smile. "You know what I mean." She searched for a conversation change when Layla continued to smile without saying anything to help her out. She really did make her feel like a horny teenager.

"Thanksgiving is next week, and I'm hosting a big get-together for a bunch of us at my place. If you don't have any plans, I'd like for you to come."

"Can I bring my friend Syd?"

"Of course. I over-cater every year in the hope that the actors who come might actually eat something substantial; they never do, so you can bring as many people as you want."

Rix's phone buzzed with news of their food delivery.

Layla checked her watch. "Wow, time flies and all that nonsense. I'll take that as my cue to leave."

They both stood, and Rix pulled back on hugging her, Layla's words echoing in her head. Not teenagers. No physical contact. "I'll see you tomorrow at the table-read."

Layla stepped back, picked up her leather bag, and swung it over her shoulder. "Thanks for the de-brief."

Rix smacked her palm to her forehead. "Oh my god, we barely talked about the reading."

"I enjoyed what we talked about instead." Layla pushed her hair over her ear and glanced away briefly. "I could come in an hour earlier tomorrow, and we could talk about it over breakfast?"

Rix would take any chance to spend more time with her. "Yeah, that'd be great, if you don't mind?"

"I don't mind at all."

Buoyed by the bright smile Layla gave her, Rix clapped her hands. "Perfect." She walked to the door and opened it just as one of the security detail approached with her dinner.

Layla slipped past them both and headed down the corridor. "Enjoy your platter," she said over her shoulder.

Rix stared after her for a moment after taking her food and tipping the guard. She tried not to grin as she watched Layla walk away, glad for the long corridor leading to the elevator. Seeing a beautiful woman walk away from her was almost as good as seeing one walk toward her. And boy, was she delighted this one had walked into her life.

Chapter Nine

"Jack said he had other queer friends you might be interested in." Syd placed the pizza box on the table mat and headed toward the kitchen. "Wine or beer?"

"White wine, please. There's a chilled bottle of something in the fridge." Layla had bought a couple of bottles and a six pack of light beer for their girls' night in. "And I don't need Jack to fix me up, thank you. I can find my own love interest." In fact, she'd already found a serious contender for the title, which she planned to share with Syd this evening.

"As long as you keep dating now that you've started again." Syd returned with the bottle and two glasses and flopped down onto the couch beside her. "I got half and half. I've got an audition on Monday, so I'll be fasting after this little blow out."

"I don't know how you do it." Layla opened the box and took a deep inhalation of the aromas that rose to greet her.

"I may not be doing it much longer."

Layla turned, her desire for food trumped by what Syd had just said. They hadn't had much time to talk in the past couple of weeks, and Syd hadn't raised the subject since the night she'd met Jack. "Is this a serious night? You sounded serious on the phone."

"I've missed you lately. Can't a girl want to spend a night with her bestie without there being a major agenda? And how can I sound serious in a text?"

"Easy. Proper grammar and no explosion of emojis. Serious."

"Fair enough. Who knew you took so much notice of how I text?"

"It's the way my editor has forced me to think. I can't read anything without seeing comma splices and run-on sentences." She snagged herself a slice of meat feast and a pot of garlic butter and settled back on the couch, scooching her legs under her so that she could face Syd. "Regardless, spill. Is this about acting not making you happy anymore?"

"It's not that I'm not happy when I'm actually acting; it's all the in-between stuff I'm growing tired of." She picked up her own piece of pizza and wafted it in the air. "It's gluten-free pizza and low-fat vegan cheese. It's sugar-free chocolate and low salt chips. It's water when I want beer." She paused to pour wine, gave Layla one, and clinked her glass to hers. She took a long drink then put it on her side table before mirroring Syd's position. "And it's the dog-eat-dog competition that's getting to me. I did Women's Studies at college, and I was all about raising my sisters to higher levels but acting is all about proving—mostly to men—that I'm better or prettier or sexier than all the other women around me."

Layla blinked, aware that her eyes had widened throughout Syd's rousing speech cum diatribe and waited until Syd took a breath to munch through her limp pizza slice. "I had no idea you were so miserable. How long have you been feeling like this?" Layla quelled her immediate self-recrimination that she'd been a bad friend not to see Syd's downward spiral over the last few months.

"I think it's been dawning on me for a while, but I've been ignoring it. I started to let it seep into my consciousness when you came to live with me. You were content in your apartment, churning out your books but you came here for me, and I saw *your* despondency every day when you were working with Mac Mitchell. I think I've dragged you into this world to keep me company."

Layla dropped the last chunk of her slice back onto the box and moved so that she could wrap her arm around Syd. "You shouldn't be giving yourself a hard time on my behalf. You've always pushed me beyond my comfort zone, and while I've often kicked and screamed my way through it, I've invariably ended up in a better place because of you." She pulled Syd in tighter when she thought of what she could've missed out on if she'd let her fears get in the way and not listened to her constant companion. "Christ, I would never even have been published if it wasn't for you sneakily sending off one of my manuscripts. I would never have become a best-selling, award-winning author. And if you hadn't insisted on me joining you here after my last break-up, I never would've gotten to work on my books being turned into movies and TV." She kissed the top of Syd's head gently. "I couldn't be the person I am today without you by my side being the pushy big sister I never knew I needed."

Layla stopped herself from continuing. The emotion of her response to Syd's guilt gathered momentum, making tears inevitable. Syd tended to be the only one who could draw that particular reaction. Her reluctance to cry in front of anyone else had often made the end of relationships sour and the accusation of ice queen a regular riposte, something that gave Syd unending mirth in Layla's retellings.

But she needed to continue. She needed Syd to know how important a role she'd always played in her life. Syd had been Layla's rock for so long and had hardly ever needed her help or support. As alien as it was, Layla had to woman up and be strong for her. "I don't think I'll ever have the words to make you understand how much you mean to me. You've been by my side and helped me so many times I've lost count. I'd probably be in rehab or worse without you, so don't you dare beat yourself up about the one time you might need me to step up and help you out for a change."

Syd relaxed into her and said nothing before she began to sob softly into Layla's chest. She placed her glass on the side table and wrapped her other arm around Syd, drawing her closer. She could count on one hand the number of times she'd seen Syd cry, and that included the death of her parents and their joint funeral. Syd had been lucky to have wonderful parents but unlucky that they'd been taken from her in her early twenties.

"Have you had any thoughts about what you might do instead?" she asked when Syd grew quiet.

"Not yet but just saying it out loud is a big step. I'll let that settle for a while and let my subconscious do the thinking." Syd took a deep breath and sniffed as she lifted her head. She patted at Layla's old MSU college sweatshirt. "I've made a Rorschach tear blot all over you. What do you see?"

Layla pulled her shirt out to get a better look. "Well, that bit is obviously the two of us, and that line of snot is a roller coaster, and this bit here—this collection of spit bubbles—they're the stars. What's your interpretation, doc?"

Syd used the sleeve of her own hoody to wipe it all away but ended up smearing it into more of a mess. "I think you're saying that we're on this ride of life together, and our universe is just an amusement park."

Layla smiled, and her heart brightened when Syd smiled too. "I like that. A lot."

Syd extricated herself from Layla's arms, retrieved her glass, and held it aloft. "A toast to you and me. Whatever life throws at us, we'll always have each other's backs."

She grabbed her own wine, completed the toast, and half emptied the glass. "And besides all of what I've just said, it's a lot nicer working with Rix than it ever was with Mac." Though it was promising to be even nicer once they stopped working together if this evening's exercise and breakfast was any indication. She pushed back into the couch and resumed her previous position facing Syd, who did the same.

"That was another reason tonight had to happen; I want to know how your first couple of days have gone, and then I want to know what happened with Ella. Jack's message about that was a little garbled."

Layla rolled her shoulders and stretched her neck. Her first tai chi class with some of the crew on Venice Beach had unexpectedly kicked her ass. She'd mistakenly thought it was just lazy arm swinging and slow breathing. She wondered if it had done the same to Rix or if she was used to it. From the sweat she broke into after ten minutes, Layla expected Rix would be aching too. "It's been brilliant. Everything I expected it to be and more. It's only been two days, but it feels like it's going to be a truly collaborative experience. The family thing that Jack talked about is real. Though she did get a little preachy at the initial table-read. She sounded more like she was giving a GLAAD speech than motivating a group of actors to do their job properly."

"There's nothing wrong with a healthy dose of activism. It's how people get the status quo changed, missy."

Layla rolled her eyes at Syd's teacher-tone. "I know, but it felt like a little too much. There are straight actors—allies probably—but you don't want to alienate them by lecturing them, do you?"

Syd got another slice of pizza and took a bite before answering. "I don't know, I wasn't there. But it's good that she's impassioned about her work, isn't it?"

Layla nodded slowly. It *was* good. Maybe her reaction was more about the guilt in her own lack of crusading than Rix's passion in hers. "You're probably right."

"So are the exercise classes part of your contract?" Syd nudged Layla's arm. "I think I've only seen you in gym gear three times throughout the whole of our friendship."

Layla shoved her back, a little harder. "That's not true," she said, feigning indignance. "I'm sure it's been five times, at least. And there are other ways of burning calories than hitting the weights, you know."

Scripted Love

She wiggled her eyebrows and laughed. "But strangely, I enjoyed it." She recalled Jack's question about the takeout he ordered for Rix and how she'd glossed over it, not wanting to discuss it. "I think Rix is on a health kick, but it wasn't compulsory. I went because I wanted to."

"*You* wanted to *exercise*? Remember, I know you. There has to be more to it than that. Who're you crushing on? What's their name?"

Layla washed down some stuffed crust with a swig of wine. "I'm not sure what her given name is. She was quite coy about that when we first met," Layla said, being deliberately obtruse and eking out the build-up. "And she's a little older than me, but you wouldn't know because she looks so good for her age, if Wikipedia has her date of birth right."

"Go on," Syd said, playing along as she always did.

"We've agreed not to do anything about our mutual attraction—"

"Ooh, so she likes you back. That's great."

Layla grinned, only just now realizing how excited she actually was to get to know Rix. "We're not going to act on our attraction until we've finished filming."

"That's impressive control on your part." Syd frowned. "Shouldn't you be looking for something a little more casual to get you back in the game?"

Layla loved Syd looking out for her, but she'd never been one to rush into things. "That's not me, Syd, you know that."

"I hope she'll be worth waiting for then." Syd narrowed her eyes. "But why do you even need to wait?"

"Because I don't want to be gossip fodder."

Syd bounced in her seat. "OH MY GOD! You and Rachel Harari? You lucky bitch. Way to go, though."

"Ha, as if." But the thought was far from unpleasant. "She's lovely, by the way. With all her accolades and talent, it'd be easy her to be a complete diva and I'd forgive her that, but she's totally laid back and nice to everyone. And not nice in that—"

"Whoa, take a step back. You can fill me in on Rachel in a moment. First, let's get to the bottom of this 'mutual attraction' thing you've got going on that you're choosing not to do anything about. If it's not the star of the show, which actor is it?"

Layla bit her bottom lip to stop a ridiculous grin. "It's not an actor."

"Then what's the prob—oh my god. The director? You've got the hots for the silver fox director?"

Layla nodded, though Syd's response had her feeling like a college student with a crush on a professor. Syd had been around for more than one of those, too. "And she has the hots for me." She made no attempt to stop the sing-song childishness in her voice. The first flushes of a possible relationship were exciting, and she wasn't about to hold them back with the person she trusted most in this world with her vulnerabilities.

"I have to say that I'm a little jealous. And I might be even more so if it weren't for Jack," Syd said.

She rubbed at her eyebrow and looked a little unsure of herself, though Layla had seen that so rarely that she wasn't certain that's what it was. "Everything is going okay with him, isn't it?"

Syd held up her hand. "Hang on. There are so many things here we both need to talk about, I feel like we should have an agenda so we don't miss anything." She refilled their glasses. "This is going to be a long night; it's good that you don't have work in the morning. Let's just go back to your headline news. Tell me everything."

It took another two glasses of wine to fill Syd in on the LGBTQ center trip, the climbing challenge, the table-reads, and the meeting in Rix's office. Syd made oohs and aahs in all the right place, as was her duty as her bestie, and had inched so close to Layla as she told her story that she was almost on her lap.

"So you're calling the shots, huh? That's very progressive for an older butch."

Layla playfully slapped Syd's hand. "Don't be such a box stuffing, label queen. And it's not like she's *that* old." Layla grasped Syd's knee. "You don't think she's too old, do you?"

"Don't be crazy. She doesn't even look forty. How old is she?"

Layla calmed a little. "Forty-five if the internet is to be believed."

Syd shook her head. "Ten years is nothing once you're out of your twenties. And fifty is the new thirty—"

"Not in this town, it isn't."

Syd shrugged. "Maybe not, but she looks younger than her years. Anyway, now that you've explained why you're waiting, it makes sense. But that's a helluva commitment to make based on one kiss."

Layla touched her lips, almost still able to taste Rix. "It was an a-mazing kiss."

"It would have to be to stop *me* from having sex for nearly six months."

"Rix says principal photography shouldn't take that long."

"Ooh, *Rix says*. Listen to you."

"Shut up. And anyway, we're practically dating without the physical stuff. And I'm happy to wait for that."

Syd arched an eyebrow. "I'll put in a regular battery order with Amazon."

It took a moment before Layla realized her friend was talking about her using a vibrator for the foreseeable future. She gave her a hard shove. "You're so rude."

"And so right."

Syd wasn't far from the truth. Layla *would* have to take care of those urges herself for a while, and if their kiss was a sign of things to come, the building anticipation could make her explode if she abstained. "Okay, that's one discussion point from the agenda, let's move onto Jack. You seem strangely unsure about just leaping in with this one. What's going on?"

"Mm." Syd knocked back the rest of her wine and set the glass on the table before taking Layla's hands in her and looking at her with a particularly serious expression. "Would you agree that you're a serial monogamist?"

Layla laughed at the moniker, but it was pretty accurate. "Sure. I'm not a player, and I'm not fond of being alone. I like being in a relationship, but I don't believe in forever and I move on when it feels like it's time. What's that got to do with Jack?"

"And you fall in love in all of those relationships?" Syd hunched her shoulders, her focused expression remaining unchanged.

"Yeah, I do."

"And when do you *know* that you're in love with them?"

Layla blew out a short breath and considered the question. "It varies. I haven't really analyzed my pattern of falling in love, but it does depend, I think." She paused in an effort to try to remember what it was that tipped her from really liking someone to loving them. "It usually takes a while. I mean, the sexual attraction is instant, obviously, but I don't fall in love with someone just because they can make me orgasm. I've been in at least one relationship where I never came when we were having sex, but that didn't stop me loving them. Though I was still giving them orgasms, so I suppose sex is a big part of it for me. I need time to get to know them, what

I believe is the real person behind the public mask they show everyone else." She squeezed Syd's hands. "And sometimes that's what ended the relationships too; when I thought I knew them but discovered they were a completely different person. Love dies a quick death for me when that happens."

Syd looked thoughtful. "What's the fastest you've ever fallen in love with someone?"

"Come on, Syd, I know I've had milk cartons in the fridge last longer than a lot of your relationships, but you've had strong feelings for people before. Wasn't that love?"

Syd tilted her head slightly and scrunched up her nose. "I *thought* it was love. It was never for long—like you unkindly alluded to with your milk analogy—but there's something different this time."

It was Layla's turn to bounce on the sofa with this revelation. Syd had never been a commitment kind of woman or had let anyone hang around long enough for Layla to get to know. That had led to more than one of Layla's partners voicing a harsh judgment, which in turn led to the end of that relationship. She'd often thought it would be easier to have a "Love me, love my best friend" tattoo. Syd deserved to have happiness, and Layla wasn't about to let anyone judge her by how she found it. She didn't care to analyze that the ease with which she parted with those people perhaps meant that she'd never been in love in the first place. "Tell me more."

Watching how animated Syd was as she talked about Jack and their "cosmic connection" was evidence enough that it was different to every relationship Layla had witnessed. Syd's disbelief and lack of trust in her own feelings made sense since she'd spent her entire adult life in bite-size dalliances with no apparent interest in settling down. After Syd had exhausted her explanation, Layla asked, "Have you told Jack how you feel?"

Syd swiped at Layla's hand as if swatting the question away. "Of course not. I don't want to scare him off, do I? He's very sweet, but if I mention the L word after two weeks…" She shook her head. "Anyone but a clichéd lesbian would run for the hills. I know I would. Hell, I've lost count of the number of times I've turned tail when things got way too serious way too fast."

Syd had a point, about the cliché and her own tendency to hit the road when her romances got, well, a little too romantic. "Has he said anything about how things are going?" There were always clues; they might be coded and vaguely offered, but in her experience, it was relatively easy to tell if someone wanted something casual or longer term.

"I don't know what I'm listening for. That's why I wanted to go on the double date with you and Ella, for you to pick up on his vibe and translate it for me," said Syd. "Which leads us nicely into the next item on the agenda: what happened with her?"

Layla grasped Syd's hand. "Oh my god, stalker alert."

"Really? That was fast." Syd pointed at Layla and waggled her finger. "You might have to get used to that kind of adoration."

Layla shook her head. "Adoration, I might be able to cope with. Obsession, not so much. A few dates do not a relationship make, but Ella had other ideas, apparently. I told her we weren't compatible and thought she was okay with it, but then Jack asked me about the double date as if nothing had changed. And she's been blowing up my phone with texts and heart GIFs since we met." Layla picked up her phone, scrolled to messages, and passed it to Syd. "See? I don't know how many different ways to tell someone I'm not interested."

Syd's eyes widened the further down she went, as the messages increased in intensity and frequency. When she finally got to the end of them, she handed Layla her phone. "Wow. That's some serious destiny and fate shit, right there. Do you want me to ask Jack to talk to her?"

"No, don't do that. I don't want to get him any more involved that he already is, and I see him at work every day; I don't want to make things awkward. You know what I'm like about mixing the personal with the professional, it's exactly the reason I'm not taking things up with Rix like I want to—like I *really* want to."

"Okay. Did you tell Jack that it was over with Ella, at least from your perspective?"

Layla dropped her phone onto the couch after switching it off, not wanting to receive another message from Ella as if she were somehow spookily tuned into their conversation. "I did. He was eager to convince me they were just work friends and not real friends. I think he might've been worried that it would affect your relationship with him if you thought he was friends with someone a little off balance."

"Well, I have told him how important you are to me."

Layla tapped Syd on the knee and grinned. "See, if he cares what I think, that's a sign that he's taking your relationship seriously. Rix invited me to her Thanksgiving party next week, and she said I could bring you. I bet Jack's going. It won't technically be a double date, like you wanted, but it'll still give me the chance to see how Jack is around you." She gently squeezed Syd's knee. "But you should trust your instincts too."

Syd shook her head. "Nope. I have no instincts. This is uncharted territory, and you're the one with all the maps. I need you to be my guide."

Syd laughed and to anyone else, they would've thought she wasn't being serious, but Layla knew she needed her help. And she'd happily give it, for what it was worth. She was good at falling in love, that part was easy. It was the staying in love Layla didn't believe in.

Chapter Ten

RIX RAN HER fingers across the first rackful of her vests and shook her head. "None of those work." She went to the next rack and scrunched her toes on the thick, soft carpet underfoot. If she could walk around everywhere barefoot, she would. The freedom and the feel of the earth beneath her toes involved no separation between her and the world, and it grounded her and induced a certain calmness. Whenever she was in conflict, which was more often than she wished, at the earliest opportunity, off came her shoes and socks. She hadn't yet done it in the middle of an argument with a fellow professional—she didn't want *that* sort of reputation—but she'd often done it when quarreling with lovers. Though that hadn't been for a while. She hadn't declared a moratorium on dating as such, but she had been taking a breather. Finding the woman she wanted to spend the rest of her life with was proving to be more difficult than the romance books would have her believe. Her puzzle piece was most definitely still missing.

Looking along the next rack, she began to fall into spiraling thoughts that she may never find the true love she'd been dreaming about. She'd always loved the movies where the prince swept the princess off her feet and rode off into the sunset for their happily ever after. Five years shy of a half century. Christ, she'd thought she'd have a wife, two kids at school, a dog, and the white picket fence by now. Instead, she had a gated mansion with all the trappings of bachelorette freedom and too many empty rooms. She didn't even have a dog to come home to, and the only woman she got to whisper to was Alexa.

Dismissing the vests and moving to the next rack, her thoughts drifted to the temporary families she created with her crews. Her Thanksgiving parties were something she looked forward to immensely. They gave people who didn't have families to go home to something to focus on, whether their solitude was their choice or not. And this year, that group included Layla Adams. When Layla had told her the sad story about her family predicament, Rix had been torn between empathy and something akin to glee and was barely able to wait to extend the invitation. She wasn't about to jinx the potential of what could be, but she'd take any opportunity to get to know Layla away from their shared work environment.

Layla's promised presence was why Rix was having so much trouble choosing her outfit. Was it crazy to want to impress Layla when they weren't officially dating? She decided it wasn't. They *were* dating; it was just top-secret and undercover, like old-fashioned courting that no one knew about. And the sanctions on physical contact made it like something from the nineteenth century, the tradition of which Rix could appreciate in a time when fast sex and loose connections were the order of the day. She enjoyed making love as much as the next red-blooded woman did, but that was just it: making love, not having sex for short-term satisfaction. Yep, she was definitely old-fashioned, and this type of dating would suit her fine. In theory, anyway.

Rix finally settled on a brocade vest in black with a silver paisley design. The shirt and tie would have to change, but that was okay. She loved this one and had watched it being made in Florence a few years ago when she was there for filming. Decision made, she quickly switched from a white to a black tank top and took a black herringbone cotton shirt from a rail on the opposite wall. She put it on and fastened the top two buttons before taking out a gray-silver tie from the top tie drawer. She took her time to ensure the Windsor knot was perfect before buttoning her shirt and tucking it into her jeans. She closed her shirtsleeves with her favorite cufflinks, pulled the vest from its hanger, slipped it over her shoulders, and fastened it closed.

She checked the end result in the full-length mirror at the far side of the closet and smoothed her hair down with the heel of her hand. She was no George Clooney, but she looked sharp and hoped Layla would think so too. Rix scanned the shelves stacked with shoes, boots, and sneakers. She wasn't going out of the house, so she didn't need to wear them. And socks and shoes separated her from the various textures of floors in her house, surface coverings she'd carefully curated for maximum enjoyment. She knew she might be considered odd, but she hadn't really cared what people thought of her bare-foot obsession before. Most of her guests would be expecting her to be shoeless; she always was in her own home, but would Layla think her too kooky? She got up to reach for a pair of matt black brogues but stopped herself. Layla wanted to get to know her, and this was who she was.

She checked herself one last time then headed downstairs to see how the caterers were getting on. If the divine smell of turkey wafting up the staircase was anything to go by, all was well.

A few hours later, and after her first few guests had arrived, Rix's anxiety was beginning to get the better of her logical brain, and her concern that Layla wouldn't show increased with the arrival of each guest. Since they'd spoken about getting to know each other after the first table-read, Rix hadn't managed much time with Layla other than a few morning exercise classes, and the group dynamic was such that it had been almost impossible to snatch any one-to-one time. She was determined that today would be different. She had the full day and hopefully the evening to make sure they got plenty of time to talk, and she'd engineered the seating plan for Layla to sit beside her at dinner.

Rix turned from the bar just in time to see Layla enter with her friend Syd. In Rix's head, her jaw dropped, and her tongue lolled out of her mouth at the first glimpse of Layla, resplendent in a ruby red, calf-length dress and matching heeled sandals that made her almost the same height as Syd, who was stunning in a traditional Hollywood way. Rix tugged at the bottom of her vest and headed toward the two of them. "You both look amazing." She made sure she acknowledged Syd, though all she wanted to do was take in every single inch of Layla's curvy feminine perfection. She air-kissed them both, taking care not to linger too long when Layla's delicate perfume hit her senses and kick-started her raging passion again.

"And you look very handsome. I love your vest; the design is beautiful," Layla said.

She ran her fingers around one of the large tear drop shapes, and the heat of the contact seared through Rix's vest and shirt as if Layla's fingers were directly on her skin. Goddamn, this woman had an unusually sexual effect on her. "Thank you. It's Italian." God, that sounded pretentious. "I meant, the design is Italian." No, that didn't sound much better.

"And your cufflinks are gorgeous." Layla took Rix's hand and turned them slightly toward her friend. "Aren't they, Syd?"

Syd looked like she was having difficulty suppressing a grin, making Rix assume Layla had told her about their arrangement. She placed her hand over Layla's and pulled Rix's hand closer to inspect it. "They really are beautiful. Are they made of some type of precious stone?"

Rix swallowed hard. The two of them were too much to take when they were clearly toying with her. Sophisticated and sexy women like Layla and Syd were her kryptonite. She stammered for some purchase in the conversation. "They look like they should be, but that's actually old car paint."

"Surely not?" Layla said.

"It's true. Black Detroit agate. My dad worked in the car industry all his life, and his buddies had these made for him when he retired. He gave them to me when I started my production company." Rix had noticed Layla's expression drop slightly as she told the story, no doubt expecting it to end with her inheriting the cufflinks when her father died. Lucky for Rix, he was alive and kicking, and on his way to her house for the party her parents hadn't missed since she'd started the tradition…which she should probably mention. Crap, should she have told Layla about them coming when she invited her? She didn't want her thinking all of this was some strange and extremely premature ploy to have Layla meet her parents. If she fessed up now, she ran the risk of Layla simply turning around and walking away. "My parents always come to my Thanksgiving party and my dad likes seeing me wear them." Once again, Layla's expression faltered slightly, and Rix had no way of telling whether it was because she felt trapped or because it made her think of her own family.

Layla hadn't let go of Rix's wrist, but she dropped it now. "That's nice. Do they live close by or are they flying in?"

Her transition from whatever Layla had been feeling to personable interest was all but seamless and so swift, it made Rix dizzy. She decided not to make a big deal of it and hope that Layla didn't walk away, though she realized she'd been insensitive. Having a great family around her made it difficult to see when others might not be so fortunate. "They've got a beachside house in Long Beach so they're only an hour away, if the traffic isn't too hellish." She held back the extra information she usually shared, which was that Rix had moved them there to be closer as they got older and would need her more.

"That's wonderful," Layla said. "I hope they have lots of embarrassing stories to tell me."

Maybe Rix was overthinking everything; Layla seemed fine. "I will *not* be letting that happen. I don't want them scaring you away." She clamped her mouth shut when Layla raised her eyebrows at her as if to say, way to go with keeping this on the downlow. "Syd knows, doesn't she?"

Layla tugged on Syd's arm and smiled. "She's my best friend, and I tell her everything. But talking like that isn't going to keep it secret for long, is it?"

Rix held her hands together and mock bowed. "Consider my wrists slapped," she whispered.

"I bet your mom will tell me your real name too," Layla said.

She looked adorably mischievous in a way that would see Rix letting her have anything and everything she wanted. Boy, she could be in real trouble here. "And I'm definitely not letting *that* happen. Mom and Dad are sworn to secrecy."

"And it doesn't bother them that their daughter doesn't want to be known by the name they gave her at birth?"

Layla's teasing apparently knew no boundaries.

Syd touched Rix's forearm gently. "I'm going to leave you two to your undercurrent of sexual banter and go see Jack."

Both of them nodded, but Rix's concentration remained laser-focused on Layla, whom she should welcome into her house properly rather than keep her standing in the hallway. "Would you like something to drink?"

Layla pulled a bottle of wine from her tote bag and held it out. "I'd love one."

Rix took the gift but shook her head. "I said you didn't need to bring anything."

"I know, but what kind of a person shows up empty-handed to something like this?"

Rix gestured to the guests milling around her home. "The kind of person who listens to instructions."

"Oh, I listened. Then I chose to ignore. My mom may not have taught me much, but she did impress upon me the importance of taking alcohol to any party, even the ones at home that no one else was invited to."

Again with the humor that Rix didn't yet know how to handle.

"Does my making light of my alcoholic mother bother you?" Layla asked.

Rix took her arm and led her to the temporary bar in the front reception room, where she deposited Layla's offering. "It doesn't bother me, no. I don't know how you do it though. I mean, you haven't told me much, but

I don't know how I'd cope with it. Probably just bury it in a mind box somewhere and try not to think about it."

They ordered drinks, and Rix led the way to one of the outdoor seating areas by the pool. The sun was already high in a bluebird sky, and there wasn't a hint of wind to temper its heat. "Sun or shade?"

Layla tilted her head upward with her eyes closed and took a deep breath. "The sun, please. I adore this heat."

Rix chose a reclining lounger in the direct sunlight and a soft seated chair beneath a parasol.

Layla placed her drink on the table beside her seat and inhaled deeply. "In answer to your question about how I do it: I didn't consciously choose humor as my coping mechanism. It's just what comes naturally to me. I feel a little like, if I didn't laugh, I might cry, and I don't want my adult life to be defined by my childhood." She shrugged. "I know some people can be shocked by my flippant comments on such a serious topic, but it's my experience, and it's my way of dealing with it." Layla leaned close to Rix and touched her forearm briefly before picking up her drink and taking a sip. "You wouldn't want to think about it, because you've had such a good childhood that you can't bear to think of your mom or dad acting that way. But it wouldn't be your mom and dad. They'd be different people." She leaned back into her chair to face the sun. "Does that make sense?"

Rix appreciated Layla's raw honesty. It made her even more attractive, if that were possible. "It does, actually. Thank you for explaining it to me."

"Now will you explain something to me?" Layla asked, still facing the sun like she was a solar panel soaking up its energy.

"Of course."

Layla pointed to the floor without looking at her. "Why aren't you wearing shoes?"

Rix laughed. She loved that Layla asked, rather than wondering and not saying anything for fear of prying. If communication between them was going to be this easy, it boded well for the future. She explained her reasons. "And this whole area is grassed so I don't burn my feet."

"That's unusual—weird, for some people—but I love that you're doing it at a party when everyone else is in heels, or sandals, or dress shoes."

"Most of these people are friends or family so I expect them to accept me and all my eccentricities. Isn't that how it's supposed to be?" Even as she said the words, she knew there were so many people out there for whom it wasn't that way for them. She made a mental note to contact George at the LGBTQ center to see how they were getting on with fundraising for the homeless accommodation he'd mentioned in passing at the end of their event day a couple of weeks ago.

"That's certainly an idyllic wish. If it were reality, there wouldn't be a need for your friend's LGBTQ center."

Rix didn't suppress the smile at having the same thought. "That's true, but we can dream, right?"

"Absolutely. Show your little piggies to the world and be damned the consequences." Layla turned and glanced at Rix's feet. "Though they are quite cute, but not so little."

Rix scrunched her toes self-consciously. "I'd fall over if I had smaller feet," she said and took a long pull on her beer.

"I could glam those big flippers up in no time with some hot pink nail polish."

Rix couldn't stop herself from choking on her drink. She was only thankful that it didn't reach Layla and ruin her beautiful dress, though helping her out of it and putting her in one of Rix's shirts held enormous appeal. The image of Layla in that and nothing else made her clench. Layla laughed freely, and Rix grabbed a napkin from the table to wipe her mouth. "That is *never* going to happen."

Layla arched an eyebrow and flashed her a wicked grin. "I'm going to creep into your house one night, tie you down to your bed, and paint your toenails with industrial paint that you won't be able to remove."

Rix swallowed hard. An unexpected twist of arousal shot from her core. Maybe she would let Layla bling her feet if that's how she'd do it. A strong hand gripped her shoulder, pulling her out of her dirty daydream. Layla smirked, clearly seeing the effect her repartee was having on Rix.

"Hey, buddy, you're falling down on the job. You've got guests arriving. Go be a good host and stop hogging this pretty lady."

Rix grabbed his hand, twisted it slightly until he yelled, and stood. "Layla, this idiot is my good friend, Luke." She tugged him into her chair and released his hand. Luke held it like she'd broken it.

"Ow. Why'd you have to be so aggressive?" Luke asked.

"You bring it out in me. I'm a pussycat with everyone else."

"I call bullshit on that one. You're more ferocious lion than domesticated feline, although you do like p—"

Rix cuffed the back of Luke's head. "Don't be an infant." She motioned to Layla. "This is Layla Adams. She's the author of the books I'm turning into a limited TV series."

Layla held out her hand, and Luke shook it. "It's lovely to meet you," she said.

"The pleasure is all mine." Luke bent to kiss Layla's hand, and Rix gave him another swipe.

"What would your wife say about you kissing other women?"

"She'd ask them to join us." Luke grinned.

"You're incorrigible." Rix turned her attention to Layla. "I'm sorry. I have to play host for a while, but once everyone's arrived, I'll find you."

Luke narrowed his eyes at her but said nothing. She'd be getting the third degree from him as soon as he had the chance.

"There's no rush, Rix," Layla said. "I'm sure Luke can regale me with some great stories about you."

Crap. "Luke will do no such thing if Luke would like to continue breathing," Rix said and squeezed his shoulder until he squealed. "And no, he doesn't know my real name."

Luke batted Rix's hand away. "I really don't. I've known this woman fifteen years, and she still won't tell me." He leaned toward Layla conspiratorially. "I can't imagine how bad it must be that she's had the internet scrubbed of all trace of it."

"The plot thickens." Layla pursed her lips. "I will find out, you know."

Rix scrubbed her hand across the back of her head. Somehow, she didn't doubt that she would. And it wasn't so bad. It just didn't fit her. Keeping it a secret was more of a joke than a necessity, but if it kept Layla's interest, she was in no hurry to reveal it. "No, you won't." She winked a good-bye when what she wanted to do was wrap her hand around Layla's neck and pull her into a deep kiss, the kind that would keep her going while she did the rounds of her party.

When she returned to the pool area over an hour later, Layla was no longer there, and Luke was nowhere to be seen either. She walked, as casually as she could manage, back into her house and wandered from room to room like a lost puppy, stopping to chat with people as she did, but feeling Layla's absence a little more with each passing minute. Where was she?

Rix heard her dad before she saw him. His booming voice greeted someone in the same jovial tone he had for everyone he met, and it was something she loved him for. He was the most evenly tempered person she knew, which was why he was the one she would always seek out in any crisis, and she'd had a few of those.

She excused herself from Rachel and her current lover and headed toward the door. "Hey, you two," she said and enveloped her mom in a warm embrace. Her dad put his arms around the two of them and squeezed so tightly, Rix's back cracked. "You're going to break us with those hugs one of these days."

He released them, and her mom swatted his chest playfully. "He's not big enough to break me," she said.

"But I keep trying," he said and winked.

Rix closed her eyes and shook her head, immediately knowing what he was talking about and wishing she didn't. "Aren't you too old for that yet?" As far as she was concerned, they'd had sex once to make her, and that was it. She never wanted to think of her parents that way.

"You won't be saying that when you're our age." He gently punched her shoulder. "*If* you make it that long."

He was joking, but her mom and Rix exchanged a quick look. She was the one Rix had spoken to after her latest consultation with her doctor. "Did you have a good drive?"

"It was fine." Her dad twitched his finger between the two of them. "What was that?"

Apparently, their glance had been none too subtle. Maybe Layla was right about her poker face. "What was what?" It was still second nature to feign innocence when her dad challenged her, even though she had long ago flown the nest. "Come on, let me get you both a drink." She took her mom's overnight bag and tried to get her dad's, but he pulled it away.

"You forget you're still my little girl, and I can tell when something's going between you two. I had years of practice. What are you not telling me?"

At five eleven, only her dad could still refer to her as a little girl. Rix made a grab for his bag again, this time successfully, and he let it go. "It's nothing much. Let me put these in your room, and I'll tell you." She cast a defeated glance toward her mom. Since they'd failed to keep the secret to themselves, there was no point trying to delay the conversation further.

Her parents followed her up the stairs with her mom giving her a blow-by-blow account of the journey, including the tale of the driver who cut them off and must've "gotten his license from Disneyland." They entered her main guest room, one of way too many and the one she'd earmarked to decorate with strong women from Disney and the Marvel universe for her first child. Five years later, and it remained the room her parents stayed in whenever they came to visit.

She placed their bags on the California King bed and dropped into the Bug armchair alongside the Juliet balcony. She looked out onto the garden and saw Layla chatting with Meg under the gazebo. Damn. Given that Layla was attracted to Rix, she could easily be interested in Meg, the high-flying, globe-trotting, sexy photographer. If Rix was ever going to be into butch women, Meg would be her first stop. And Layla fit Meg's type in every way. Damn, damn. She should make this quick and get back to her before Layla's interest turned to Meg.

"Earth to Rix?"

"Sorry, Dad." When she looked back at him, she saw the worry in his eyes and pointed at him. "That is exactly why I told Mum not to say anything."

He crossed his arms and gave her one of his most stern expressions. "I'm allowed to be concerned about my daughter. Now, what's wrong?"

"I haven't been feeling great for a few months, some chest pain and fatigue, but I figured it was just part of getting older and didn't really think anything of it."

"You had chest pains and didn't get them checked out immediately?" Her dad shook his head. "That's crazy, Rix. Your grandfather on my side died of an early heart attack."

"Well, I didn't remember that until Mom reminded me." She sighed. Her mortality wasn't something she wanted to confront in her mid-forties. Christ, it wasn't something she ever really wanted to confront. "Anyway, I went for a routine check-up, and my cholesterol is a little high. I called Mom to check family history, and that's when I told her. I wasn't going to bother either of you with it. I've just got to make some changes to my diet and exercise more." When her dad raised both eyebrows, Rix threw up her hands. "Fine, exercise at all. I'm always working, Dad, I don't have time to—"

"Live? It's that simple, honey. You have to make time if you want to keep living. I thought you'd taken up surfing. What happened to that? And have you stopped smoking?"

She rolled her eyes, feeling like fifteen-year-old Rix, caught smoking with her friends after lacrosse practice. "I haven't surfed for a while, but yeah, I could get back to that." She could make it a group activity for the crew. She'd like to be out on the ocean with Layla too. "And I don't smoke." *Very often.*

Her dad harrumphed. "Oh, really? Then who do those Cohibas belong to in your study?"

Damn his memory. The box of Behikes were a gift to herself when her first movie made the studio a few million dollars in profit, and she wasn't about to give them up. "I only smoke one of those when I've finished a project."

He put his hands on his hips and glared at her. "And how many projects do you finish a year?"

"It depends, two or three, I suppose."

"Then that's two or three more than you should be smoking, isn't it?"

"Go easy, honey," her mom said and took his hand. "She's a grown woman. She knows what she has to do."

He visibly softened, and his towering six-foot-four height didn't look quite as intimidating. "I worry about her is all." He put his arm around her mom and pulled her close. "Both of my parents died before their time, so I know grief, but I can't imagine what it would be like to lose you."

"Jesus, Dad, there's no need to pile dirt on my grave just yet."

"Promise me you'll do whatever the doctor's advised." He fixed her with his most serious expression. "You're not as invincible as you might want to be, Rix. You spend a lot of time taking care of other people and making their lives better. If you want to continue doing that, you need to take care of yourself too."

She pulled herself up from the chair and hugged them both again. "I promise." She let them go and headed toward the door. She needed to go to Layla before she fell for Meg's considerable charms. "I have to get back to the party and check everything's on schedule for dinner." She opened the door and paused in the entrance. "When you've got yourself a drink, come find me. There's someone I want to introduce you to."

"Ooh, that's exciting. Someone special?" her mom asked.

"I hope so. But it's complicated, and we're not dating. Yet. Just be cool." She left them to it and made her way as quickly as possible to the gazebo, again stopping for a few swift greetings. "God damn it," she said when she could see her destination. Layla had disappeared again but, much to Rix's relief, Meg was still there so they hadn't hit it off and ducked out. She admonished herself for her train of thought. She had no reason to think Layla would do that and couldn't understand where her usual self-confidence had gone.

Meg spotted her and waved before walking over.

"Wonderful party, as always, Rix," she said after they'd exchanged a bro hug.

"Thanks for coming. No beautiful woman on your arm today?"

"Unfortunately not, but it looks like there are plenty of single ladies here so I'm planning not to be solo for much longer." She motioned over Rix's shoulder. "In fact, here's one such beauty coming our way."

Rix turned, hoping to see any woman other than Layla.

"Your house is a maze. I feel like I've been lost for hours," Layla said when she reached them. "Is there any chance you're giving private tours later?"

"Sure," Rix said.

"Oh." Meg wiggled her eyebrow and nodded at Rix.

She appreciated Meg recognizing that she might be interested in Layla, but the agreed pretense was that they were just friends. How was she supposed to handle this? She certainly didn't want to give Meg the green light to pursue Layla, but she also couldn't declare her own interest. "Have you two met? Layla's the author of the project I'm working on, and Meg is an all-star, amazing photographer." Christ, did she have to sound like she was matchmaking? That was a step too far.

Meg widened her eyes and grinned, indicating that's how she'd taken Rix's introduction too. Damn.

"We have," Layla said.

"Maybe I could give Layla the guided tour? I've been here so many times, I know it as well as my own place anyway."

Meg didn't need any further encouragement. What did Rix expect? Layla was a beautiful woman and single. Of course she'd get hit on, and Rix couldn't do a damn thing about it.

"Perhaps later," Layla said and gave Meg a dazzling smile. "I need to warm up. All that A/C air has chilled me to the bone. Rix, please stop me if you don't want to talk about filming, but while I was wandering, an idea hit me about a subplot that I took out of the overall screenplay. Would it be okay to sit down and discuss it before the muse leaves me?"

"Will it take long?" Rix played her part of reluctant director and kept her excitement from her expression. Or at least she thought she had. Thanks to Layla's comments, she now doubted her ability to keep her emotions from showing. But Meg was one of the poker buddies Rix always left penniless at the end of the night. She was probably safe.

"No, I promise I won't keep you from your guests for long."

Rix patted Meg on the back. "Sorry, buddy, duty calls. I'll catch you later."

"No problem." Meg caught hold of Layla's wrist as she turned. "Don't forget about that offer of a guided tour, Layla. I'd love to show you around."

Layla put her other hand over Meg's and gently removed it. "I'm sure you would," she said with a sweet smile, before walking toward the table they'd been sitting at earlier in the afternoon.

Meg whistled under her breath as Layla sashayed away. "She's a fiery one, bud. Totally our type. Why aren't you going there?"

"We're working together, and it's one of her first projects. I don't want to make things awkward."

"So you would?"

"See you later, buddy," Rix said over her shoulder as she headed over to join Layla, who was already seated and waiting for her. Mission accomplished. She knew Meg would back off now that Rix had delicately declared her interest in Layla. She probably didn't need to have said anything. Layla had extricated herself from Meg perfectly well herself and in doing so, had unknowingly buoyed Rix's ego. Before she tucked into the turkey later, she'd be giving thanks to whatever fates had led Layla into her life.

Chapter Eleven

"Judging by your cat on a hot tin roof impression, we should have had the discussion about exclusivity during our getting to know each other period," Layla said as Rix sat down beside her.

Rix looked surprised that Layla had picked up on her discomfort with Meg. "Was I that obvious?"

Layla nodded. "It was to me, but then I'm paying attention, and Meg probably isn't." Watching Rix squirm her way around figuring out how to get Meg to back off had been fun, but she had to intervene before Rix burst a blood vessel with worry. Meg was certainly appealing, and on another day, Layla would be interested, but she was giving Rix her full attention and wouldn't be looking at other people that way.

"Thanks for coming to my rescue." Rix gave a sweet half-grin. "It's kind of impressive how well you already seem to know me after only a couple of weeks."

She clasped her hands together so tightly Layla saw her knuckles whiten. She'd seen her do it a couple of times on set, usually before she gave an actor some criticism or direction when they were going off on the wrong track. Layla was beginning to understand Rix, yes, and she was enjoying learning. She'd been in a couple of relationships with people who labelled themselves butch, and she'd loved discovering their unique vulnerabilities under the bluster and strength. Rix was no different, but then altogether different. "Is there something you want to say?"

"The…exclusivity thing," Rix said after a long pause. "You're okay with that?"

Layla wanted to hold Rix's hand as they spoke. Their agreed physical contact prohibition was making her realize how much of a touch-dependent person she was, and how much she craved to explore Rix's body and caress her skin, to slowly undo her tie and unbutton her shirt, to rake her nails across Rix's shoulders as she pulled it off.

"Layla?"

Layla jumped, and heat flashed up her neck. She could only hope that the wonderful LA sun would cover up the inevitable blush.

"Are you okay?" Rix's brow creased. "You're really red. Maybe you should get out of the sun? Do you need some water?"

Layla smiled at Rix's concern and complete misinterpretation. "Sorry. I drifted to thinking about how much fun I'd have undressing you. Slowly." The resulting coloring of Rix's face gave her the courage to keep going. "I feel like we're at that moment when we've built a fire and lit the match, but the flames haven't caught yet. Do you know what I mean?"

Rix's nostrils flared slightly. "I know exactly what you mean. Being close to you and not being able to touch you is driving me crazy."

She'd almost growled the words, her voice dropped deep and low, and her eyes half-lidded. None of which alleviated Layla's current state of intense arousal. "I need to find Syd and spend some time with her and Jack. It's that or I'm taking a dive in your pool."

Rix bit her lower lip and arched her eyebrow. "That's got me wishing you were a lady in white instead of red. I like your sophisticated version of a wet T-shirt competition."

"Would I win?" Layla whispered.

"Every time."

Layla took a deep, cleansing breath, trying to force the unhelpful urges from her being. She stood. "In answer to your question: yes, I'm okay with being exclusive. It's a deal breaker for me, so you should say now if that's going to be a problem for you."

Rix gazed up at her, an unusual thing since she had six inches over Layla. The gentleness mixed with raw sexuality in Rix's eyes took Layla's breath away. It was a look she could easily get used to seeing.

"I want the same thing." Rix moved as if to take Layla's hand but leaned back in her chair and loosened her tie a little instead. "I've been desperate to start this project for over three years, and now I'm torn because I love what's happening on set and don't want it to end, but finishing it means I get to touch you." She closed her eyes briefly and sucked in a breath. "And boy, do I want to touch you. For days."

Layla felt exactly the same. Having her books turned into TV for a wider audience was amazing, and she wanted to fully immerse herself in the experience and enjoy it while it lasted. Similarly, the first flushes of a new relationship were to be savored while *they* lasted. Anticipation was a great aphrodisiac, but patience had never been one of her fortes. "I like the sound of that. Hold onto that thought." She picked up her phone and fired off a quick "Where are you?" text to Syd. "See you at dinner?"

"You're seated next to me on the top table," Rix said. "Bring your appetite."

Layla smiled. "I always do." She winked and walked away to find Syd and Jack, knowing that Rix would be watching her leave. She put an extra swing into her hips for her benefit.

Her phone pinged with a text and location from Syd, so she headed inside to the library. A library? That sounded impressive. She hoped it would be a real one, rather than a showcase of pristine books that had clearly never been removed from the shelves once placed there. Rich people had an annoying habit of buying old and modern classics in the expectation that their mere proximity would achieve intelligence via some sort of non-fluid osmosis. She suspected that wouldn't be the case for Rix, but it was an easy trap to fall into.

Syd jumped up from her chair and pulled her into a hug. "She's got every single one of your books in hardback," she whispered.

"Wow." Layla hadn't expected that. She'd hoped, maybe, that Rix had a few of her books, probably from the Lane Roberts series given that's what they were filming. Rix had said she was a fan, but Layla had taken the flattery with a large pinch of Hollywood salt.

"Look."

Syd dragged her into the library, but Layla pulled back to appreciate the absolute glory of it and let out an awestruck gasp. The room was completely circular with a vaulted ceiling. There was a semi-circle of windows taller than Layla, with a stunning view of LA that was made even more beautiful by the falling dusk and twinkling city lights. Above the windows and along the rest of the room, the walls were lined with simple, stained wooden shelves. Each shelf was packed with books of all sizes and jackets, paperbacks, hardbacks, and leather tomes with ornate spines. Access to the higher books was provided via a chrome ladder on a circular track embedded into the floor, and Layla had the urge to step on the lower rung and push herself off so that she could fly around the fascinating library on a literary merry-go-round. The glass ceiling gave the room an almost unearthly feel, and a deep sense of calm settled in Layla. Surrounded by the words of so many authors helped her remember why she'd started writing. A place so clearly dedicated to the written word and its enduring longevity felt so incongruous to be located in Hollywood, a place of transience and impermanence. Layla closed her eyes. She hadn't been prepared for an almost spiritual reaction to this library, and its presence drew her closer to Rix, its creator.

Layla had asked Rix for the guided tour and wished that she'd been the one to show it to her. She had so many questions about it.

She felt the tug of Syd's hand again and brought herself back into the room. "I don't think I've ever seen a library this beautiful."

Syd pulled her toward the window and pointed at a head-height shelf. "There you are."

Sure enough, every one of her books were in date order. She allowed herself to feel a little proud and perhaps overwhelmed. She'd never seen all of her books together like this on any shelf but her own and the one in her editor's office, not even in the public libraries or bookstores that stocked her novels. And somehow this felt different to the homes of women in her past who had Layla's books on their nightstand or stuffed between a collection of movies and magazines. This felt more like a privilege. "That is so cool."

"Didn't you believe Rix when she told you she was a fan of your work?"

Layla turned at the sound of Jack's voice. He stood behind Syd with his arms wrapped around her waist and his head peering around her shoulder. Few people were tall enough to stand behind Syd and put their chin on her shoulder, but it was cute that Jack had tried. "If I say that I didn't, will you tell her?"

"I've told you already, I'm not a spy."

"In that case, no, I didn't believe her. When I moved here a few months ago, Syd briefed me on what to expect and what *not* to expect. Strangely, brutal honesty was on both of those lists. But still, it didn't seem possible that Rix would have read my work and have all my books."

"Now you know it's true. Between getting Rachel Harari to take the lead and you to write the script, this series is a dream come true for her."

Layla wondered what other dreams of Rix's that Jack knew about, but she held back the question. She'd sworn Syd to secrecy and that included not discussing it with Jack. If anyone was going to tell Rix's assistant, it should be her. Syd flicked her eyes to a few free chairs, reminding Layla why she was here with them and not using the party to continue getting to know Rix. She was desperate to know more about this library, but she'd made Syd a promise. "Is that a bottle of wine you have over there?" she asked.

Syd pulled away from Jack, hooked her arm into Layla's, and headed toward the empty chairs. "It is. Care for a glass?"

"Uh, I'll go do the rounds for a while then?" Jack said, though it was clearly more of a question than a desire.

Layla turned and grabbed his hand. "Don't be silly. I want to get to know 'out of the office Jack,' please." Which wasn't a lie. The guy who'd pulled her into the building for her initial meeting with Rix was a far cry from the one Syd had been telling her all about. "And I've been wanting to thank you for whatever you said to Ella. She texted me and apologized. I haven't heard from her since."

Jack blushed. "I know you didn't want me to say anything, but I didn't want to be responsible for giving you a stalker. I think she just got caught up in the possible romance of it all, you know?"

Layla nodded. She *did* know.

The next hour or so passed pleasantly enough. It was blatantly obvious that Jack was besotted with Syd. He complimented her constantly, maintained some form of physical contact with her, and he made moon eyes at her whenever she spoke, and whenever she didn't, for that matter. Several painfully beautiful women came in and out of the library, and while Jack acknowledged them because he knew them from work, he returned his focus to Syd as soon as was politely possible. And he was charming, and engaging, and funny. She could see why Syd was so taken with him. What was more revelatory about the time she spent with them was Syd. Layla had never seen her with anyone like she was with Jack. She clearly reveled in his adoration and attention, and she was attentive to him in ways she'd never been with her previous lovers. More than that, she looked relaxed and was being the Syd that Layla knew her to be. Which wasn't to say that she'd been false or disingenuous with previous partners, but more that she held much of her true self back, though Layla had never truly understood why. Syd had said it wasn't for fear of being hurt, because she wasn't interested in long term relationships anyway. Whatever it was, it was absent with Jack, and if he made Syd happy in new ways, then he had her best friend seal of approval.

Jack tapped his watch. "I hate to break up the conversation, but it's four o'clock, and that's when Rix likes to serve dinner." He looked at Layla. "And you know how she likes everything to run on time."

That was something Layla had learned early, even after their first meeting. Everything on set had run like clockwork so far. No delays and no wasted time. No tantrums or temperamental actors hanging around in their trailer while everyone else waited on them. It made Layla wonder if Rix allowed any chaos or spontaneity in her life, or if neat and ordered was everything to her.

They picked up their glasses and Jack led them out to the terrace. Everyone else had had the same memo because they fell into a line of people finding their way to the tables via helpful wait staff. Four large tables, seating around ten people each, were placed beneath a white marquee decorated with orange fairy lights. Oak leaf garlands hung from the ceiling and the uprights of the marquee had been wrapped in autumn leaves and berries, and each table had a large centerpiece of orange roses. Rix couldn't have known that roses were Layla's favorite flower, could she? Aesthetics were clearly important to her, as evidenced by her clothing and home in general. Layla wanted to see beneath this production though. What did Rix wear around the house, or to go to a ball game, or to the beach? Did she even do anything to relax, or was her world a constant whirl of work and fundraising?

Layla saw Rix at the head of the top table and waved. Rix beckoned her over. She gestured to Syd and Jack, and Rix nodded and waved them all to her.

Layla overheard Jack whisper to Syd that he'd never sat at Rix's table before. If he suspected Layla, and thus Syd, might be the reason for his upgrade, he didn't reveal it. As she approached, she saw the empty seats Rix had pointed to, and she saw an older couple on Rix's right, both of whom looked to be as tall as Rix, if not taller. The parents. Rix had her dad's eyes and her mom's stocky build. It dawned on her that she was meeting the parents. Shouldn't this be a much later step in the dating game? It wasn't a part of the process that bothered her. Generally, she liked meeting new people, but there was usually so much expectation from all parties and sometimes anxiety. Maybe this was better, though she didn't know how much Rix had told her parents about them. She should've asked when Rix told her they'd be here.

Rix stood when she got to them. Layla smiled at the chivalrous gesture. "Layla, this is my mom and dad. Mom and Dad, this is Layla Adams, the award-winning, best-selling novelist working with me on the TV series I'm directing."

Her dad stood and held out his hand. "Well, that's a mouthful, isn't it? I'm Dexter Reardon."

She shook it and smiled. "Hi, Dexter. It seems to be a Rix thing; most people just introduce me as Layla."

Her mom offered a little wave. "And I'm Millie. It's lovely to meet you, Layla. Rix has been telling us all about you and your books. She says she's been wanting to make them into this TV series since she read the first one."

"It's a pleasure to meet you too." Layla took her seat and placed her wine glass on an oak-shaped coaster.

"And this is Layla's best friend, Syd. She's an actor. And you've met Jack before."

The little group exchanged more pleasantries and greetings, and Layla emptied her wine glass. She'd barely replaced her glass before it was refilled by a stealthy waiter. Moments later, there were plates of turkey in front of everyone and tureens of all kinds of potatoes, vegetables, and side dishes.

"This looks almost as good as my turkey," Millie said as she spooned a healthy amount of sweet potato casserole onto her plate.

"Do you miss it? Cooking holiday dinners, I mean," Layla asked and put a dollop of cranberry sauce on her turkey.

"Oh no, not at all. I welcomed releasing the reins to my lovely daughter. When she first floated the idea, I was relieved that I wouldn't have to cook another turkey ever again." She patted Rix on the hand. "You were worried I wouldn't be happy though, weren't you?"

"Yep. But it was about time I got to look after you both."

"You've always been such a wonderful daughter." Millie turned to Dexter. "We did good, didn't we, honey?"

Dexter beamed with obvious pride. He took Millie's hand and kissed her knuckles. "We certainly did, sweetheart. Though you were the one who raised her. I spent most of her childhood working double shifts at the paint factory."

There was a certain ruefulness in his voice that Layla interpreted as his desire to have been around more. A sharp pang of envy that her father hadn't felt that way took Layla by surprise. Though he'd worked long hours too, he'd spent the rest of his time at the local bar with his friends. He saw Layla and her brothers as little more than time and money pits. Layla went to pick up her wine glass to drown the niggle but thought better of it. That was her mom's way of coping, and she'd worked hard at therapy to make sure it didn't become hers too. She pulled her hand back and glanced across at Rix, who was looking at her parents adoringly. What did that kind of love even feel like?

"Oh, honey, without you doing that, we wouldn't have had a roof over our heads." Millie looked across at Layla. "We lived in Detroit when Rix was a child. Hard times, you know?"

Layla shook her head. "I can't even imagine, Millie. You said you worked at the paint factory, Dexter. I love the cufflinks your colleagues had made for you."

On cue, Rix lifted her arms to show she was wearing them, and Dexter smiled widely.

"I was so proud of her for following her dreams and taking a risk to start her production company." Dexter gestured around him. "And look how well it turned out."

"I got my work ethic from you, Dad." Rix raised her glass and her voice so others could hear her. "I'm thankful for that and for everything else you taught me, as well as for the people I work with."

Rix's Thanksgiving kicked off everyone else on the table doing the same, and to a person, first thanks went to people's families. Syd squeezed Layla's hand under the table, knowing the pressure this ritual put on them both. Layla had nothing to thank her family for other than giving her life, and Syd had no living family to thank. As the thanks continued, sound began to swim, and Layla couldn't make any words out. A dull ache pressed on her chest, as if something were trying to get out. She wanted out, to run away. All the love in Rix's family, and with Rix's chosen family, and the friends who surrounded them was so overwhelming. It suffocated Layla while giving oxygen to everyone else around her, and she felt like she was struggling to keep her usual cool and easygoing façade in place. Layla pushed away the panic, imagining herself doing the new Tai Chi moves and breathing she'd been learning and calmed herself.

"I'm thankful to be here among friends, new and old, experiencing the biggest Thanksgiving celebration I've ever been to." Layla smiled and raised her glass toward Rix. "And I'm thankful to be working for such a talented director and to have the chance to make my words part of something truly special. I'd like to give thanks to everyone involved in that process." She took a sip of wine to signify the end of her speech and focused on the plate of food in front of her rather than make eye contact with Rix as she invited everyone to dig into the feast. That hadn't been so hard after all. What was that anyway? A panic attack? She'd never had one of those in her life. Maybe too much sun and the wine had combined to upset her system.

She asked a nearby waiter for a glass of mineral water and began to regain an equilibrium of sorts.

"Are you okay?" Syd whispered.

"Yeah, I'm good."

"A little too much wine?"

Layla nodded. "Must've been. I felt a bit disoriented and dizzy." She picked up her knife and fork. "I'm sure I'll feel much better when I've had something to eat."

Syd topped up Layla's glass with the bottle of chilled water the waiter had left on the table. "Nudge me if you need me to go to the bathroom with you."

"I'm sure I'll be fine." Layla scooped a forkful of mashed potato and had just popped it into her mouth when Rix touched her other hand gently and all too briefly.

"I'm sorry. Is all of this a bit too much?" she asked softly.

Layla took a moment before answering. She didn't want to make Rix feel bad; the party was wonderful, as were her parents, and up to the individual speeches, Layla had been having a lovely time. And she felt more herself again now, so maybe there was little point in attracting attention to her discomfort now that it had passed. But Rix had been attentive enough to notice something was wrong, and Layla didn't want to dismiss that accurate observation by not telling Rix how she felt. And how did she feel? Rather silly now, and also, not sure how she could explain it. "I don't know," she whispered, not wanting Rix's parents to overhear. "Everything closed in on me a little bit." It surprised her that she was instantly more honest with Rix than she had been with Syd.

"Are you okay to stay?"

The concern in Rix's eyes was so clear and genuine that it made Layla's heart bounce. Rather than be inconvenienced or conclude that Layla was being overdramatic or ungracious, Rix showed nothing but compassion.

"I am. I want to be here." She meant it. Despite the unexpected disquiet, she didn't feel the need to escape. Instead, she was drawn closer to Rix, safe enough to simply feel and to sit with her emotions without fear of judgment. And that was both a special and significant realization.

Chapter Twelve

Rix took a step back and examined her progress before she took another look at the large poster of the eagle's anatomy on her workshop wall. With the main shape complete, it was time to begin the more delicate work, where any mistake would mean she'd have to start all over again. She switched out to a quarter tip carving bar and took a deep breath.

Her phone vibrated in her thigh pocket. Usually, she would've ignored it. *Usually*, her phone would be in the cabin. When she was out here, she liked to forget about the city and her work, and to have any chance of that, she couldn't be within fifty feet of her phone. But she was hoping Layla might call. Even though she'd said she was okay yesterday, Rix was worried about her. Layla had been her usual charming self throughout dinner and during the ball game, but Rix had sensed a reflective quiet about her. She'd controlled the urge to check in with Layla earlier and decided to leave it until mid-afternoon. A quick check of her watch showed it was before noon. It probably wasn't Layla anyway.

She placed her saw on the workbench beside the carving and retrieved her phone. Her heart lightened when she saw it was Layla, and she was video calling. *Crap*. She tugged her ball cap down slightly then brushed off the saw dust from her shirt. Deciding she was respectable enough, she answered the call and grinned when Layla's face came into focus.

"Hey you," Layla said. "I wanted to thank you for yesterday, and also to apologize again for going a little weird on you."

Rix shook her head. "Not weird at all, and you're very welcome. Did you have a good time?"

"I did. And I enjoyed meeting your parents and more of your friends. All of them told me how amazing you were; did you pay them for that, or did they already owe you something?"

Rix laughed, relieved that Layla seemed to be her usual light-hearted self. "Assume that everyone owes me something, and you won't go wrong."

"If that's how they talk you up to a work colleague, I'd be interested to hear what they'd say if they knew they were talking to your girl—" Layla took a breath, censoring herself, and pulled her ponytail over her shoulder.

Rix took the opportunity to tease her. "Is that what you are? My girl?"

Layla narrowed her eyes, but her ice queen expression just made Rix's hormones kick in. Again.

"I don't know if a thirty-six-year-old woman can be considered a girl. Why? Do you like the sound of it?"

"Would you hold it against me if I said that I did?" Rix asked.

"Because 'girl' is patronizing and sexually suggestive?"

"Only if a man says it, no? But yes."

Layla stretched and yawned. "Since I said it first, I can't really judge, can I?"

"Not really. So do you think I'm as amazing as my friends and family think I am, or is it too early to tell?"

"I don't have enough quantitative or qualitative data to make an informed opinion yet." Layla was clearly trying hard not to smile. "But early indications are positive."

"I like the sound of that." She liked these playful exchanges that reminded her flirting wasn't just the purview of the young. "What do you need to get closer to your conclusion?"

"More interactions with the subject. More you."

Layla's husky voice notched up the sexual tension. Rix shrugged. "I could help with that, but you've forbidden any non-group gatherings."

"Where are you anyway?" Layla pointed over Rix's shoulder. "I didn't see a wooden building at your home, or did I miss it because I never got the guided tour?"

Rix clutched her heart. "Ow, you wound me. You could've taken Meg up on her offer."

"Is that right? And you would've been okay with that, would you? Because I remember you bristling a little at that suggestion."

She wasn't wrong. Meg would've wasted no time encouraging Layla to try out one of her guest beds. "I believe that would compromise the boundaries of our exclusivity agreement, so no. Not okay with that. At all. Ever." Rix ran her fingers along the peak of her ball cap as if she were underlining her words. "I'm at my lodge in Big Bear."

"You must've had an early start. Did you kick your parents out at six a.m.?"

"Of course not. They're still at my place, house-sitting and enjoying the pool."

"Sounds wonderful. Are you hunting?"

Rix caught the slight judgment in Layla's tone. "What if I were? Do you want me to bring you the head of a mule deer?"

"No! God, no. What am I supposed to do with that?"

"So you'd like some fresh venison instead?"

"Again, no."

"But you're not vegetarian, are you? I'm sure I saw you eating turkey yesterday."

Layla gave a tiny harrumph. "But *you* hadn't killed it."

"I'm confused. You're okay to eat a turkey bought from the butchers, but you won't eat venison from a hundred-and-twenty-pound deer I shot with the compound bow."

"You hunt with a bow?"

Rix chuckled. "You sound surprised."

"A little. I imagined you'd use a rifle, that's all."

Rix wiggled her eyebrows. "You've imagined me hunting? Was that just now or have you been dreaming about me in some kind of feral warrior state?"

"Someone's full of pep and vinegar this morning."

"And someone else is not answering the question."

"Yes."

"Yes to just now or yes to dreaming about me?"

"Both."

Rix propped her phone on a shelf and leaned against her workbench. "Is it your intention to get me so riled up, I won't be able to see straight? Whatever the female equivalent of a hard-on is, I've got the worst case of one in the history of lesbianism."

Layla didn't look in the least bit contrite. "The worst or the best?"

"Depends on your perspective. It'd be the best if you were here to take care of it. It's the worst because you're not, and you won't be for a while."

"Are you trying to guilt me into giving you an orgasm?"

"If I am—and I'm not admitting that's the case—I feel like you should shoulder some of the blame due to you *deliberately* making me feel like a highly-sexed twenty-something. I haven't thought about sex so much in a long time. I wake up turned on, I walk around turned on, I go to sleep turned on."

"I'm going to take that blame, but only because you're absolutely right, and I'm winding you up intentionally."

"Have you ever waited to sleep with someone you were dating for this long?"

"Rix, it's only been a couple of weeks."

That wasn't an answer, and it made Rix narrow her eyes slightly. "It already feels like months. I don't know how I'm supposed to hold out until the end of filming."

"Can't you take care of yourself?"

"Mee-maw told me I'd go blind if I did."

"And you've never tested her authority on the subject?"

Rix grinned. "Maybe."

"I suppose I could help you out…from a distance."

Now she was talking. "How so?"

"I've written a lot of sex scenes in my books, and you've got my whole back catalogue in your very fancy library. Book in one hand…"

A small twinge of disappointment settled when Layla neither finished her sentence nor offered phone sex, though Rix hadn't done that in a decade or so either. "So, you're coping just fine with the lack of physical contact? Am I not attractive enough for you to be fantasizing about?"

"I thought you were hunting deer, not fishing for compliments?"

"I'm not hunting," Rix said.

"Didn't you say you'd just killed a deer?"

"God, no. I've never killed anything larger than a spider. You assumed I was hunting, and I just played along."

"Huh. Well, if you're not hunting, what are you doing in the forest all by yourself? Assuming you are alone, that is."

"Of course I'm alone. And I'm working on a carving." Rix heard the desire for Layla's approval in her voice. Would she be impressed?

"Carving?"

"Chainsaw carving, actually."

"Ooh, how very butch. Now I know how you've developed such broad, strong shoulders."

Yep, even through the light mocking, Layla sounded impressed. "Have you been ogling my body, Miss Adams?"

"If I said yes, would you hold it against me?"

Rix laughed and shook her head. "Oh my god, that was cheesy. I don't think anyone has ever said a line like that to me."

"You get picked up a lot, do you?" Layla took a sip from a mug emblazoned with the words, "Go away, I'm editing."

"That would be a no. I'm usually the one who makes the first move."

"Why doesn't that surprise me? I suppose I should get off the phone and let you get back to your carving."

"Do you have plans?" Rix asked, enjoying the conversation too much to get off the phone just yet.

"Not really. But inspiration has just struck, and I've got an idea for an erotic short story about a woodworker in a forest lodge who takes in a lost hitchhiker. I'll probably get my laptop out and hammer it out while it's fresh in my mind."

Rix liked the idea of being Layla's muse. She liked the idea of reading an erotic story by her even more. "Can I read it when it's finished?"

"I don't know. It feels like this one might be too personal for me to share."

"Oh yeah? Are we the main characters?"

"What do you think? This could be my way of dealing with our sexual tension."

"Maybe you've hit on the perfect way for both of us to deal with it. You write it, and I'll read it. If it's going to be personal, I could pick up some good tips for when I do finally get you in my arms."

"You want me to make it easy for you?" Layla asked. "Isn't most of the fun in the discovery?"

She heard a door close loudly in the background and Syd called out.

"You have a point, and it sounds like you have company. I'll let you get to it."

Syd appeared on the screen and waved. "Hey, Rix, thanks so much for letting me come to your Thanksgiving yesterday. It was an awesome party, and you have a beautiful home."

Rix noticed Syd was wearing the same clothes as yesterday but didn't comment. She was glad Jack had found someone to date, and Syd seemed like a lot of fun. "You're very welcome, Syd. Thanks for coming."

Syd retreated, and Layla took up the screen again. "I have to go. Syd likes to give me a full debrief."

"That doesn't sound weird at all. Jack would be mortified if he knew Syd was discussing his sexual prowess with a work colleague."

Layla smiled. "Okay, not a *full* debrief. And you've just proved my worry about keeping personal and private lives separate."

"Damn." Rix smacked the hell of her palm to her forehead. "Hang on, were you coming around to an earlier liaison?"

"Speak soon, sexy woodworker." Layla waved and cut the video feed before Rix could respond.

Rix took her phone from the shelf, slipped it into her pocket, and picked up one of her carpenter's pencils. She caressed the lines of the wood slowly and earned herself a splinter, which she tugged out with her teeth. Switching between glances at the eagle and the carving, she lightly etched the outline of the bird's feathers and wondered what it might be like to sketch Layla in the nude. Rix didn't profess to be an artist of any caliber, but she'd enjoy simply staring at Layla's body for hours. Maybe when their physical relationship began, Rix would invite Layla over to the house to do exactly that. She tried to breathe away her arousal and concentrate on the wood. The way Layla made her feel, sketching her would be the last thing on Rix's mind when that time eventually came.

Chapter Thirteen

LAYLA WALKED INTO the changing room she'd been directed to and scrunched up her nose. Rustic would've been a generous way to describe the rotting lean-to space lined with neoprene suits of torture and degradation. The wetsuit. She wasn't a big fan of wearing suits; she never had been, and these contraptions were the worst of the lot. At least with a skirt suit, there were places for her body to take cover, though not to hide. Even if she had a Hollywood-approved body, parading herself around in skin-tight clothes wouldn't be her style. Form-fitting, she could do, and she liked her curvy edges. Angular bones covered with nothing but skin wasn't an ideal she would ever strive to emulate. Syd had a nice body, and it suited her, but Layla wasn't envious of it. And even Syd would struggle to make a wetsuit sexy.

Rachel and several other members of the cast filtered into the room. They consulted a dog-eared poster on the wall, selected their suit, and began to pull them on.

"How am I supposed to know which size I need?" Layla quietly asked Rachel. She'd already got hers up over her muscular thighs and the rest was folded down over her waist. How had she managed to make it look cool?

"Check out that guide." Rachel pointed to the poster then caught Layla's wrist. "It's warm enough to stay in what you're wearing, if you'd prefer."

"Okay." She very much would prefer that, but she didn't really want to be the odd one out. This was another group activity Rix had organized, and if everyone else was encased in the tortuous material, she should be too. She followed her chest and waist measurements to a recommendation, then went to the rack marked large. Neon pink, canary yellow, and fluorescent green were her options. The extra-large rack offered far more preferable black and gray harlequin efforts. She took one of those instead, deciding that a little extra room couldn't be a bad thing when the instructor would be expecting her to jump around. Ah, jumping around. The bikini she had on beneath her board shorts and T-shirt was designed for comfort and looks, not support. If she was going to have to be up and down like a yo-yo, she didn't want to be jiggling around all over the place.

She huffed as she swapped out her sedate costume for a large, bright green one. At least if she fell in, she'd be easy to spot in the dark waters of the Pacific. Who was she kidding? *If* she fell in? The better question would be how many times she'd fall in. She found a free spot on a decrepit looking bench, kicked off her flip flops, took off her water shorts, and sucked it up.

A few arduous minutes later, and thanks to Rachel helping zip her in—because Layla wasn't a Cirque du Soleil contortionist with bendy toy arms—she was ready to go. She headed outside and joined their group of ten. Rix, who had been catching some early morning waves, smiled as she approached. Slick and wet, her surfboard under her arm, she looked every inch the ad for hot lesbian.

The three instructors, in matching white and blue wetsuits, arranged the group in a circle, and they stood in the center to demonstrate how to lie on the board and how to pop up from it. Pop up? Now *they* were kidding.

"Are you ready for this, city girl?" Rix asked as she took a spot in the circle beside her.

"Why are you so hell bent on making me do crazy, life-threatening activities?" Layla asked. "First the climbing and now this." She gestured at the piece of foam on the floor, already doubting its capacity to keep her afloat even before she started "popping up."

"The tai chi wasn't life threatening."

Rix grinned mischievously, and Layla shook her head. With a smile like that, Layla would probably follow her into a dark, foreboding cave without a flashlight. "You should tell that to my screaming thighs and ass."

"I'd love to have a conversation with your ass," Rix whispered.

Layla gave Rix a playful evil eye and shushed her. "I'm trying to concentrate, and you're distracting me. Shouldn't you be standing in the center with those three showing us all how to do this?"

Rix shook her head. "Nope, it's better this way. And just because I can surf doesn't mean I can teach someone else to do it."

Layla rolled her eyes. "Don't tell me. This is the part where you say how you feel the power of the ocean under your board, and it rises up beneath you. You become one with the board, and you ride the wave all the way to the shore, not quite knowing how you managed it." She gave Rix a sideways glance as she unsuccessfully tried to focus on the instructors.

"No. This is the part where I tell you I'm really impatient and can't teach anyone anything."

"Ha. I don't believe you. Look at Jack." Layla motioned toward him as he lifted himself into a push up position on his board. "You're teaching him everything about the business, he says."

"I'm mentoring him, that's different."

"It's Layla, right?" one of the young instructors asked as she approached. Layla nodded. "Your turn."

Her turn to what? She hadn't done a push up since college. "I'm really sorry, but my boss keeps talking to me, and I didn't really catch what you were saying."

The instructor turned to Rix and raised her eyebrow. "Is that right, Ms. Reardon?"

"Snitch," Rix said to Layla then clasped her palms together in apology. "I'm sorry, Ann. I'll be quiet."

Judging by the expression that accompanied Rix's words, Layla wasn't convinced she meant it.

Ann smiled and shook her head. "You should know better by now."

"By now?" Layla asked. "How many times have you made your employees go through this torment?"

"Torment?" Ann managed to look unimpressed and good-natured at the same time. "Is that what you think of surfing?"

"No, not at all," Layla said, eager not to irritate the person who might have to dive to her rescue, drag her to safety, and resuscitate her. Although perhaps Rix could do the final part. "It's not the surfing. That looks amazing and I've always wanted to try it." She pinched at the stretchy material her body was clad in. "It's these things. I feel like I've dressed for a fetish sex party without the payoff."

Ann laughed. "Well, I won't say that riding a wave is as good as riding a woman, but it's a good runner-up. Let's have this same discussion after you've caught a few breaks."

So, Ann was family. Layla liked that the things she was doing with Rix all seemed to be with LGBTQ people. The tai chi guy was an impressively hirsute bear of a gay guy, and now that she paid attention to the other two instructors, she'd bet they were queer in one way or another too. She'd save the query for later lest Ann reprimanded them again. "I like your optimism, but I don't share it. I was watching some surfers earlier, and there's just no way I can get upright on that board and balance on a moving carpet of water that fast."

"The people you were watching have probably been surfing since they were babies." Ann put her hands on Layla's shoulders. "Don't worry. I'm going to show you how to get up sure and steady."

Layla wished she could suck in some of Ann's confidence through her shoulders. "I promise I'll give it my best shot," she said, somehow wanting to do it for both of them.

"Good." Ann released Layla's shoulders and took a half step back. "First, we need to find out which foot is dominant. Relax and face me. I'm going to push you, and you need to keep yourself from falling over. When I push, your dominant foot will naturally step back to save you."

Layla planted her feet and waited. A couple of pushes determined she was "goofy-footed," so she'd have to plant her right foot at the front of her board.

Ann positioned her board in front of Layla and demonstrated what she wanted her to do. "Okay, Layla, lie down on your board for me as if you're floating on the water."

Layla did as instructed and even managed the push up as directed. After a few attempts, Ann seemed reasonably happy with her efforts.

"Keep practicing. We'll be hitting the water soon," Ann said and moved onto the next learner.

Layla turned to Rix. Her body needed a break from all the jumping, bouncing, and dragging. "I wanted to ask if it was coincidence that all the things we've done so far have been with queer businesses or if you make a point of supporting them?"

"It's not a coincidence." Rix uncapped her water bottle and offered it to Layla.

"How did you come to choose them?" she asked when Rix didn't offer further explanation.

"Do you want the short version or the long version?"

Layla handed Rix her bottle back after taking a long drink. "The long version. Always the long version."

"Then we should sit for a minute or two." Rix laid down on her board, and Layla rested on hers. "All the businesses we've used started at the LGBTQ center, under their start-up program. They're led by young people who ended up there because their families rejected them."

Layla thought about the martial artist who led their morning classes. "But the tai chi guy was in his early thirties, wasn't he?"

"Nah, all the hair makes him look older than he is," Rix said and smiled fondly. "He's only twenty-five, and he landed with George when he was fifteen."

Rix's expression had softened and become almost wistful. Her passion for her work with their community was clear, and it reminded Layla that she'd once been a bit of an activist herself. But her life had taken her in a different direction, and her writing career gave her little spare time. Given Rix's schedule, she wondered if her logic was more of an excuse than an actual reality. "Have you been involved with the center that long?"

"Longer." Rix leaned back on her board and laid flat. "I started volunteering there when I first got to LA. I soon got chatting to George, and he had such huge plans and ambitions. He's a real visionary. I'd wanted to do something that made a difference since Matthew Shephard was murdered. I'd marched in Prides, but it wasn't enough. When I met George in my late twenties, he inspired me to do more, and the LGBTQ center was the perfect place to do it for thousands of my community."

Rix's dedication was impressive, and it was another thing that made Layla like her even more. True altruists were a rare breed. Today's society, while connected digitally in unprecedented ways, had never been more self-absorbed. But Rix's activism and generosity forced Layla to turn her attention to her own life. A quick examination had her coming up very short on any kind of pay it back scale. Uncomfortable with the comparison to Rix, she decided to park the self-flagellation.

"What's Ann's story, if you're allowed to tell me?"

Rix put her hands behind her head and looked up at Layla. "Ann has shared her experience at a lot of the center's conferences and training workshops. She's very comfortable with people knowing her story, but it's nice of you not to expect me to be able to tell you."

Layla shrugged. "Everyone owns their own story, and I think they should choose who gets to hear it and how. It's not always the case, and that's probably why I hate gossip so much." But her main reason for disliking it was far more personal than that. "My family and I were the epicenter of our small town's gossip mill."

"Because of your mom?"

"Mom. Dad. My brother. They had plenty of fodder." She dismissed the maudlin thoughts. "But tell me about Ann."

Rix seemed to hesitate. "It's not a regular gay kid rejected by parents story, Layla. Are you sure you want to hear it?"

Layla never *liked* hearing or reading about the kind of thing she was expecting Rix to tell her, but that didn't mean she shouldn't be exposed to it. "I am."

"Ann is from Knoxville, where her father was a hardline Baptist pastor. Bastard was a police officer too."

Rix's language sharpened Layla's focus. In almost a month of knowing her, Layla hadn't heard Rix raise her voice, let alone curse. She prepared herself that the tale she was about to hear wouldn't be as inspiring as everything else Rix had shared with her today.

"Ann realized in her early teens that she liked her best friend in ways she didn't like her other friends, and in the ways she was supposed to like boys. She kept a lid on it for a while, but then her friend confessed she had similar feelings, and they started to play around a little. Her mother caught them in her room."

Rix took a deep breath, as though it was physically painful to retell the next part of the story. Layla could guess what the end result was, but Rix's words were far worse than she'd imagined, and nausea gripped her stomach when Rix had finished. She thought about all the crap in her own family history and how she'd escaped it to lead the life she wanted to, away from the shadows and sorrow, but all of that felt like nothing in the face of Ann's story.

"Are you okay? You've gone pale."

Just as the color had apparently drained from her face, so had her energy and her words. She shook her head and swallowed hard as she picked up Rix's water bottle and took a long, cooling drink to wash down the bile that had risen in response to the story.

"That's the kind of stunned, sickened silence Ann gets at talks when she finishes that part of her life experience," Rix said.

"Monsters." Who did such things to their own flesh and blood? Layla looked around the circle of people jumping up and down on their boards, some of them queer, some of them straight. She'd talked to all of them but didn't really know any of their backgrounds. She looked across at Ann, smiling and laughing with Rachel, who seemed to have grasped the principles easily and was up on her board looking like she was born to surf. It would be impossible to know what she'd been through just from looking at her, and though maybe a closer inspection would yield physical scars, the emotional scarring she simply had to have was hidden from view. But here she was now, in LA teaching people to surf, hundreds of miles away from her history and seemingly happy.

Layla looked at Rix, who hadn't tried to speak or infringe on her thought process. "How did she get from that to this?"

"That's where it gets better. She managed to escape the conversion camp and hitchhiked her way to LA, because she'd read on the internet about the center and George's work. She showed up on the center's doorstep emaciated and lost, and George took her in. He found her a foster home with a lesbian couple, and she started to rebuild her life. George and I started an initiative that provided seed funding to young entrepreneurs with big ideas about three years after Ann got to LA, and she was one of the first beneficiaries. The surf school is her baby."

Layla felt the tear on her cheek before she realized she was crying. Rix wiped it away with her thumb then seemed to catch herself and apologized. Layla shook her head and cleared her throat. "I can see why you'd have her speak. That's a hell of a story with a happy ending."

Rix smiled. "Not a happy ending: a happy beginning."

"Very poetic. Have you ever thought of being a writer?"

Ann returned with Rachel and Dewy, the make-up artist. Layla tried to keep her expression neutral. Rix said she didn't mind her story being told, but she was working and probably didn't want to be suffocated by the admiration Layla had for her.

She squatted down to Layla on her board. "Are you ready to give it a go on the water? The waves are nice and gentle at the moment."

"Sure," Layla said, picking up her board as she stood. "Let's see if I can win your trophy for worst surfer ever."

Rix joined her, both her and her surfboard towering over Layla. "If I can do it, I'm pretty sure you'll be able to."

"How long have you been surfing?" Layla asked as they walked toward the water's edge.

"Only about six years. I had a mini mid-life crisis approaching forty when I realized I had a long bucket list of things I hadn't even begun to tick off. Surfing was one of them, and it was an easy one to start with since I was living so close to all of these amazing beaches."

Ann nodded. "And she's pretty good for her age." She jumped out of reach when Rix made a grab for her, but Rachel swatted Ann's shoulder.

"Cheeky," Rachel said and smiled.

"You won't make it to my age saying things like that. I'm not too old to kick your ass." Rix grimaced and rubbed her chest.

Ann laughed. "Did you pull a muscle?"

"It's nothing." Rix strapped her board rope to her ankle. "Come on, let's catch your first waves."

Layla, Rachel, and Dewy secured their boards to their legs as Rix had done and waded into the ocean.

"Ooh, that's cold," Dewy said.

Layla shivered. "I'm wishing I chose a full body suit now."

Rachel laughed. "What are you talking about? It's like bath water."

"I don't know who's been drawing your baths, Rachel, but you should fire them if this is their idea of a warm one." Layla dropped her board onto the water and hugged herself.

Rix was already up ahead of them on her board and paddling out. Ann followed her and encouraged them to get on their boards.

"Show this trio how it's done, Rix," Ann said.

Layla tentatively sat up on her board and watched as Rix paddled toward the shore, popped up on a wave, and rode along it before jinking back and taking it all the way in. She jumped rather than fell into the shallows. Layla led the group appreciation by applauding, though she stopped when her enthusiasm started to rock her board.

"You're up, Layla." Ann had paddled behind her. "There's a nice gentle one coming up. Let this one go, then get flat to your board and start paddling as fast as you can. I'll call out when you need to pop up."

Layla got down on her board. "Okay, lovely ocean. Be nice." She began to paddle as fast as she could without splashing so she could see where she was going. "Good ocean."

"Go, go, go."

Ann's call made her jump, but she stopped paddling, put her palms flat and pushed up. She pulled her left leg up but wobbled as she tried to draw her right foot to the front of the board. She over-corrected and tumbled headfirst into the wave. Water invaded every open orifice, and she emerged to the surface, flapping like a baby bird. Her feet found purchase on the sand bed, and she felt a little silly when she realized she could stand up and was only waist deep.

"Watch out!"

Layla heard the call too late as she reached for her board and was knocked off her feet by another wave. She took on a mouthful of sea water and retched it out as she broke the water's surface once again. She felt strong hands on her upper arms as she struggled to stay upright.

"It's okay. You can stand now," Rix said. "Just make sure you face the ocean as soon as you come up, so you know what's coming your way."

Rix's hands felt reassuring and safe, and Layla spat out the last of the salty water. "Attractive, huh?"

Rix grinned. "More than you know." She pulled Layla's board in using the ankle tether and handed it to her. "Ready to go again?"

"I think I'll paddle some more before I try again. Me and the ocean need to come to an agreement. I have to convince it not to try to kill me."

They walked back into the Pacific until Layla was waist height in it, and she pulled herself onto her board.

Ann was busy helping Rachel catch her first wave which, of course, she did with the elegance of a swan, and stayed perfectly balanced and upright all the way in. Layla didn't envy her body, but she did covet her poise.

"You will get it."

Rix must've read her expression. Layla sighed. "I hope so. I love being out on the ocean. It's so calming and surfing properly looks like a lot of fun."

"You were close to a good pop up, and that's impressive for a first attempt."

Layla didn't know if that was true or if Rix was just humoring her, but she appreciated it either way. Rix sat up on her board, and Layla noted she clasped her hands together the way she did when she had something to say. "Is something on your mind?"

Rix nodded. "What you were saying earlier, about your family and gossip mongers… I want you to know that I understand why you don't want to make us official until after we've finished filming. We're not under the same kind of scrutiny as the actors, but there's still interest in what we get up to and with whom, possibly more from the inside than the paps."

"I appreciate that. And I'm glad that we're getting to spend so much time together, even though it's in groups." She leaned closer to Rix though no one was near them to overhear. "Which is probably for the best, because it's not getting any easier to keep my hands off you."

"I hope you'll think I've been worth the wait."

The seriousness of Rix's words was clear beneath her jovial tone, and her small insecurities revealed themselves to be the same ones Layla held. She hadn't had complaints before, her sex life had been pretty good, although she hadn't had or given mind-blowing orgasms. She constantly returned to the night of their first, and only, kiss. The heat rating had been off the scale, and she tried to commit every single aspect of it to memory: the softness of Rix's lips, the tender but firm pressure when they kissed, the sweet taste of her. She used all of it to kickstart the fantasies she'd been creating in the privacy of her bed each night. Going home alone after spending a full day with Rix was becoming harder to bear. The more time she spent with her, talking to her, seeing her in action with other people, the more she craved.

But not being talked about, by anyone, was important to Layla, so she wasn't about to give into her sexual urges, as ridiculously strong as they were. "If that kiss is an indicator of how amazing it'll be when we finally get together, I'm almost one hundred percent certain that you have nothing to worry about."

She looked back across to their group just as Dewy emerged from the water looking like a drowned rat. It seemed mean, but Layla was glad she wasn't the only one who sucked at this. Ann waved at her to come closer. "Looks like it's my turn again. Wish me luck." She paddled over and spent the next energy-sapping thirty minutes popping and falling, popping and falling, until things finally clicked into place, and Layla rode her first baby break without crashing into the ocean. Everyone in their group, on the water and the beach, hollered and clapped, and Layla saw Rix taking it all in as the little TV family she was building came together. For someone who'd never really appreciated group dynamics, Layla was beginning to see the appeal.

Layla walked back out and sat up on her board to watch as Rix started to paddle to catch a wave about fifty yards away. But just as she pushed up from her board, Rix clutched at her chest, throwing her off balance and into the surf. "Ann!"

Ann looked to Layla then across to where Rix had been. "She'll be fine. She probably got caught off guard by a surprise wave."

"No, she held her chest and fell in." Layla started to paddle toward where she'd last seen Rix just as she came up, but she looked flustered. Another large wave submerged her, and Layla thought she saw Rix's surfboard pop up behind her head. "Ann, she's in trouble."

Ann had obviously seen Rix's distress this time and began to swim toward her. Layla continued to paddle, but Ann overtook her, and Rix's board bobbed up to the surface. Ann dove under a wave and remained submerged. Layla's heart pounded against her board, and time seemed to slow. She kept her eyes fixed on the spot, praying for them to emerge.

Ann came up with Rix under her arm. Layla was close enough now to see that Rix's eyes were closed. Was that blood on Ann's wetsuit? Layla paddled toward shore parallel to Ann and Rix. After Ann got into shallow waters, where her other two instructors waited, the three of them carried Rix onto the sand.

Layla's arms weren't cooperating, and she lost all coordination and speed. When she finally got out of the water and tore off the ankle strap to her surfboard, she saw Rix was on her side, still unconscious, and Ann was kneeling on the floor beside her. It was a good sign she wasn't performing CPR, wasn't it? As she got closer, her knees buckled beneath her. Ann held a small towel to the back of Rix's head, and it was soaked with her blood. Jack paced back and forth with his cell phone pressed to his ear. The rest of the group milled around at a polite distance, looking like they didn't know how to react. Layla became hyper aware of her own reaction. She hadn't gone so far as to wail and sob, but she was the only one on her knees.

She put her hands on the warm sand and pushed herself up, willing her legs to support her. She slowly walked to Jack.

He looked up and grimaced. "The ambulance is on its way."

The color had drained from his face, and he looked like she felt. Kicking her own emotions into touch, she went into care mode. Rix was like a mother or big sister to him, and they'd known each other for several years; he was far more distraught than she had a right to be. She put her arm around his shoulder, hoping he wouldn't baulk at the gesture. "She's strong. She'll be okay."

He cleared his throat and stiffened under her arm. "Did you see what happened?"

He did a decent job of trying to cover the tremble in his voice, and she pulled him in a little tighter as she described what she'd seen.

Jack pulled away from her embrace and looked at her, his expression deadly serious. "She clutched her chest. Are you absolutely sure?"

"I'm positive, and she did it briefly before getting in the water too. Why?" Layla wondered if it had anything to do with the doctor's orders Rix had shrugged off in an earlier conversation.

Jack held up his index finger to indicate she should be quiet and went back to his mobile. "Hello? Yes. Ms. Reardon may have had a heart attack… Yes."

What? Why hadn't Rix mentioned she had heart problems? Wasn't she too young for that? She was about to grill Jack when the ambulance came down the jetty. In the blur of activity that followed, Layla realized that she wouldn't be able to accompany Rix to the hospital. As far as anyone else was concerned, she was just another one of Rix's colleagues, just like everyone else standing around on the beach looking shell shocked. But inside, she was reeling.

Chapter Fourteen

WHEN RIX WOKE, the first thing that came into her awareness was the sharp, throbbing pain in the back of her head. The second was the various spots of tightness on her arms and chest. She opened her eyes slowly, looked down her body to see multiple needles in her veins, and followed the lines up to bags of fluid. Wires from her chest led to a monitor with a colorful and spiky display of her vital signs. *I'm in the hospital?* She slowly raised her right arm, lifted her head slightly, and felt the back. She discovered a padded bandage that wrapped all the way around her skull and then she sighed, remembering what she'd been doing. Rookie mistake. She relaxed back onto her pillow gingerly and took a deep breath, concentrating on the rest of her body to find any other sore spots. Everything else seemed normal.

The door to her room opened, and a white-coated woman entered. She picked up Rix's chart and flipped through it before looking up and making eye contact. "Good afternoon, Ms. Reardon, I'm Doctor Jephson. How are you feeling?"

"Embarrassed, mostly." It'd been at least nine months since she'd last surfed, and she'd gone straight back into it, expecting to be the same standard. Which wasn't high in the first place, but she'd appreciated Ann's comment about her skill level even though it was tempered with a reference to her age. An age she felt right now, lying prone in a damn hospital bed. The last time she'd been in the hospital, she was being born, and she was proud to be able to say that. No broken bones, obviously no pregnancies, and no health scares. She'd broken a perfect record as well as her head.

Dr. Jephson smiled, a perfectly fake smile where the emotion stopped way short of her eyes. "The good news is that it wasn't a heart attack. Your ECG and blood tests were clear. Your assistant tells me you gripped your chest before you fell into the water. On a scale of one to ten, how bad was the pain?"

Rix had been hoping to keep that to herself, but Layla had probably seen her do it and told Jack out of concern. She was aware of the futility and counter-productiveness of her thought process, but she hadn't wanted to give credence to her health issues by acknowledging them herself, let alone sharing them with other people. "Two."

Dr. Jephson arched her right eyebrow and tapped on Rix's chart with her pen. "There's little point in not being honest with me, Ms. Reardon. I can only help you if you wish to help yourself."

Suitably reprimanded, Rix amended her answer to a five.

"And the pains you've been having, they've been around the same level?" Dr. Jephson asked.

"Yes."

"And they haven't been getting progressively worse since your own doctor diagnosed your angina?"

"No."

"Well, that's one good thing. If you take steps to alter your diet, and you exercise more, the pains should reduce over time. But you won't ever be able to go back to your previous lifestyle. What about smoking, drinking, and drugs?"

Wow, the bedside manner on this doctor was seriously lacking in subtlety. "I smoke the occasional cigar, and I drink most nights. I haven't done drugs since I was at college."

"Good. But you'll need to take the smoking and drinking down to zero if you want to get serious about your health…unless you're interested in more regular and prolonged visits to my hospital."

No, Rix didn't want that. She'd be happy never to see this doctor again.

Dr. Jephson flipped over another page. "It looks like you bashed your skull with the surfboard, but the CT scan shows no swelling around the brain. We'll keep you in overnight for observation, but I expect you'll be free to go in the morning." She replaced Rix's chart. "I noted that your doctor advised you to exercise more too. Perhaps you should try something a little less dangerous."

This time, her smile was more genuine, but she'd turned and left the room before Rix could respond, leaving her staring at the door and wondering why the woman had chosen the caring profession when she seemed better suited to something requiring less actual care.

Jack leaned in around the doorjamb and knocked. She waved him in.

He pulled up a chair to sit beside her after placing one of her overnight bags on the drawers under the window. "I collected your emergency bag from the office."

"Thank you," she said, once again reminded that Jack was a great assistant. But he looked pale, and his concern was painted in the lines around his eyes. "I'm okay, Jack." She could see his internal struggle in his expression, as he strived to maintain a professional appearance when all he probably wanted to do was give her a hug. She knew that's what he'd be feeling because she was feeling exactly the same.

"What did the doctor say?" he asked.

She appreciated the caution in his voice. There was no expectation that she should share her medical details with him, but he clearly hoped she would. If Rix wanted him to continue being a great assistant, he had to have all the information, particularly since he was responsible for feeding her most of the time. She gave him a quick rundown of what Doctor Ryan had said, and he made notes on his tablet.

"No more steak meals with Mac then? You've got a dinner date coming up next week. Would you like me to cancel or shift to a different restaurant?"

Did she want Mac to know about her health issues? Or could she change venues without the Spanish Inquisition? Sure, she had to make some changes, but both her own doctor and Dr. Personality here agreed she could mostly go back to normal. There was no need to worry anyone else about it. "See if you can find a new restaurant opening with a good buzz. If we swap to that, I won't have to mention the real reason."

Jack nodded. "I'll contact a dietician and get a special meal plan worked out for you."

She rolled her eyes. "If it's possible, I'd really like it if every meal wasn't either bland or liquid."

"You got it." Jack looked up from his tablet. "What do you want to tell the cast and crew?"

"Who saw me fall?"

"Just Layla, I think, and she told me when I was on the phone to 911."

She didn't want to make a big deal of this, but she also didn't want to lie. Rix rolled her neck and grimaced at the pain in her head. "Let's stick with the obvious: I fell in, and my board smacked me in the head and knocked me unconscious. The doctor said they'd release me tomorrow so

I can be back in the studio on Monday."

"And what about Layla?"

That was a good question. Would she be mad that Rix hadn't told her about any of this? The getting to know each other had to include health too, but they hadn't really gotten to that yet. It wasn't like they were using a questionnaire and ticking off information as they went. "I'll talk to her. Do you know—"

Jack pulled her phone from his jacket pocket. "Here it is. She seemed quite worried about you, the whole group was. I'll send an email out to reassure everyone you're okay."

"That'd be great." Rix glanced at the time on her phone. "Thanks for checking in on me, but you can go home now. I'm sure you've got far more interesting things to do on a Saturday night than hang around this hospital all night."

His responding grin was a dead giveaway. Things must still be going well with Syd.

"Thanks, Ms. Reardon." He finished tapping away on his tablet, presumably firing off the email to the team, then slipped it into his shoulder bag. "Are you sure there's nothing else? Would you like me to contact your mom and dad?"

"No, definitely not." It'd only been a week since her dad had given her hell for not telling him what was going on with her. She'd call him in her own time and stick to the official story. He didn't need the hassle or the worry. "I'm all good. Off you go." She waited until he'd left before picking up her phone and pressing the speed dial to Layla, voice rather than video call. She hadn't looked in a mirror yet, but hospital gowns and full head bandages were on no one's list of attractiveness. Layla picked up on the first ring.

"Rix?"

"Hey, Layla. Are you okay?"

She let out a short laugh. "Am I okay? Let's talk about you first."

Rix smiled. Hearing Layla's concern gave her comfort that she cared. "I'm fine. A bit of a gash on the back of my head from my board, but that's all."

"That's all?" Layla's voice sharpened a little. "If that's all, why did Jack tell the paramedics that you might have had a heart attack?"

"He overreacted. I've been having some chest pains. Jack put two and two together and came up with six."

"I saw you hold your chest, Rix. I don't think Jack overreacted at all. And he probably has more information than I do."

"Honestly, I'm fine. And I'm sorry I didn't tell you. It really is just a few chest pains and a higher than desirable cholesterol level. The doctors have told me what I've got to do, and Jack is all over it. But I'll be at the studio on Monday, signed off with a clean bill of health. If it was something more serious, they wouldn't release me, would they?" She flinched a little at the small white lie, but there was no need to worry Layla unnecessarily. Despite having to explain herself, Rix's heart hummed in a good way. She was usually the one who cared too much.

Layla huffed. "I suppose not."

"Were you worried about me?" Rix couldn't resist teasing her a little.

"*Everyone* was worried about you."

"But you were extra worried."

"Did you want me to be extra worried?"

"Maybe."

"Why?"

"It shows me you care. You know, that you really care."

Layla sighed. "If you wanted to know how I feel, maybe you could just ask next time rather than facilitating a near-death experience."

"That's a little over-dramatic, isn't it?"

"You were unconscious and would've drowned, had it not been for Ann pulling an amazing Baywatch-style life-saving feat and dragging you to safety. You were bleeding everywhere. A shark could've come and eaten you. There are sharks here, aren't there? Big, giant, woman-eating sharks. I feel like I should've asked about those before I dangled my legs in their territory and offered them human sushi."

Rix laughed and had to hold her head. "Don't make me laugh; it hurts."

"Good."

Beyond the vague humor of the situation, Layla's point was sobering. Rix could've been out there on her own with nobody to save her. If Ann hadn't been there, or if she hadn't been quick enough… That was a thought she didn't want to entertain right now. "You're mad at me for having an accident?"

"Apparently, I am."

"You sound surprised."

"That would be because I am surprised."

"Because you like me."

"Are you asking me or telling me that I like you?"

"I'm asking you how you feel about me." Though Rix had no idea how she'd gotten around to that question. The ensuing pause was longer than Rix had hoped for. Did it take that long for Layla to answer because she didn't know how she felt about Rix, or because she didn't want to say that she didn't like her all that much?

"Like is such a wishy-washy word," Layla said, finally. "I like a lot of things: smoked hickory nuts, cinnamon coffee, making snow angels. But the other L-word is a little premature. The things and people I love have been around for a long time, but you've only been in my life for a couple of months. Is there a word for the middle ground, do you think?"

"You're the writer. Don't you have license to create new words?" Rix tried to keep her reaction under control when what she wanted to do was a little Irish jig around her room. It would be impulsive to talk about being in love, but it certainly seemed like they might be heading in that direction.

"Okay. It's not very clever, but I loke you."

"I love it," Rix said, deliberately used the L-word.

"Can I bring you anything?" Layla asked. "I'm at Nazu. It's only a few minutes away, and they do takeout."

Rix grinned. Her day was getting better and better. "Really? Do you go there a lot?"

"Don't be an ass. I'm here because it's close to the hospital you were rushed to, and I didn't want to go home without knowing you were okay. And by that, I mean seeing for myself that you're okay. I can come empty handed, if you're going to be obstreperous, but I am coming."

"That's another thing *I* love: you use words I've never heard of even though I consider myself well-read."

"Now you're getting crazy with the L-word. I'm going to bring you a selection of low-fat, super healthy, and surprisingly tasty options, okay?"

"I'd love that." Rix liked this take-charge, bossy britches version of Layla looking after her. And it'd be very easy to get used to.

Chapter Fifteen

AFTER LEARNING HOW much Rix loved steak and burgers but that she couldn't eat any of it now, Layla was sure she'd found the perfect way to soften the blow. She'd wanted an excuse to visit the Sugar Baby Farm near Boise since she'd first heard of it, and this was it. Layla had also booked them an overnight stay in a nearby B&B even though the flight was only two hours. All she needed to do now was get Rix to come with her.

"Cut. That's great. Let's call it a day."

Rix stood from her director's chair and after stretching, she shared a few words with Rachel. Rix was still sporting a sizeable Band Aid at the base of her skull where her surfboard had done its best to give her a lobotomy. Layla had to make light of it, or she'd drift into a darker scenario where Rix had been seriously injured. Since that eventful weekend, Layla had woken in a cold sweat on several nights, with nightmares varying from Ann not being able to find Rix at all to a shark attack. One thing was certain, Layla wouldn't be surfing in the Pacific any time soon, and neither would Rix if she had any say. And if Layla had any say in Rix's overall health, she'd be making changes. Rix was somebody special, someone different to the partners of Layla's past. She couldn't lose her when she'd only just found her.

She waited until Rix had finished then wandered over casually. "Do you trust me?"

Rix turned around and frowned. "That's a strange way to open a conversation."

"I don't ever consider our conversation closed. We've never said good-bye to each other yet."

"Huh, I suppose we haven't." She shrugged and gestured to the studio exit. "Shall we walk?"

"Sure." Layla decided to wait until they'd exited the studio before she spoke again. She took a moment to allow the winter sun to warm her after being in the dark, air-conditioned building all day. She still missed

Denver, but the hotter temperatures in LA made up for it for the most part. "Do you trust me?" she asked again as she slid into the passenger seat of the golf buggy Rix used to zip to and from her office.

"Yeah." Rix got in the driver's side and set off. "Why do you ask? Was there something you didn't like about the dailies?"

"No, it's nothing to do with filming." After her experience with Mac, being on set with Rix was wonderful. She listened to all of her advice, especially on dialogue, and she treated everyone with complete respect. She was the perfect director, as far as Layla could see. "I want to take you somewhere this weekend, but I don't want to tell you where it is."

"Alone?" Rix gave her a sidelong glance.

Very much alone. "There are people where we're going, and we need to get there on a commercial plane, so not alone as such. There are no group plans you haven't told me about, are there?"

Rix shook her head. "I thought people might appreciate some time to do their Christmas shopping, so I didn't organize anything." She turned into her allotted spot outside her building, turned off the engine, and swiveled in her seat to face Layla. "Why don't you want to tell me where we're going?"

"Don't you like surprises?" Layla hadn't taken that possibility into account. She'd come to think of her as a spontaneous person and liking surprises came with that territory.

"I love surprises."

There was the L-word again. Even Syd had used it last night. She was convinced she was in love with Jack and wanted Layla's advice on whether to tell him or whether to wait for him to say it to her, as if it was some sort of weakness to admit it first, like a guilty secret. Didn't most people just want to love and be loved by someone? However transient the love was, it was still important in that moment. Layla saw no point in waiting or playing games. If the person didn't say it back, so be it. Pack up your heart and move on. It would end eventually anyway, better simply to enjoy the emotion while it lasted. "You might not agree to go if you know where I'm taking you."

Rix frowned. "It's not a nice place then? Are you taking me to rehab for red meat?"

"Something like that. But a lot more fun. And there'll be a reward at the end of it." A reward they'd both be able to enjoy. "It's somewhere I've always wanted to go, but no one would ever go with me."

Rix dropped her hand to the seat and discreetly touched Layla's thigh. "I'd go anywhere with you, but if you want it to be a surprise, I'm okay with that too."

Layla looked for any tell-tale signs of an untruth, but Rix's expression was open and genuine.

"And if it's a public place, we can stick to our rules of conduct," Rix said, withdrawing her fingers.

Layla liked that Rix called them "our rules" even though she was the one who had been insisting on no real physical contact while they were working together. She also liked that Rix didn't know Layla was about to change those rules. A near-death experience tended to change a person's perspective and putting her life on hold for fear of judgment by other people who didn't really matter now seemed ludicrous. "You'll come?"

"Of course. When?"

Layla slipped out of the buggy and slung her messenger bag over her shoulder. "Meet me at the JetFast concourse, LAX at nine tomorrow morning." She began to walk away but called over her shoulder, "And bring a warm coat and an overnight bag." She resisted the pull of looking back to see the expression on Rix's face. Her phone pinged when she reached her car, and she pulled it from her bag to see a text from Rix.

I'm going to assume that you've booked separate rooms. I couldn't handle sharing a room, even with twin beds x

She turned back to see Rix holding her phone in the air, as if she were waiting for an immediate response. Layla made a show of putting her phone back in her bag and placing her bag in the trunk. She waved, got in her car, and reversed from her spot. In the rear-view mirror, she saw Rix waving her fist at her, but her grin took any sting from the playful threat. Layla honked her horn twice and drove off with a huge grin of her own. Tomorrow night, she'd finally get her hands on Rix. To hell with judgment and gossip. This was her life; it was too precious to waste, and she'd lead it any way she damn well pleased.

***

Syd pulled up to the gates serving the JetFast airlines and turned to Layla in the passenger seat. "You're sure about this?"

Layla sighed and shook her head. "I was sure the first time you asked me, and the second, and the following fifteen times. Rix could've died last week, and I would never have known what it might be like to love her and have her love me. You know me, Syd; whether it lasts fifteen weeks or fifteen months, I don't ever want regrets. I like being in love."

"I know you, yes, but I still don't get you. You like being in love, but you don't believe in forever love?"

Layla pulled her carry-on bag from the back seat. "Hey now, Ms. Judgy McJudge Nut, you didn't believe in love at all until you met Jack."

"And maybe that's it. Maybe you just haven't met the right person yet either. Or maybe Rix is that person, and that's why you're doing this and going against your professional and personal boundaries rule."

"Oh my god, have you turned into a Born Again Romantic?" Yes, she was falling for Rix. She knew herself well enough to know that, and she wouldn't deny it. But that didn't mean she saw them together in their dotage, swinging on a porch seat sipping iced tea. She'd never seen or imagined that for her future with any one of her previous partners. Love was too intense to burn brightly for any real length of time. And after the flame went out, what was the point of staying together? Wasn't it best to move on and give each other the chance to find love again? "Don't force your newfound, fanatical beliefs on me just because you're in real love for the first time." She pulled Syd in for a hug. "The only person I'm going to love until I die is you. Bestie love is the only kind of love that lasts forever."

Syd hugged her tightly then pushed her away. "Go, or you'll miss your flight, you heartless wench."

"I'm not heartless, or I wouldn't be able to fall in love at all, would I? My heart just bounces back for the next adventure. Happy for now has worked fine for me all these years, so why change for inevitable heartache?"

"That's cynical, especially for someone who peddles purple prose and happy every afters."

"I'm open for love. How is that cyn—"

A sharp tap on the window glass cut Layla short. "You need to unload or move on, please."

Layla held up her hand in apology, opened the car door, and got out. She leaned back in to grab her ski jacket. "Have a lovely weekend with your boy toy."

"Have a lovely weekend with your sugar daddy."

Layla laughed. "Touché." She closed the door and waved as Syd drove off. She took one last breath of fresh air and made her way into the airport.

Rix was already waiting at the JetFast concourse with an impossibly small leather roll bag.

"Is that your overnight bag?" Layla asked, pulling the retractable handle and wheels into action so her heavy carry-on was easier to handle.

"Yeah, why?"

Layla shrugged. "And there are clean clothes in it?"

"Are you questioning my packing prowess or my hygiene?"

Layla tried to keep a neutral expression when the image of Rix packing something entirely different flashed into her mind. That could be an adventure for another weekend. "Both."

Rix huffed and pouted, something Layla couldn't honestly say she'd seen a butch woman do before, but Rix pulled it off with aplomb.

"Since we're not sharing a room, let alone a bed, that's not something for you to worry about."

"I'll be alongside you on the plane and in the rental car, but I'll let you use my deodorant. I have two." Layla tugged at her luggage.

"Number one, why do you have two for such a short trip, and," Rix indicated the winter jacket slung over her shoulder, "number two, I'm unlikely to sweat if we're going somewhere that I need a heavyweight jacket."

"I've got one in my handbag and one in my carry-on, in case either go missing or get stolen."

"Do you have two of all your clothes for the same reason? At least your sweat won't get through when you're walking around naked then. Though that's now tempted me to steal your carry-on bag."

Layla swatted Rix's shoulder, though she was now considering blowing off the farm to spend the whole day in bed with Rix instead. She wheeled her bag to the check-in machine. "I can buy new clothes easier than I can find my deodorant brand." It was a poor excuse, and she sensed she was far from convincing. "We're going to a farm near Boise."

Rix arched her eyebrow, clearly seeing right through Layla's subject change, but she simply smiled. "A farm? And it's somewhere you've always wanted to go to but hadn't gotten around to?"

"Yes." Layla zipped through the check-in, scanned their driver's licences, and turned to Rix. "Shall we head up to the departure lounge?"

"Sure." Rix tapped the button when they got to the elevator, and they got in. "You know, we could've made this a group trip if you'd told me about it. Who doesn't love a farm when you live in LA? Some of our crew have probably never even see a pig, let alone know that it's hairy."

"Pigs are hairy?" Layla tugged her wheels over the gap as she exited the elevator and headed to security. "I thought they were smooth like dolphins. Why would you know that?"

"We had some on set for a movie I directed."

"Oh, I see. And would you rather have come in a group? Would you feel safer?" Layla glanced over at Rix and tossed her hair over her shoulder, shampoo commercial-like for maximum femme effect.

Rix blew out a breath and shook her head. "Well, you probably wouldn't pull stunts like that in a big group of your colleagues." She pulled at the collar of her shirt, as if she were hot.

"True. But that would be far less fun."

Layla loaded up the security conveyor belt and sashayed her way to the full body scanner. She waited at the other side of security after she'd passed through in seconds, but Rix was held up and patted down after the machine's alarm went off.

"It was the jeans," Rix said after picking up her bag and re-joining Layla.

She headed toward a coffee house. It was early, and she needed a caffeine boost. "They look good on you, I meant to say." They looked better than good. Rix looked like a brick wall with solid tree trunks for thighs. Layla had always been a sucker for a strong woman. "And I like your polo shirt. It's nice to see you in something a little more casual."

"Wetsuits, tracksuits, and hospital gowns don't count as casual?"

"Nope, they were outfits specific to your activity. I'm seriously concerned about how many thousands of silkworms have died for your seemingly endless tie collection."

"You don't like the way I dress?"

Rix stuck out her bottom lip just enough to be adorable. Truthfully, Layla loved Rix's wardrobe. She found the whole shirt, tie, belt buckle, jeans, and brogues ensemble very sexy indeed. She imagined it took a long time to put together, and she vacillated between wanting to remove each item exceedingly slowly and ripping them all off in seconds. "I certainly wouldn't say that."

Rix grinned and looked suitably appeased. "Phew. It took me a while to find my look. I've been through a lot of phases."

"I can't imagine. Do you think you take longer than me to get ready?"

Rix pursed her lips and shook her head. "Oh no, you're not catching me out with trick questions like that. If I say yes, you'll be offended that I think you don't take enough care in getting ready, and if I say no, you'll be offended that I assume you take way too long to get ready. It's a lose-lose situation."

Layla frowned and wheeled her bag to an empty table at Moondeers. "Wow, you must've been with some high maintenance partners to predict my responses would be so negative."

Rix dropped her bag onto a chair and held up her hands. "Sorry, that's a bad habit. Borne from a little too much undesirable experience, as you astutely deducted, but totally unacceptable to assume the same from you." She dropped into the adjacent chair and sighed. "Especially when you've been so far removed from any woman that I've ever spent any serious time with."

In context, Layla very much liked the sound of that. And who didn't like being told they were different in a good way? "I'm going to take that as a compliment," she said and sat opposite.

Rix widened her eyes and nodded. "You should. You're the most interesting, straight talking woman I've had the privilege of meeting. And you're uncomplicated but complex in the nicest of ways. It's mind blowing, really." Rix fiddled with the sugar packets on the table. "I'm sorry if I offended you."

"You surprised me; you didn't offend me." Layla reached across the table and took Rix's hand in hers. "And I like that I'm nothing like the women you're used to. What I like even better is that I know it's genuine and not just a line." Layla traced a raised vein along Rix's hand and forearm, enjoying how Rix flared her nose, a sign she was coming to understand signified her arousal. Layla's answering response throbbed between her legs, unbeknownst to Rix.

"I should get us some coffee," Rix said but didn't move.

Layla released Rix's hand and smiled slowly. "Full fat, double shot latte, please."

Rix sighed deeply and nodded before she joined a short line to order. Layla pulled out her phone and busied herself by skimming the latest news rather than simply staring at Rix and imagining all the things she'd like to do to her. If it weren't for how long Layla had wanted to visit these Highland cows, she'd drag Rix straight into her hotel room, and they wouldn't leave until they had to be at Boise airport for the return flight.

Chapter Sixteen

Rɪx ᴛᴏᴏᴋ ᴏɴᴇ more look at Scotty, the unimaginatively named Highland calf she'd just "adopted" and waved. Yep, she'd waved to a cow. At least adopting it didn't mean she had to make room at home and give it a bedroom. She wanted the patter of *tiny* feet in the house, not tiny hooves, even though the baby Highland cows were the cutest animals she'd ever seen. "This was quite an imaginative way of getting me to stop eating red meat." Rix offered her arm, and Layla hooked in and cuddled up. Rix could feel her shivering from the cold.

"I figured that once you looked into their beautiful brown eyes and saw how sweet and gentle they were, you'd never want to eat another steak again. I mean, how could you after connecting with the amazing animals it comes from? They're like a bovine boy band with their bangs and flowing locks."

Rix laughed. "Really? What do they sing?"

"How about '*Moo*-ve like Jagger' or maybe 'I Feel the Earth *Moo*-ve'?"

"Were those pre-prepared answers? I feel like you had them in your pocket, ready to serve up if I gave you the right opening."

"I told you, I'm obsessed with these big boys and gals. I've got a hundred more titles, but your lackluster response leads me to believe that you're not worthy of hearing them."

Layla scrunched her nose and looked away briefly, but Rix could see she was trying hard not to laugh. "Does your list include 'S-*moo*-th Criminal'?"

Layla smiled and slapped her hand across Rix's chest playfully. "That's a good one. I take it back. You're ready to become a card-carrying member of my Cow Club."

Rix placed her hand over Layla's, liking the way it felt and not wanting her to move it. "I should hope so since I've just sponsored one of them. How long do they live anyway?"

"Over twenty years if people like you don't slice them up for dinner."

Rix held up her free hand in mock surrender. "I'm a changed woman. I promise I won't touch another steak or burger in my life." She closed her eyes and tried not to imagine her last steak and how it had melted in her mouth. God, not to have that taste ever again. She wished she hadn't inherited her family's heart weakness or that she'd eaten in moderation before and kept herself healthier. If she could maybe just have it on special occasions like birthdays and holidays…

Layla smacked her palm against Rix's chest again. "You're thinking about eating steak, aren't you?"

Rix opened her eyes and tried for a poker face, but since it'd been established that Layla could see straight through any of her expressions, she quickly gave it up as a lost cause. "I'm *trying* not to. That's got to count for something, doesn't it?"

"I suppose I can't ask you to reform your character flaw instantly."

"You're saying that my dietary choices represent a character flaw? I thought they had to be traits like arrogance, and pig-headedness, and jealousy. I don't think I've ever come across a person's food choices being viewed as a defect before."

"You have now."

Rix sighed. Layla could twist her in knots with her crazy logic if she wanted, as long as she was giving Rix her attention. Speaking of which, she checked her watch, wondering what else Layla had scheduled. "It's a little too early for dinner. Have you got any other surprises planned for this trip?"

Layla flashed her a wicked grin. "Actually, I do. But we should check into our B&B first."

"Are you taking me to a barley farm to show me the cruel and unusual punishment of crops to warn me away from alcohol?"

"Damn, you've spoiled the surprise. We may just as well skip to an early bird dinner and find a flight home." Layla nestled her head against Rix's chest and hugged her. "This is nice," she said quietly.

Rix took a deep breath and sighed at the delicate scent of tropical fruits emanating from Layla's body, a refreshing change from the overbearing smell of cow manure that had assailed her nostrils for the majority of the visit. This was more than nice. This was pretty much perfect—Layla was perfect. And Rix wasn't about to question the sudden change in Layla's perspective on keeping their relationship under wraps, though she supposed the likelihood of anyone knowing who they were here was zero. No one she knew had ever expressed a desire to come to Boise. Maybe there were other Highland cow farms closer to LA, but Layla had chosen to bring Rix here so they could get a little closer without the threat of gossip that Layla feared.

She wrapped her arms around Layla and pulled her closer, ignoring the little voice that told her she shouldn't get too carried away with how good Layla felt in her arms, about how easily she fitted against her body, and how right all of this seemed. They'd established a wonderfully open sense of communication, but there was nothing wrong with keeping her overactive imagination and enthusiasm under wraps, for now. She didn't want to scare Layla off with talk of picket fences, dogs, and children. Hell, she didn't want to scare herself with talk of that just yet. That had only led to broken dreams and heartache.

But if Rix stopped dreaming, she may as well stop breathing. And her heart had always bounced back, ready to continue her lifelong search for the elusive perfect woman. In reality, no one had really come close to being that woman, and she was the one who had put an end to most of her previous relationships. This already felt different, the way she hoped every relationship would be different but never had been. She certainly hadn't expected to fall for someone over a decade younger than her. She'd always thought cougar territory wasn't for her… Perhaps that's where she'd been going wrong all these years. She always felt younger than her years but supposed everyone did; every year older, going to the mirror and beginning not to recognize the person staring back at them. Wasn't that simply part of the human condition?

Layla gently pulled away from the embrace and smiled, with a hint of shyness. She pulled the keys to their rental car from the pocket in her coat sleeve. "Let's check out those heated seats and get warmed up."

"You go. I need to nip back into the gift shop for a few things," Rix said.

"You mean you didn't get everything you needed in the two giant bags of gifts already in the trunk?"

"Nope, I've been thinking about that Highland cow version of Monopoly."

"That's about the only thing you didn't get, isn't it?" Layla rolled her eyes when Rix simply shrugged and smiled. "Okay, big spender. I'm going to defrost myself."

Rix watched her half-run to the car before she turned and went into the shop. She selected a cute twelve-inch-high cuddly cow and a tiny keychain cow and had them giftwrapped, in tartan paper, of course. She paid, thanked the cashier, and headed back to Layla with the sealed paper bag tucked under her arm. She indicated to Layla to pop the trunk and made sure that her gifts were hidden under her bag. Her seat was already warm when she got in, and her frozen legs were grateful for the feature.

"Do you know if the hotel has a shower or a tub?" Rix asked. "I'd love a nice soak before dinner."

Layla shrugged and looked non-committal. "I think there's a spa bath. Even my bones are cold; a soak sounds good."

Rix arched her eyebrow. "Are you saying what I think you're saying?"

Layla pulled out of the lot and got back on the main road. "A hot soak sounds amazing considering how cold I feel. What are you hearing?"

Idiot. "Nothing, nothing. Sorry." She'd gotten carried away with the intimate hug and what it might lead to, and now she'd opened her mouth. "I don't think I've ever been this cold. I feel like ski pants might've been a good call. My thighs feel like a thousand needles are sticking in them."

Layla glanced at her and smiled. "I thought you'd be a little hardier, given you spent your childhood in Detroit. Don't they have freezing winters?"

Either Layla hadn't registered Rix's misinterpretation, or she was ignoring it. Whatever it was, Rix was grateful for the change in topic. "Ha, it's been nearly three decades since I lived there. I'm an LA woman now, and my body is very attached to a much warmer climate, thanks."

"Don't you miss the beauty of real winters though?" She gestured to the landscape on each side of the road they were on. "I can't believe that I'm going to have to make sand angels on the beach instead of snow angels this Christmas. Do you think Santa has to wear Bermuda shorts when he's delivering gifts in California?"

Rix grinned at the images of Layla lying in the sand to make angels and Saint Nick in board shorts. "I'll ship some real snow to my backyard just for you."

"You'd do that?"

"I'm starting to think I'd do anything for you." They drove in silence for a while, and Rix stared out the side window. Layla was right. Real winters were all about frosty days and open fires. "Maybe one Christmas you could come to my cabin. We could ski all day and make s'mores all night." Rix didn't vocalize her train of thought as to what they could get up to on a soft fleece blanket in front of the log burner.

"I'd like that. I skied a lot in Colorado. Vail is so pretty; it's like a model Scandinavian town, and there are lots of tree-lined runs. Have you skied a lot?"

"That depends on what you mean by ski. I have skied a little, here and there, but I don't know if that translates to 'I ski.' I can just about stay upright, but I'm a blues skier. Though I tried a red once on a European resort, and it took me an hour to come down the slope on my ass, because it was too hard." She shook her head, both at the memory and at sharing something that made her look so weak. "Reds in Europe—"

"Are like our blacks, I agree." Layla placed her hand on Rix's thigh and squeezed gently. "I like that you shared that with me. Not many people would be so comfortable telling a new lover something that they might see as embarrassing."

"Who said I was comfortable?" Rix asked, determined not to latch onto the clear mention of Layla being her lover accompanied by the physical contact. If this was a game, Layla wasn't playing fair. "You seem to have a habit of getting all sorts of truth from me even when I really should keep my mouth shut. Couple that with your uncanny knack of knowing what I'm thinking through my expressions, and I'm truly screwed." Bad choice of word and most definitely a Freudian slip. It'd been difficult enough to keep her hands off Layla in the presence of their colleagues, but with no one around to see what they were getting up to, this was double black diamond territory.

"Do you want to keep secrets from me?"

Christ, Layla practically purred that question, her tone all velvet and silk. Rix switched off her heated seat function, no longer needing the extra warmth. She unzipped her coat and tugged it off, a task made difficult around her seatbelt, but she managed it. "If you know everything about me, I can't surprise you, and there's no mystique to the relationship, is there? Wouldn't you get bored?"

"Stability isn't boring. And I'm sure you could still surprise me for a long time to come. I don't profess to know nearly enough about you yet."

"Yet?" That sounded promising. "You're interested enough to want to know more then?

"Absolutely. Fact-finding was my secondary reason for this trip." Layla took a hard left, and the car snaked a little in the gravel parking lot.

Fact finding? Rix failed to hold in the chuckle when she read the sign. "The Anniversary Inn. Was I in a nine-month long coma after I hit my head?"

"See? You can be a smart ass; that's surprising." Layla gave Rix a sidelong glance and rolled her eyes. She parked and turned off the engine. "Celebrating an anniversary isn't a pre-requisite of staying here. It's just the most interesting place I could find in the area for an overnight stay, and I want it to be memorable."

Rix's heart skipped and other places on her body reacted accordingly. Or was she hearing what she wanted to hear? If Layla had decided to change the rules of their engagement, this was a subtle way of telling her. She said nothing for a moment, wavering between an outright question and keeping her mouth shut to see how things played out. She'd know soon enough once they were at the reception desk.

Layla got out of the car and popped the trunk. Rix grabbed her coat from the rear seat and quickly tugged it on before going back into the cold. By the time she got out, Layla already had her own bag out and on the ground.

"Can I carry that for you? I don't think the wheels will work so well on the rocks." Rix took her own bag from the trunk and slung it over her shoulder. She left her gift bags in there. If this trip *was* about to get intimate, a fluffy toy didn't portend romance. There were some chocolate cows in one of the other bags; they could melt them all over each other.

"Sure. Obviously, I could carry it myself, you know, me being a strong and independent woman etcetera."

Layla's mischievous grin set all kinds of happy synapses firing in Rix's head. She tilted her head. "Absolutely, m'lady. But why not exercise these strong shoulders you commented on?"

Layla's gaze flicked up and down over Rix's body, as if appraising her. She wiggled her eyebrows. "Why not, indeed?" Layla closed the trunk and locked the car.

Rix walked by her side and opened the reception door with her free hand. As she followed Layla in, a forbidden feeling swept over Rix, like she was a gigolo and Layla was taking her to a hotel to use her for the night.

She almost laughed out loud at the ludicrous thought and couldn't fathom where it had originated. She wouldn't call herself vanilla in the bedroom area, but role-playing was something she'd never thought possible before. How could she know how adventurous Layla was without asking? Having read all of her books, and guiltily pored over the sex scenes, she knew Layla's characters liked all sorts of sex, rough and ready, soft and gentle, and downright filthy, but that was fiction…wasn't it?

Rix ran her hand through her hair as if that might brush out the base thoughts. She was getting ahead of herself. Any second now, Layla would ask for the keys for two rooms, and they probably wouldn't even be adjoining rooms. A place like this shouldn't really have adjoining rooms, Rix thought then admonished herself again. She hadn't been this obsessed with sexual connection since her late teens and early twenties.

"I have a reservation under the name Layla Adams."

Rix blew out a breath. She wasn't preparing for bad news, because there'd been no explicit promise of anything. The trip was about deterring Rix from eating the tasty rumps of pretty cows, nothing more. Layla had mentioned "fact-finding," but that's what getting to know someone involved.

Still, Rix edged toward the desk as the man smiled and checked his computer.

"Ah, yes, Ms. Adams and Ms. Reardon. Welcome to the Anniversary Inn." He ran his finger over the screen and squinted. "I see you're staying the one night in the one room."

He prattled on, but Rix couldn't focus on anything after hearing "one room." Surely a hotel like this wouldn't have twin beds. Rix made a note to ensure Jack kept her updated with the modern lexicon; fact-finding was apparently a new euphemism for sleeping together.

Chapter Seventeen

RIX DIDN'T SPEAK on their way to the elevator. Once they were inside and Layla had pressed the button for the top floor, she turned to face her. "I haven't taken too much of a liberty, have I?"

Rix grinned widely. "You've got me hoping you're going to take *all* the liberties."

That was the response Layla had prayed for. Her stomach had been in metaphorical knots since she'd gotten on the plane with Rix this morning. The anticipation of finally being in a room alone with her, of getting to touch and be touched, had driven her a tiny bit crazy. And each time she made physical contact with Rix—her powerful chest, her thick thigh— Layla had wanted to fast forward the day to this moment: riding up in the elevator to their hotel room.

"Can I ask how long you've had this planned?" Rix stepped out into the corridor after Layla had exited the elevator.

"Only since the beginning of this week." Layla hoped Rix wouldn't push for the reasoning behind her change of heart. Talking about heart attacks and mortality would hardly elevate the sizzle of a sexual encounter. She scanned the board on the wall which signposted the rooms and headed toward the Captain's Quarters. She flashed the card on the wall sensor beside the handle and opened the door. Rix followed her in and put the bags on the table with legs made from old fashioned wooden beer kegs.

"Wow. When you said memorable, you weren't kidding."

Layla walked slowly over the wooden planks suspended over a small strip of shallow water, in which toy sharks and boats bobbed around. "In a good but completely cheesy way, yes?" Without waiting for an answer, she wandered past walls adorned with all manner of flags, replica flintlocks, and fake cutlasses—or at least she thought they were fake. It wouldn't do for a hotel to provide the weapon in a domestic disagreement. The corridor opened up into a large area with the bed on one side of the room and a sunken tub on the other, with a door which she expected would lead to a bathroom. She'd seen the bed in pictures, but they really didn't do justice to the sheer size and scale of it. And the tub was bigger than the whole bathroom at Syd's apartment.

"Is that half the hull of a ship?" Rix put her hand on the small of Layla's back.

Layla pushed into her touch, her body's immediate reaction a fierce reminder of why they were here, and it wasn't to admire the structural engineering of a nautically themed bed. "I think that's what they were going for." She turned into Rix's embrace and pressed her hand against her chest. "Do you want to see how she sails?"

"Are you still talking about the bed?" Rix moved closer so their mouths were mere inches away from each other.

"No," Layla whispered. "Now I'm talking about us." She stroked Rix's cheek and ran her thumb across her bottom lip slowly. The memory of their first and only kiss a couple of months ago flooded back, making the distance between them and the bed far too great. She wanted Rix, and she wanted her now.

Rix put her hands on Layla's shoulders without pushing her away. "I've got the self-control to ask this question only once: are you sure you want to do this?"

Layla nodded slowly. "Thank you for asking, but I'm more than sure." She traced her fingers down Rix's neck to the buttons of her polo shirt. "And we can figure out the logistics of what this means, but for now, I need you to take me to bed…if you want to, that is."

"As if there'd ever be any question of that." Rix slipped her hands from Layla's shoulders to the base of her back and pulled her close, so their bodies touched. "I've been thinking about this moment since we kissed in my office. And I've been happy to wait, but now all I want to do is strip you naked and make love until you tell me we've got to stop."

Layla sighed deeply and tilted her head. Rix dipped down, and they kissed, not tentative, or slow, or mediated in any way. It was raw and ripe with the desire of anticipation. Rix pulled Layla's coat off and tossed it on the leather Chesterfield sofa in the center of the room, where it was quickly joined by her own. Layla tugged Rix's shirt from her jeans, and Rix stripped it off before she guided Layla up the three steps to the bed and gently pushed her backward onto it.

The comforter enveloped Layla like a cloud, giving her a feeling akin to weightlessness, and she put her hands behind her head, happy to allow Rix free rein. Rix got to her knees and unzipped her boots before pulling them off. She frowned as she tried to pull off Layla's socks, and they didn't budge.

"They're ski socks. They go all the way up to my knees." The days of sacrificing warmth for sexiness were long gone. "My jeans'll have to come off first."

Rix raised her eyebrows briefly. "Won't that be a shame."

She inched forward, pushed up the hem of Layla's sweater, and slid her fingers inside the denim that trailed along Layla's panties; she hadn't sacrificed sexiness there and had worn one of her favorite silk and lace twin sets. Rix let out a low breath, and Layla took that as a sign of approval. Layla put her feet on the edge of the bed and pushed up her hips so that Rix could take off her jeans.

"Are you in a hurry?" Rix asked, her voice soft and deep.

"Yes. I want your skin on mine, and all these winter clothes are in the way." She flopped her arms onto the bed, a tiny bit exasperated. "Maybe I should've taken you somewhere hot."

"This place was perfect." After pulling off Layla's jeans and socks, Rix stood, toed off her boots, and climbed on top of Layla, straddling her. "You're perfect."

Layla smiled. That was one thing she was certain she wasn't, but this wasn't the time to correct her.

Rix peeled Layla's sweater from her body and moaned as she ran her hand lightly over Layla's bra. "You're so incredibly sexy."

Layla glanced away briefly, the intensity in Rix's eyes almost too much to bear. "I'm glad you think so." She ran her fingers along the edge of Rix's tank top and started to pull it off, but Rix put her hand over Layla's.

"I'd prefer to keep it on," Rix said.

Layla pushed out her bottom lip. "But I don't want any barriers between us." She waited a few beats, and when Rix said nothing, she chose not to push it and slid her hands onto Rix's hips. "It's okay, you don't have to."

Rix focused slightly beyond Layla. "Thank you."

Layla lifted her head from the pillow and pressed her lips against Rix's, hopefully showing her acceptance of Rix's boundaries with the unspoken passion of her kiss. She moved her hands down to Rix's jeans. "Take these off?" she asked, hoping it wouldn't be an issue. The speed with which

Rix jumped up, stripped them off, and laid back on the bed showed that it wasn't, but she noted Rix hadn't taken the opportunity to shed her boxers.

Rix shifted onto her side and trailed kisses along Layla's neck and down to her breasts. Her hand rested on Layla's waist before she drew abstract patterns on her stomach, slowly making her way down to the band of Layla's panties.

Goddamn, Rix had some self-control. Hadn't she said she was desperate to make love to her? Layla pushed up her hips to meet Rix's hand. "Please." She placed her hand on Rix's and pushed her down until Rix cupped her pussy.

Rix flared her nose. "You want me inside you?" When Layla tried to take her own underwear off, Rix gently tapped her hand. "You might be in a hurry, baby, but I want to go nice and slow. We only get one chance at the first time."

"And the sex after that will bore you?"

Rix shook her head. "If I got to make love to you for a million years, I wouldn't get bored."

The concept of any fire burning bright longer than a decade was alien, but Rix's notion was wonderfully romantic. "I like your confidence, especially since we haven't done it once yet." Layla pouted and bounced her hips on the bed. "I could be a terrible lover."

Rix laughed. "I doubt that very much, but what's terrible to one partner can be fabulous to another." She ran her fingers along the inside of Layla's thigh. "And I'm sure I could teach you how to please me; you're a very smart woman."

Layla caught Rix's hand and flipped over so that she was straddling Rix's stomach. She pressed down, and Rix's eyes half-lidded.

"You're also surprisingly strong." Rix placed her hands on Layla's thighs. "And really hot—do you have a furnace down there?"

"Why don't you put your hand down there and find out?" Layla had a feeling Rix would want to pleasure her before she'd even entertain the possibility of Layla touching her, which she hoped she'd allow.

"Kiss me," Rix whispered.

Layla leaned down and traced her tongue along Rix's lips. Then she kissed her, hard and full of yearning. Layla's core throbbed in response, and she ground herself against Rix's stomach. Figuring she might be able to get a sneaky release, she stretched herself out along Rix's body, straddled her thigh, and began to rub a slow rhythm against her. Layla deepened the kiss, and Rix grasped her waist and dug her fingers in, gasping into Layla's mouth. Layla pressed her whole body against Rix and put her hand around the back of Rix's neck.

Rix broke off from the kiss. "I know what you're doing," she said, breathless.

Layla pressed her fingers to Rix's lips. "Don't worry, I've got plenty more; I recharge pretty fast."

Rix caught Layla's wrist and flipped her with her body weight, leaving Layla on the precipice of pleasure. She wriggled beneath Rix and nibbled her neck. "That's so mean."

Rix laughed gently. "*I* want to be the one making you come."

"Your thigh was doing a very good job of doing exactly that until you rolled me over." Layla made a show of checking the time on her watch. "I was hoping we could work up a real appetite before dinner."

"We've got hours until dinner."

Rix pinned Layla's wrists above her head with one hand and used her other to squeeze Layla's breast. She squirmed beneath Rix's weight and moaned when Rix palmed her breast harder. This was a kind of exquisite torture, where the pleasure transformed to painful longing, only to return to perfect pleasure…eventually. "I thought you'd be desperate to have me since I've made you wait this long."

"Oh, I'm desperate, babe. But desperate doesn't mean I have to go from zero to sixty in record time. I want to treasure every second of the build-up." Rix flicked the front clasp of Layla's bra open with one hand and shook her head slowly. "So beautiful."

She lowered her head and sucked one of Layla's nipples into her mouth. Layla had no idea if she was using her tongue or her teeth, but the pleasure was incredible. She pushed her hips upward, but Rix put her hand on Layla's stomach and pressed her down to the bed.

Rix flicked her eyes up at Layla and released her nipple. "Patience, baby," she said before pulling Layla's nipple back into her mouth.

"I should've mentioned patience and me aren't the best of friends," Layla managed to say between ragged breaths as Rix flicked and teased her nipple.

Rix pulled up again and shook her head. "You're going to have to hash it out, because I'm not rushing this."

Before Layla could say anything more, Rix crushed her lips to Layla's, and she softened into the kiss. Maybe she could wait a little longer; Rix's kisses were sensational. Layla relaxed into the bed as Rix ran her fingers from her collarbone, over her breasts and stomach, and down to her lacy panties. Her breath hitched when Rix hooked her finger under the delicate fabric and traced a line along the top of Layla's hair. Rix broke from the kiss, released Layla's wrists, and trailed soft kisses along the same path her fingers had gone.

"I need you so bad," she whispered.

Without responding, Rix flipped Layla onto her front and began to stroke her back, her touch feeling almost reverent. Layla couldn't think of a first time with a previous lover who had taken such care and been in no hurry. It had always been frantic and desperate, but Rix seemed to be mapping her entire body as if committing it to memory.

"Your tattoo is beautiful," Rix said.

Layla felt Rix's hot lips at its tip before her tongue traced its lines around and around.

"I didn't see it when we surfed," she said as she continued her exploration.

Layla couldn't respond. Rix's tongue and fingers were everywhere and nowhere, in the perfect place and yet not, because every sizzling contact made Layla all the most desperate to have Rix inside her. She began to rise and fall against the bed, the phantom of Rix's fingers exactly where Layla needed them.

Rix pressed the small of her back to the bed. "You're a horny little minx, aren't you?"

"Not a bad thing." Full sentences were no longer an option.

"Not a bad thing at all."

Rix's hot breath on her neck and ear made her bite into the comforter and let out a small scream. Rix laughed gently, apparently enjoying Layla's unbearable state of arousal.

"You're driving me insane."

Rix's response came in more feathered kisses and trails of touch so light they were like the heat of a candle held almost too close. Layla surrendered to the erotic expectation. Rix would need to be make her come soon enough, and since all this foreplay was making her incredibly wet, she'd be ready. Rix trailed her fingers along Layla's back to her ass and down her thighs. When her short fingernails grazed the underside of Layla's foot, she bucked. "Sorry. My feet are really ticklish."

"So if I kiss them, you're likely to kick me in the head?"

That wouldn't be a desirable direction for this to take. "There's a fifty-fifty chance, yes." Layla buried her face in the bed.

"How about if I do this?"

Rix wrapped her hand around Layla's ankle, and Layla felt Rix's tongue glide over her ankle bone. Then she planted small kisses along the arch of Layla's foot and kissed each toe softly. Layla moaned, the sensation traveling directly up her leg and into her core. Few lovers had managed to take advantage of that connection, but Rix was doing exactly that, and Layla writhed beneath her expertise, giving her a preview of what was to come when Rix finally made it between her legs. "Uh-huh, that works."

"Yeah?" Rix moved to Layla's other foot to do the same.

Layla scrunched the sheets in her hands. Rix's mouth felt like it was on her feet and her pussy at the same time. Surely she wasn't so revved up that she'd come just from her feet being teased? But the way her whole body thrummed in pleasure right now made Layla think anything was possible.

For a moment, she felt nothing but a wisp of a breath on her foot. Rix was neither touching nor kissing her. Layla remained still and waited. She hadn't felt Rix move from the bed, but everything had gone so quiet. "Are you okay?" Layla turned over slowly, and Rix came into focus.

Rix laid down beside her and sighed. "I'm more than okay."

She cupped Layla's face and kissed her, somehow making it feel like the most precious kiss Layla had ever had, like it could be the first, or the last, or every kiss in between. "Please make love to me," Layla said softly, her desperation to come replaced by a longing to connect with Rix in a primal and deeply emotional way.

Rix smiled. "That's what I was looking for."

"Did you just Yoda me?" Layla asked, feeling strangely serene and highly sexual at the same time.

Rix trailed her fingers along Layla's body until she got to her panties. Layla lifted her hips slightly to allow Rix to push them down.

"I'm not sure that's a recognized verb."

"I'm a writer; it's my job to make them up." Layla wrapped her hand around Rix's neck and pulled her in for another intense kiss, happy to let Rix's lips answer her question wordlessly. Yep, she'd been Yoda'd, for sure; her carnal need for an orgasm was still very much present, but it had been joined by a tranquil desire to bond in a way that transcended mere sexual gratification. This was love territory.

Rix placed her hand between Layla's legs. She pulled from the kiss and let out a breath when she slowly separated Layla's lips. "You're soaked."

"You're surprised?"

Rix inched inside her, and Layla moaned as she clenched around Rix's fingers. She'd barely exhaled when Rix added a second and third finger and began a steady rhythm. Layla rocked her hips in time with Rix's movements, and when she pushed deeper inside, Layla dug her nails into Rix's back. Rix made a guttural growling sound and seemed to lose her pacing for the briefest of moments.

"Don't stop," Layla whispered and raked her nails along Rix's shoulder. She growled again, and Layla looked into her eyes, darkly swimming with desire. Layla wrapped her other hand around Rix's neck and pulled her back into a kiss. She closed her eyes and simply let herself *feel* what was happening in her body. All sense of solidity slipped away, and all that remained were Rix's lips crushed to hers and Rix's fingers deep inside her. Any consciousness of the rest of her body fell away as the powerful waves of pleasure began to surge and slip away, surge and slip away, each time building higher and higher.

When she opened her eyes, Rix was staring into them, her expression one of yearning and passion and expectancy.

"I love you," Rix said and thrust deep and hard.

Rix's words, her rhythm, and her final drive combined with the precipice of Layla's last surge, and she crashed into a cavernous orgasm which immersed every conscious cell in her body in a pleasure so intense, it ached and throbbed against her skin. She shuddered and shook, and Rix pressed her body against hers, as if to share the experience. Layla eventually stilled, and her breathing returned to normal. She didn't speak. She couldn't find words that wouldn't sound trite or cliché.

Rix began to move inside her again.

Layla wrapped her hand around Rix's wrist. She couldn't take anything else right now, and her body and mind needed time to process what had just happened. "No, not yet."

Rix grinned and looked mighty pleased with herself. "I thought you said you were quick to recharge?"

"Usually, I am. But usually, I don't have orgasms that reach deep inside my very soul and turn my emotions inside out." Layla turned onto her side to face Rix and put her hand on her waist. "Can I touch you?"

Rix placed her hand over Layla's. "Next time."

Layla saw the flash of vulnerability in Rix's eyes briefly before she pulled Layla into an embrace. She rested her head on Rix's chest, content, sated, at peace. And completely comfortable in the knowledge that she'd just fallen in love. The fluttering in her heart was something more, but she put it down to Rix's declaration of love during an orgasm rather than a hint that this love might be something different.

Chapter Eighteen

"YOU KNOW THAT we'll have to come back here every year on the anniversary of this, don't you?"

Layla didn't want to think about something like that right now, because it couldn't possibly last, and all she wanted to do was enjoy life as it was happening right now, rather than thinking about a future that may or may not exist. But it was a nice sentiment, and she didn't want to ruin the moment, so she said nothing. Last night had been about just that: last night. There was no need to get bogged down in the mists of maybes and fleeting heart flutters; Layla was all about how good everything felt right now, and good god, Rix had made her feel something far beyond good in a clichéd earth-moving kind of way. And not just once, but all afternoon and into the early hours of the morning, so they'd missed dinner entirely. Twenty-four-hour room service had been a life saver at two a.m. *If a fire burns bright, it doesn't burn long.* She shooed the unwelcome thought away. It didn't matter how long this lasted, as long as she was experiencing it. "There are too many fabulous hotels in the world to keep coming back to just one."

Rix frowned and clicked her seatbelt closed. "What about celebrating important moments in your life?"

Layla shrugged. She'd never understood the attachment people formed to places, and their enjoyment in the safety of the known. "I'm all for that, but you don't have to do it in the same place every time, do you?"

"The place was a big part of the moment. I think going back to the location where things happened is like a pilgrimage for your memories."

"I'm going to have start recording what you say and using it in my books." Layla's deflection seemed to have worked, and Rix didn't say anything else, but she still looked as though she was confused by Layla's stance.

The air steward greeted them and checked everything was as it needed to be. A few minutes later, they were in the air and headed back to LA.

In her peripheral vision, Layla could see Rix wringing her hands.

Surely Rix wasn't upset by their conflicting views? Lovers rarely agreed on everything and weren't the best relationships fueled by healthy disagreement and discussion? Unless it was something to do with the take-off, and Rix was anxious. Layla reached over and put her hand over Rix's. "Does flying bother you?"

"No." Rix turned her hands over and held Layla's. "I can't say that I enjoy it, and I'm glad that people tend to travel to me for business meetings, but it doesn't scare me, if that's what you're asking."

"You seem tense."

"I'm not. It's just that we haven't talked about what last night means for us, or how it even came about, and I guess I'm not looking forward to going back to hiding what I feel for you."

Ah, there it was. Layla had been blown away having the most intense sexual experience of her life, and words had been too smoky a concept to grasp so when Rix had said the L word, Layla simply didn't have the tools to reciprocate. Add that to how Layla had sprung the surprise sleepover on her, and there was little wonder that Rix was a little discombobulated. "I did kind of trap you into having sex with me, didn't I?"

Rix grinned and wiggled her eyebrows. "We can safely say you made a sound prediction of my response, and I can say, without prejudice, that I didn't feel trapped. I was surprised that you'd changed your mind about waiting to take us to a physical level until we'd finished filming, and you didn't explain why."

Layla pressed her lips together and wrinkled her nose, and a little guilt crept in unannounced. That, and discussions about death were never her favorite topic. "I decided that I shouldn't let fear stand in the way of what I wanted, and I wanted you. I feel a little silly about imposing that rule in the first place. I felt insecure about being in a new environment and out of my comfort zone, especially with everyone talking about what happened with Mac. I've spent the last decade holed up in my apartment, not needing to worry about what people think of me and my relationships, because they were focused on my words, and suddenly, it felt like there was simply no privacy."

"And your decision was all about that and had nothing to do with my impromptu hospital visit last weekend?"

Layla blinked and tilted her head slightly. "It *may* have had a little to do with you almost dying, yes, and that *may* have nudged things into a different perspective for me in a 'life is precious, don't waste it' kind of way." She shifted so that she was sideways in her seat and faced Rix, not wanting to have this conversation with the seat in front of her. "It's not me being morbid. I listened to what your doctor had told you, and I know that you're not going to have a heart attack and die, but life can change on a dime. You could've drowned. This plane could crash and burn. I could get caught in the crossfire of a drive-by shooting on the way home. I've always been about living life for the here and now, and this fear I've held since I was a kid got in the way of that for a while, and I'm not going to let it do that anymore."

Rix grinned. "I feel like I should stand up and applaud you. That was a hell of a speech."

Layla pulled her hand away and slapped Rix's shoulder. "Asshole."

"Guilty." Rix tucked Layla's hair behind her ear, wrapped her hand around Layla's neck, and kissed her gently. "What does all that mean for us when we go back to the studio?"

"Well, it doesn't mean that you get to woman-handle me all day long and slap me on the ass as I pass you on the set."

Rix chewed on her bottom lip and looked adorably petulant. "Are you sure? That seems mean. Is it non-negotiable?"

"It's a deal breaker, yes." Layla was good with public displays of affection—she saw it as something necessary to make sexuality a non-issue through exposure—but she still wanted to be professional at work. The way she felt around Rix might make it hard to stick to her own rule. "I don't want to hide us though; if people ask, we tell them the truth, and I'll be happy to come to work with you in the same car if I've stayed at your house."

"That's presumptuous of you. Why can't we stay at your place?"

"Because I live in a crummy two-bedroom apartment in a rundown part of town that's waiting to be gentrified, while you live in a mansion. And because Syd and Jack are *not* quiet when they have sex…and they're having a lot of sex." Layla had been playing music and audiobooks so loudly to mask the noise of their nookie that her ears always hummed when she took the buds out. "Jack shares his apartment with three other queer peeps, and Syd's funny about her sex screams with anyone but me." Layla raised her hand before Rix could comment. "I know that sounds incredibly weird, and it is, but c'est la vie."

Rix nodded but looked like she was trying not to laugh. "Does that mean I get to call you my lover? Partner? Given our ages, I've never been comfortable with girlfriend. It offends my feminist sensibilities."

"And mine. Most of the time. There are times and places where you calling me your girl might be acceptable, but it's never in public and almost always in the bedroom. I'm not sure we need a label. Isn't it just enough that we love each other?" Layla smiled when Rix's jaw comedy-dropped open. "Yes, I love you. I would've said it last night, but you kind of took away my power of speech for a while, and you orgasmed me into an exhausted sleep."

Rix glanced away then refocused on Layla and took her hands. "It kind of freaked me out that you didn't say it back, but I wasn't going to say anything." She lifted their hands and kissed Layla's knuckles. "I love you so much, and this," Rix took a deep breath and kissed Layla's knuckles again, "feels so perfect."

There it was again; Layla was beginning to think it was Rix's favorite word. *Perfect*. It didn't exist, did it? She leaned across the seat and kissed her. "So, given that momentous milestone, I don't care who knows."

Rix looked almost disappointed. "You're absolutely sure that you don't want to keep us a secret?" she asked. "Because I could get on board with sneaking off for sex weekends in themed hotels across America. I hear there's one in New Hampshire where the bed is a giant circle and it's suspended from the ceiling by chains—not that I'm into chains, of course."

Layla smirked. "Of course. Unless you count chainsaws."

"Huh, you remembered. Maybe this weekend, I could take you to my lodge and show you my carvings."

Layla smiled at Rix's switch to a child-like excitement. "You light up when you talk about that. I noticed that when we FaceTimed after Thanksgiving. Seems like you're as passionate about chainsaw carving as you are about filmmaking. What are you working on?"

Rix looked off into the distance for a moment, as if she were contemplating Layla's words. "I suppose I am. They're both creative processes but in a totally different way."

Layla nodded. "You make your studio a collaborative process, but your carving is—"

"A solitary pursuit, yes." Rix straightened up in her seat. "If I make a mistake with the wood, it's all on me, and maybe that's why it appeals to me."

She was silent for a moment, and Layla didn't interrupt her thoughts. Instead, she took the time to think about making love in Rix's log cabin in the woods in front of an open fire with nothing but the wind to compete with her cries of pleasure. Or *their* cries of pleasure; Rix had said she'd let Layla touch her next time, and Layla couldn't wait.

***

"You're meeting Matt again? You're starting to get more calls from our agent than I do." Syd flopped onto Layla's bed and propped herself up by bundling three of her pillows. "Why do you have so many cushions? Won't you need the space in here now that you're back on the horse?"

Layla slapped Syd's thigh as she passed her bed on the way to her dressing table. "I'd ask if you were jealous, but you're thinking of giving it all up, so you're probably not. If you are still thinking about it, that is." They hadn't talked about Syd's future plans since their last night in together. They hadn't actually talked much about anything other than who wanted what for breakfast lately; Layla had been engrossed in her TV work, and Syd had been enthralled with Jack, which had taken up all the time when they might have otherwise gotten together. That was unfair; Layla had spent a lot of those nights over at Rix's and had been pretty much unavailable due to inordinate amounts of sex. The "next time" Rix had promised Layla that she'd get to touch Rix had yet to come however, but she'd chosen not to push it. Whenever Rix was ready, Layla would be waiting. In the meantime, she was loving the way Rix made her feel.

"I've been thinking about more than that." Syd winked and grinned, obviously ready to spill a secret.

Layla ran a rake through her hair and whistled. "Really? Are you going to make me play the guessing game you love so much, or are you just going to tell me?"

"I *was* going to just tell you, but now you've made me want to play the guessing game. We haven't done that in ages." Syd bounced on the mattress and clapped like an excited kid.

"That's because I'm bad at it." But Syd's enthusiasm for it did make it slightly more entertaining. "Do I get any clues?" Layla checked her watch and continued applying her make-up; she had to be at the Nut Hatch restaurant to meet with Matt by one, and she always liked to be on time.

"No clues, but you can ask closed questions."

"That's strangely specific, but okay. Is it to do with the conversation we had about your work?"

"No."

"Is it do with Jack?"

Syd's eyes lit up and smiled so big, Layla could see all her teeth. "Yes."

"Are you investing in his and hers gags so that I can sleep when you're busy having sex?"

Syd clamped her hand over her mouth. "God, are we *that* loud?"

"You are *that* loud."

She frowned and looked partially unconvinced. "But our bedrooms are at separate ends of the apartment."

"When you're having sex, I wish they were at separate ends of the earth."

Syd giggled. "I'm sorry about that but also not sorry for having such amazing sex that he makes me scream bloody murder. And no, though Jack does have an impressive collection of sex toys which includes a ball gag. We just haven't gotten around to using it yet."

"TMI." Layla looked around for something to throw at Syd, but everything was breakable or too big. "Having newly discovered the concept of love, have you declared your undying love to him?"

"Pah, I did that two weeks ago when you went for your dirty weekend with your sugar daddy, and Jack said it first."

Layla thought it funny that Syd felt that the order of declaration was important. "Ha, so we both said it on the same weekend."

"That's cool. And I'm assuming by the amount of time you're spending at her place that Rix loves you too?"

"She does," Layla said, not feeling the need to mention Rix had said it first too.

Syd wrapped her arms around herself. "I'm hugging you from a distance. I don't want to mess up your hair. But anyway, back to me."

Layla nodded. "Of course. Back to your interminable guessing game." She applied her lipstick and dabbed the excess with a tissue then turned in her chair to face Syd. "I give up. I thought the love thing would've been it. I really can't see what else it could be."

Syd swung her legs off the bed and got up. She walked over to Layla, held out her hands, and pulled her upright. She held Layla's hands to her chest. "Jack asked me to marry him…and I said yes."

Layla squealed and began to jump up and down. Syd joined her, a huge smile across her face. God, it was so good to see her so free and happy. "You're lying! Are you playing a trick? It's not April Fool's. Oh my God." She had so many questions, not least how such a huge change in Syd's outlook had occurred. A few months ago, Syd was an avowed bachelorette, enjoying the whole smorgasbord of people that the world had to offer, always happy to let a new lover go just as easily as she'd picked them up. Layla had lost count of Syd's sexual encounters early in college and of the number of times Syd had lectured her on how boring Layla's serial monogamy was. "Jack must be a hell of a lover." But surely it wasn't just that.

"Layla, what we've got is about so much more than mind-bending sex."

She laughed at Syd vocalizing the exact thoughts in her head. "That's good news." Layla didn't want Syd to find a way into her head to vocalize Layla's worry that she was rushing into marriage. To go from someone who enjoyed the full range of Ben & Jerry's to one flavor for the rest of her life seemed like a huge step. And she hated to admit that she had concerns for Jack too. Had he been carried away with the allure of an older woman and was more enamored with that than with Syd herself? She shook the negative thoughts away and concentrated on the look of unabashed joy on Syd's face. She was practically effervescing with elation. "It's wonderful news, Syd."

"I was hoping you'd say that. You're the first person to know." She pulled Layla in a little closer. "I want you to give me away."

Tears burned Layla's eyes as the gravitas of Syd's request settled. While she didn't personally know the pride of a father in walking his daughter down the aisle, she'd interviewed many fathers and written the wedding scene in her books enough times to know its joy. And that it was further enhanced by the heart-rending absence of Syd's own father or mother. "Syd…it would be an honor." She pulled Syd in for a hug and held tight, and once she heard the smallest of sniffles and felt the tiniest heave of Syd's chest, Layla released her own tears, and they cried together. "Stop it, you're going to make my mascara run."

Syd pulled away and turned Layla's face side to side, inspecting her.

"You're good to go." She let her go and flopped back onto the bed. "It must be an important meeting if our cheap agent is taking you to the Nut Hatch. Did he say what it was about?"

"No." Layla returned to her dresser to pick up a tissue, and she dabbed the excess moisture from her eyes. Syd's ability to switch from emotional to all business impressed and exasperated Layla in equal measure. "He said that he wanted to see my face when he talked to me—oh God, you don't think he's cutting me loose already, do you?" She'd just about gotten over the worry that her relationship with Rix could affect her career. Had she relaxed too soon?

Syd threw a pillow at her. "Why would you go there? Of course he's not cutting you loose; you're doing well, and you're only going to get more popular as more of your work comes out. Remember that studio executives get to see the movie rushes long before it's released. You've got a buzz going on around you, so it's likely that people will be checking out your work and lining you up for their future projects. Popular writers get booked up months, and sometimes, years in advance. Ride that wave, babe. I said you could do this, and I'm so proud of you."

Layla wadded the tissue into a ball and dropped it in the waste basket beside the dresser. She never tired of hearing Syd say the words none of her family had ever said to her. "And I'm so lucky to have you as my friend."

Syd threw another pillow at her. "Let's just say that we're lucky to have each other. Now shut it, you soppy git. Enough tears for today, thank you very much."

Layla checked herself in the mirror one last time. "Fine." She picked up her handbag and her heels and strode out of her bedroom but stopped in the doorway. "I'll go and see which Hollywood superstar wants to work with me now."

Syd applauded her. "That's the spirit. Walk into that restaurant like you own it and don't look surprised at anything Matt says. This town is yours for the taking, hotshot."

Layla smiled at Syd's unerring confidence, and thus far, her predictions for Layla's success had been infallible. Now though, Layla was beginning to find that her ambition was overtaking even Syd's expectations. She was done doubting herself and thinking moderate achievement was good enough. She wanted everything this town had to offer, and she yearned for her star to burn bright.

Chapter Nineteen

R<small>IX</small> <small>TURNED UP</small> the dirt road and smiled. It wasn't until Layla had asked about the cabin that she'd realized she'd never taken anyone there before. As they'd enjoyed the quiet drive into the mountains, Rix had mulled over her past relationships and was surprised to recall that she hadn't ever invited anyone to join her there. She had no idea when it had become her sanctuary, or if that's what it had always been, but it now seemed strange that she'd been the only one to enjoy it. Or maybe it wasn't strange, and she'd been subconsciously saving it for when she had someone really special to share it with. She glanced at Layla, whose focus seemed to be on the big reveal as the road twisted this way and that, and her smile broadened. Layla *was* special, and Rix couldn't wait to share this place with her.

"Wow."

Rix pulled her truck to a slow halt in the parking area in front of the lodge and turned off the engine. "You like the look of it?"

"It's beautiful."

Rix got out, jogged around to the passenger side, and opened Layla's door. "Wait till you see the inside." She held out her hand, and Layla stepped out onto the gravel.

"I'm glad you told me to wear sneakers," Layla said and gestured to her feet. "I've worn these more in these past few months than in the previous three years I've had them."

Rix offered her arm, Layla hooked in, and they headed toward the cabin. "Maybe we can get you to invest in some hiking shoes for your next visit. There are some wonderful trails we can pick up close by that aren't too strenuous."

"I think you'll be quietly impressed to find out that I've already done that for this trip." Layla squeezed Rix's arm. "I thought we might need the occasional break from the bedroom to enjoy the surroundings. The sales assistant talked me into a whole outfit to go with the boots, so I need to show willing and go out at least once."

Rix unlocked and opened the door. "That is impressive, and it's also slightly disappointing that you're already thinking of leaving my bed."

"I have to give you some time to recuperate." Layla winked and stepped inside.

Rix followed and watched as Layla walked around, taking it all in. Rix loved being out in the wilderness, but she also loved her creature comforts and that was reflected in the way she'd had the cabin furnished.

"Whenever I imagine a cabin in the woods, I always think basic and rustic." She turned in a circle. "This is neither of those things, but I'm not really surprised given that it's yours. Are you going to give me the grand tour?"

"Is that a bad thing?" Rix went to Layla and pulled her into her arms. "You make it sound like it might be a bad thing."

Layla kissed her and put her finger on her lips. "No, it's a you thing, and I like your neat luxury. I'm not a muck and grit kind of girl." She kissed Rix again and put her hand on her chest.

"Maybe not, but you're my kind of girl." Rix placed her hand over Layla's, her heart beating hard against it. Layla's proximity, her touch and her voice made all sorts of things flip and somersault in ecstasy. The last two weeks had been a whirlwind of making love and laughter, and the ease in which they'd fallen into a relationship rhythm had amazed Rix. She'd had far longer relationships that had never come close to what they'd found in such a short time. Everything about them was almost poetic in its simplicity, and their lives had entwined as easily and naturally as their fingers did when they held hands. Rix had been looking for perfection, and this had to be it; she was sure she'd found the one in Layla.

Still holding Layla's hand, Rix showed her the rest of the lodge. They got waylaid christening the bed, and Rix would've been happy to have stayed there for the rest of the day, but Layla bounced up from her quick orgasm as if it had given her energy. The different ways Layla was affected by her orgasms—sometimes energized and others exhausted—baffled Rix, but she was having a damn good time learning every aspect of her.

"Will you show me your workshop?" Layla fastened her jeans and belt then held out her hand.

Rix took it and pulled herself up. She wrapped her arms around Layla's waist and kissed her. How was her kiss so perfect too? And how could it feel so different from the women Rix had kissed before? It was just their lips meeting and moving, so much less complicated than sex and yet, Layla's communicated their love for each other, its symmetry absolutely unique, and its chemistry unfathomably flawless. "I'd love to."

She led Layla downstairs and out through the kitchen into the adjoining workshop. She switched on the light and allowed herself a small smile. She hadn't worked on the eagle for a few weeks, mostly because Layla had been keeping her extremely busy back in the city, but she was pleased with how it was coming along. Sometimes she found that a longer break between carving sessions allowed the sculpture to settle, both in the wood and in her mind. Her smile grew when Layla gasped.

"That is stunning, Rix." Layla walked toward the carving before looking back. "I thought this was just a hobby, but you're a bona fide artist."

Rix laughed gently and glanced away, a little overcome with the strength of Layla's reaction. "You flatter me."

"It's not flattery when it's the truth." She reached out and slowly ran her fingers across the feather detail of the eagle's wings. "This is incredible. Does carving run in the family?"

"Nope."

"Then how did you learn how to do this?"

Rix watched as Layla continued to trail her fingers over the eagle and began to feel a little envious of the wooden bird, but mostly she was relieved and pleased that Layla liked her work. "Mainly from online videos. It's amazing how much time people are willing to give away to share their talent and knowledge."

Layla shook her head. "No, I don't accept that. You can show someone how to do a lot of things, but then there's just God-given artistic ability, and you've got it in spades." She took a step back as if to appraise it from afar. "If ever you get bored of Hollywood, you've definitely got a fallback career. People would pay thousands for something like this."

Rix joined Layla and tugged her into her arms, any distance between them feeling too great right now, especially after they'd just made love. "You really like it?"

Layla swatted her chest. "Don't play the coy creative with me; you've got to know how good you are." She looked around the workshop's walls. "Did you make everything on these shelves?"

"Yeah, that's almost everything I've made since I started. Learning to wood carve was another one of the things on my bucket list, but I really took to it."

"Almost?"

"Mom and Dad bought me a dog when I was a kid, and we went everywhere together. I was a loner at school, and Dex was my best friend. When I thought I was good enough to do him justice, I carved him. Mom loved it so much that she came up here and *woodnapped* it for their house. He's in their hallway, lying near the door like he used to do when he was waiting for me to come home from school." Rix cleared her throat and looked up to the roof in an attempt to pull back the tears edging her eyes.

Layla gently cupped her face. "Dex sounds like a perfect pooch."

"He was the best." She couldn't say anymore, and she definitely didn't want to talk about how he'd died. Over three decades, and his loss could still choke her up.

"Have you ever thought about selling any of them?" Layla asked.

Rix took Layla's hands and clasped them to her chest, grateful that she'd changed the subject. "Nah, I just do it for fun."

Layla gently pulled away and went to one of the shelves. She pulled one of the hearts from a selection of them and turned around, a gleam in her eye. "What about auctioning them at your charity events? Then other people would get to enjoy them, *and* you'd raise money for the center."

Rix raised her eyebrows. That wasn't a bad idea, especially since she was beginning to run out of room and was getting more ambitious with each one bigger than the next. "You really think people would buy them?"

"Absolutely." Layla replaced the heart and turned back to Rix. "Your work is wonderful; you really should be sharing it."

Rix pressed herself against Layla and hitched her up onto the workbench running along the length of the wall. "I'll think about it, but ever since you walked into my workshop, I've been thinking about making love to you on this bench."

"Really?" Layla ran her hand through Rix's hair then began to unbutton Rix's shirt. "It's funny that I've been thinking the exact same thing." She dragged her lips over Rix's, barely touching them. "All these amazing sculptures…" she took one of Rix's hands and traced light patterns in her palm, "created by your strong, sexy hands kind of makes a girl go weak at the knees." She lifted Rix's hand to her mouth and drew her tongue along the inside of Rix's wrist, over her palm, and up to the tip of her middle finger. She pulled Rix's finger into her mouth and sucked on it.

Rix's breath escaped in a moan. "You're making *me* go weak." The sensations from Layla's tongue zipped at the speed of light between her legs, and she clenched her thighs together to stem the throbbing. God, if she could make her feel this way from just playing with her hand, what could she do with the rest of her body? When they'd first slept together, Rix had promised Layla she could touch her the next time, but that next time had never arisen and Layla hadn't pressed the issue. But now, Rix was almost wondering why she'd delayed at all. Almost… She knew damn well why; she needed to trust a woman completely to allow her to touch her that way, and those women had been few and far between. It was a vulnerability she'd never allowed to happen freely. But Layla was special. Rix dared to believe that she might even be *the one*.

Layla released Rix's finger and laid back on the bench. "I want your mouth on me," she whispered.

"Fuck, you're too sexy." Rix squatted so that Layla's legs rested on her shoulders and then lifted her up to pull her jeans and panties from her ass. She tugged them all the way down to Layla's sneakers and let out a husky breath as the scent of Layla's sex, already strong from their quickie in the bedroom, drifted into her senses. Rix gently pushed Layla further along the bench then bent down to put her mouth exactly where Layla wanted it.

"Oh, yeah. That's it, baby." Layla balled her hand in Rix's hair and pressed her face down harder.

The breathiness of Layla's voice coupled with her forceful actions made Rix crazy with lust. She ran her tongue over the length of Layla's lips before she sucked her clit into her mouth and circled it with her tongue, in precisely the way she'd recently learned drove Layla wild. Layla's hand tightened in Rix's hair as she led her up the path to what Rix knew would be an explosive orgasm. Rix put her arms underneath Layla's thighs and placed her hands on her hips, keeping her in place as she began to grind and writhe beneath Rix's mouth.

"Oh, damn, you're so good."

Rix looked up over Layla's stomach and breasts to her face, but her head was flat against the table, making it impossible to see her expression. Watching Layla's body dance under her tongue would have to be enough. Rix's own sex was hard against the seam of her jeans, desperate for release.

She moved her right hand from Layla's hip and shoved it inside her jeans and boxers.

Layla lifted her head. "What are you doing?"

Rix reluctantly broke contact and her gaze met Layla's, whose eyes swam with desire. "I need to come."

Layla shook her head. "Let it build," she whispered.

She removed her hand and put it back on Layla's hip, though her mind screamed at her for doing so.

"Take care of me," Layla said before she dropped her head back to the bench.

Rix's hips began to rock, and she struggled to stop them. She had to concentrate on Layla's pleasure first, but goddamn, as soon as she came, Rix wanted Layla's fingers on her own rock-hard clit.

Layla's moans and gentle cursing slowly increased in frequency as Rix resumed her rhythm. She tongued beneath Layla's soft hood and circled her clit, hard and smooth as a polished marble. Layla pushed her hips upward, and Rix held her down firmly so she could maintain the flow that had Layla writhing under her hands.

Rix slipped her right hand beneath Layla's shirt and caressed her breast. Layla's hardened nipple pushed against the padding of her bra, eager for attention. Rix ran her finger over it, mirroring the movement of her tongue until Layla arched her back, the first sign she was about to come. Layla dipped and rose, and Rix pressed against her hip with one hand, keeping her mouth fixed on Layla's sex.

"God, I love you."

Layla whispered her words between husky breaths that hardened Rix's clit and made it throb so hard, she'd soon be prepared to beg for release. Layla grabbed one edge of the workbench, and her other hand grabbed at the wall as her grinding quickened. Rix held on, keeping her tongue steady until Layla cried out and bucked wildly beneath her. Rix licked and sucked every last joule of energy from Layla's outpouring.

"Damn, you're good at this." Layla slowly sat up on the bench. She grabbed Rix's shirt and tugged her in for a hard kiss. "You taste of me."

"You taste good." Rix took Layla's hand and pressed it against the crotch of her jeans. "I'm hard for you."

Layla's eyes shone. "Do you want me to do something about that?"

Rix averted her eyes briefly, unable to hold Layla's tentative gaze. "I do."

Layla tilted her head slightly and looked serious for a moment. "Are you sure?"

So perfect. The fact that Layla had asked to make certain this was something Rix wanted made her even more sure. She nodded then opened her belt and jeans. Layla gave her a dirty, wicked smile and slipped her hand inside Rix's boxers. Her smile broadened when her fingers slipped over Rix's clit so easily because of her wetness.

"You're soaked," Layla whispered and pressed against Rix's clit.

"Oh fuck." Rix jerked away under the pressure, the stimulation too intense to bear. "That's all your doing." She moved back into position, allowing Layla back into her shorts.

"Is this how hot you've been for the past few weeks?" Layla asked as she began a slow, teasing exploration.

Rix nodded and didn't speak, knowing that words would fail her right now.

"And you haven't taken care of yourself?"

Layla bit her lip, and Rix could see she wanted the answer to be no, which it wasn't, of course. She'd tried to abstain, but the frustration had been too much, and it had become a daily habit, often more than once a day if they'd spent the night together. Rix pressed her lips together and tried to express her penitence silently.

"Were you thinking about me when you were fucking yourself?"

"Oh god," Rix whispered, her arousal reaching new heights with Layla's filthy interrogation. "Yes. Always."

Layla thrust her finger inside Rix, and her legs buckled. She held onto the bench for support while Layla slid off the edge and slowly moved around. Rix had little choice but to follow, ending up with her ass against the countertop. Layla grasped a fistful of Rix's shirt with her other hand and drove her fingers in deeper.

"Fuck, that's perfect."

Layla laughed softly. "Mm, my handsome butch likes it hard."

She increased her pace and added a second finger. She ran her tongue along Rix's collarbone and bit into her neck as she pushed in harder and faster. Rix curled her fingers around Layla's hair and pulled her up. Their mouths smashed together in a collision of craving; Rix, starved of Layla's taste, held her there though her ability to kiss was suddenly lost as every ounce of awareness focused on the feeling building between her legs. There was nothing else, and everything seemed to slow as her crescendo came, and she screamed her release into Layla's mouth as the waves of pleasure pulled her under into a blissful abyss.

After Layla held her for a while in complete silence, Rix took a deep breath. She wondered if she could ever get used to this part, the awkwardness that followed allowing herself to be one hundred percent vulnerable and hoping that she'd be accepted for *all* that she was. If it could ever happen, Rix felt sure it would be with Layla. "I needed that." Simple words, but she hoped that Layla would grasp the subtext and multiple meanings. She needed to let go and allow Layla to touch her, and to show how much she'd come to need Layla, emotionally as well as sexually. This was Rix's final barrier to access all areas of her heart and soul. To be who she was, to be butch, and to give complete control of her body over to Layla was to be fragile in a way she wasn't comfortable with and could only allow with someone she trusted unconditionally.

Layla zipped Rix's jeans, buckled her belt, and tucked the front of her shirt in. "Happy to oblige. Thank you for letting me. Now that you've given your body to me, don't you think you should tell me your real name?"

Rix sighed. She would've legally changed her name if she didn't know that would break her mom's heart. "I can't just tell you my real name. There's a whole story behind it that you have to understand before I can do the big reveal."

Layla fixed her clothes, hitched herself back onto the workbench, and swung her legs from side to side. "Okay, I'm ready."

Rix opened Layla's legs, situated herself between them, and put her hands on Layla's waist. "When my mom was carrying me, I started to kick a lot after four months, particularly at night, and that kept her awake. Dad was working hard and needed his sleep, so she'd go downstairs and sit on the sofa while drinking a glass of milk. To distract herself, she started reading the children's books she'd gotten from the thrift store—"

"Are you telling me that your mom and dad called you the Lorax? You dropped the lo and changed a vowel? That's clever."

Rix clasped her hand over Layla's mouth. "Shush. If you interrupt again, I won't tell you now, and I'll never tell you. Deal?"

Layla rolled her eyes but nodded, and Rix removed her hand.

"Deal. But if I'm right, I get to choose any one of these carvings to take home with me."

"They're safe, but I might let you take one home just because I love you." Rix kissed her gently and pulled back. "Anyway, Mom tried all these stories, Roald Dahl, Kipling, Dr Suess, but it didn't change anything. I was still kicking. Then she tried *Peter Rabbit*."

Layla raised her hand and bounced on the bench. "Can I guess now?"

Rix laughed gently. "Sure."

"Is your real name Mrs Tiggy Winkle or Hunca Munca?"

Rix pulled Layla closer, and she wrapped her legs around Rix's waist. "That's amazing. How'd you guess it was one of those from all the characters in that series of books?"

Layla tapped her finger to her forehead. "Intuition, baby. Seriously though, you were named after Beatrix Potter?"

"Yep. Mom read those books, and I stopped kicking. It worked every time, she tells me—and anyone else who'll listen. Once I got out into the world, I started reading anything and everything, and I started with the books that had calmed me even before I was born. It's why I've got such a lavish library. I love the written word."

"Do you have the full set of her books?"

"Of course, how could I not? But it took a while to collect the whole set of first editions." And a lot of money, but every time Rix walked into her library, seeing that full collection on her shelves still made her smile.

"I bet your mom's glad you didn't change your name. Does it bother her that you hide it like you do?"

Rix shook her head. "She understands that the full version of my name doesn't fit with who I am, but she's happy that I settled on Rix because it's just shortened."

"Thanks for telling me."

"I love you. I'll tell you anything you want to know." She ran her fingers through Layla's hair, enjoying its silky caress between her fingers. "But if you tell anyone, I'll have to cut out your tongue."

Layla arched her eyebrow and pouted. "Hold fire on that proposed punishment until you've found out what I can do with my tongue."

Rix growled and pulled her in for another kiss. If the earlier effect of Layla's tongue on her hand was anything to go by, she was very much looking forward to finding out. And they had all weekend for that discovery.

Chapter Twenty

LAYLA RAN HER fingers over the finely polished willow tree wood carved into a heart. *Keep it safe.* Rix's words ran on repeat. It wasn't just the sculpture Rix had given her; it was *her* heart. When Rix had finally allowed Layla to touch her properly, she'd somehow said more than I love you without saying a word. Then the rest of the weekend had blurred into a bounty of sex, food, cuddles, and conversation, and it had been the right balance of everything, as close as she'd ever experienced to the romances she wrote in her books.

"Are you ready?"

Layla placed the heart back on her bedside table and stood. "As ready as I'll ever be." She picked up her handbag, and they headed out to her car.

Syd swung her door closed and sat up straight in her seat so that her head was above the convertible roofline. "Are you ever going to spend some of your new money on a bigger car?"

"I only need a bigger car when you're in the passenger seat, which is infrequent."

"Is that a no?"

Layla started the car and pulled out. "For now. You know me, I'm a saver, not a spender. This ride will end, as do all things, and I'm saving now so I don't starve later."

"You're such a pessimist."

"I'm a pragmatist. I believe every ending is a new beginning. That's not pessimistic, but the next one might not be as cash rich as this particular journey."

"Speaking of journeys, how's it going with Rix?"

Layla shook her head. "Nope, let's not talk about me. Today is all about you. Have you had any more thoughts on quitting acting?" Saying it out loud rammed it home for perhaps the first time. Everything was changing. New beginnings were everywhere for both of them. She hoped none of it would mean changes to their friendship, but now wasn't the time to be selfish and talk about that. They were solid. Layla could never have imagined that either of them would get married, but she'd certainly never envisioned Syd pairing off with a romantic notion of a forever love nor to have jumped into a shotgun wedding. Yet they were on their way to a bridal dress store. Regardless, they'd be there for each other as they always had been, and Syd getting married wouldn't change that. Syd was her rock, and she couldn't lose her. She'd be having a serious conversation with Jack about taking good care of her best friend, her chosen sister. Syd might've asked Layla to give her away, but she wasn't giving her away; she was just letting someone else have the opportunity to love Syd too, and she deserved that.

"I've been thinking about going back to school. I'd like to train to become a college lecturer in Women's Studies. A lot has changed since I did my degree, especially around the gender binary and what it means to be a woman. I want to be on the academic edge of that again. You're the fiction writer, but I've always loved academic writing. I want to research, and publish, and teach."

Layla reached over and squeezed Syd's hand. "It's so good to see you so enthusiastic about something again. You glow when you're inspired like this." She didn't ask what Jack thought about Syd's plans. Whatever Syd set her mind to, it would happen, regardless of what anyone else thought. Her single-mindedness and confidence in her decisions was something Layla loved about her. But it was possible things had changed on that score too. Syd was hurtling headlong into coupledom, where joint decisions were the order of the day. "What does Jack think?"

"He loves the idea, and he said that he'd support me no matter what I want to do. I haven't got a huge amount of money saved, and I'm going to try to get a scholarship at CalTech. But Jack said he doesn't mind going into debt if I'm following my heart."

Layla glanced at Syd. She really was glowing with positive energy and hope—and love. Yeah, there was lots of love mixed in there. It was obvious in the lilt of her voice. Jack sure had cast his spell on her. "That's amazing. Your life is changing so fast."

"Do you think I'm rushing into all of this?" Syd asked.

God, how was she supposed to answer this and not upset her? Syd and Jack were the stuff of romance novels; lightning had struck and within months, they were committing the rest of their lives to each other. *The rest of their lives*. Was that what Rix wanted? Layla couldn't even grasp what forever would feel like. Living in the moment, making sure she never let chances pass her by; that was Layla's motto. But everything ended, despite the best of intentions, and that applied doubly to relationships. And she'd witnessed firsthand how destructive it was for two people to stay together when the love and spark were long gone. The excuse of staying together for children always seemed to backfire and prolong the agony for everyone. And what was with the obsession of finding forever anyway? Much better to enjoy the here and now than fixate on an ideal that might never be reached. "Does it feel like you're rushing into it?"

Syd scrunched her nose. "Logically, yes, of course it does. We only met a few months ago. But here," she clasped her hands to her heart, "I can't rush it enough. I know that doesn't make sense to you. Hell, it doesn't make sense to me given how I've always been about relationships, but this is like nothing I could ever have dreamed, let alone be in the midst of." She shook her head. "I feel like I'm in one of your romance books. Damn it, Layla, you write them so well, how come you don't feel it?" Syd laughed and shoved Layla's shoulder lightly.

"Hey, no messing with the driver." She pulled up into a parking spot, unfastened her seatbelt, and turned to Syd. "I'm happy being in love for as long as it lasts, but let's not make this about me. You're sure, and that's all that matters. You have to trust yourself, like you always have in the past. And you've never steered yourself wrong." Layla took Syd's hands in her own. "I'll be right here with you, babe. Always."

Syd uncoupled her hands and pulled Layla into a tight embrace. "I love you, Layla."

She held on for longer than she might have otherwise. "I love you, too, but I'm still not paying for your dress."

They parted and got out of the car. As they headed toward the bridal store and Syd's new life, Layla didn't envy her strength of emotion or conviction in her relationship with Jack. She hoped it would be enough and that they would live happily ever after, just like in one of Layla's books, but what was so wrong with the happy for now Layla had been content to find? It had always been enough before. Surely that wasn't changing.

***

In her last meeting with Matt, he'd talked about the intense interest her work was getting, that the buzz around the big five production studios was building to a crescendo, and that there might be something huge in the pipeline for her. Seven figure huge. Life changing huge. Career making huge. But she hadn't let herself get caught up in the notion, and she was telling herself that's why she hadn't mentioned it to Rix.

Layla took a longer sip of her wine this time. She couldn't have heard the number right. When she put her glass down and focused on her agent, he grinned and nodded slowly, as if knowing she needed affirmation of what she'd just heard. If the number was right, he had plenty of reason to be smiling since his twelve percent fee would engorge his checking account very nicely. Jaimie sat back in her seat and looked completely unfazed by the offer she'd just made, her relaxed and elegant pose the antithesis of the warring emotions in Layla's mind. She wanted to jump up from her seat and run around the restaurant, screaming at the top of her lungs. She wanted to call Syd and yell down the phone about the unbelievable contract that had just been put on the table. But a tiny niggle tapped on her brain for her attention. What was Rix going to make of this? Would she see it as Layla selling out or would she understand that it was the opportunity of a lifetime and one she couldn't possibly turn down?

"I've had the contract thoroughly vetted, Layla." Matt tapped two fingers on the pile of pristine white paper. "There's nothing in there that isn't industry standard. I know that it probably looks daunting in comparison to your previous contracts, but Universal *is* the biggest fish in this sooty little pond so everything they do is big," he tapped the pages again and revealed his teeth, "including your remuneration."

His teeth were brighter than the paper. She hadn't noticed that before. Maybe he'd just had them treated in anticipation of her signing this deal.

"Layla?"

She looked across at Jaimie, whose silky voice matched her general demeanor. There was a vague look of concern in her expression, but while Layla didn't think her disingenuous, she wasn't fully buying it. "Yes?"

Jaimie pulled her phone from her handbag. "I sense some hesitation. Would you like to speak to Kurt before you make a final decision? I can check his calendar." She swiped the screen and looked up expectantly.

Final decision? She hadn't made any decisions. And was she supposed to know who Kurt was? This was the first she'd heard of the offer and the contract, and she'd never been one for spontaneity when it came to financial commitments. The number of zeroes Jaimie was talking about sounded almost alien and couldn't possibly be correct. Someone had made a mistake somewhere.

And yet, it seemed like everyday business for her agent and this studio executive. Okay, so the process had been similar to her only two other experiences with Matt, but the contract hadn't been physically on the table. That had come after the discussion, after the deliberation and negotiation. It seemed incongruous that she should take less time over a decision worth more money than she thought she'd earn in a lifetime, let alone for a three-picture deal.

"I'm going to need some time, Jaimie." Layla hooked her fingers over the contract pages and pulled them toward her. When Jaimie's brow arched and disappeared under her bangs, Layla understood she'd need further explanation. "This has come out of the blue. Matt told me there was some interest in my work, but I never imagined that would materialize into…into this." She laid both hands on the contract, perhaps a little too concerned that her hesitation might be taken as rejection and that Jaimie might remove the offer forever. While she wasn't sure about accepting it, she *was* sure she wanted to be the one making the decision. "I'd like to read through the contract myself." Layla ignored Matt's expression. Whether he was questioning her competence to understand the legal jargon or her sanity for not signing immediately, it didn't matter. She wasn't about to make arguably the biggest decision in her life without serious consideration or without talking to Syd, and not under pressure from Matt or Jaimie.

"That's perfectly understandable."

Jaimie said the words, but Layla doubted her conviction. She was clearly not accustomed to having to wait for anything.

"Do you have any questions that spring to mind now?" Jaimie asked and made an effort at a smile, but the corners of her mouth simply twitched like she had a tic.

"I suppose I'd like to clarify the premise of the trilogy you're proposing. You want to take *Selected* as the basis for the first film's plot, and you want me to write the screenplay, then you want me to write two more original screenplays for movies two and three."

"Yes. We don't want to drag the first book out over three movies. That wouldn't work, but there's clearly so much story left at the end of the book. We feel you easily have enough material for a trilogy, with the second film both on the new world and Earth, and the final film with everyone returning to Earth triumphant."

Layla held the scoff that almost jumped up her throat to get out. *Easily have enough material?* She'd always envisaged the book as a standalone. The story had been told. But that wasn't a problem. She hadn't killed off her heroes, so she could find new threads for them to weave. The problem was that they wanted to turn one of her heroes into a guy. "But you don't want my book as it stands?"

Jaimie blinked and looked almost less than comfortable for a millisecond before her mollifying mask slipped back into place. Layla held her gaze. If Universal wanted to monochrome her work, they were going to have to say it out loud and explain themselves.

"Audience testing shows that heterosexual couples are still the most popular leads for major movies, just as it is for color of skin. The voices may be loud purporting equality, but it doesn't translate to commercial success." Jaimie clasped her hands and shrugged slightly. "I don't like it any more than you do, but it is still the way of things."

"Isn't the Panther Marvel movie one of the highest grossing movies of all time?"

Jaimie nodded. "Indeed it is, like a black cherry on an ocean of vanilla ice cream."

Layla couldn't argue with that, nor could she dredge up a single highly successful movie with queer leads. She thought again of the money they were offering, the opportunity this represented, and the future it laid out in front of her. She wanted commercial success, and that's exactly what they were offering. All she had to do was make a sacrificial offering of one of her book babies.

"We adore the concept of your book, Layla, and it would be easy for us to have someone write a similar screenplay, but we don't want similar. We want the original, and we want you to write it." She glanced at the contract beneath Layla's hands. "And we're offering you a rather handsome sum to do it."

"I understand." Layla put her satchel on the table and slid the contract into it. "But I need some time to think about everything. Can you give me seventy-two hours?" That was very specific. Not three days, or overnight, or the weekend. What was she going to do in that exact time period that she couldn't achieve in a day or so?

"Of course," said Jaimie.

As Layla said her good-byes and promised to call, she knew she wasn't stalling the studio; she was giving herself time to find the courage to talk to Rix about it.

Chapter Twenty-One

RIX TILTED HER head to get a better view of Layla in her walk-in wardrobe.

"If I mixed all your shirts up while you were making me breakfast, would you have a meltdown?" Layla unbuttoned an apple red shirt, pulled it from its hanger, and slipped it over her shoulders. She fastened the middle button and padded barefoot back into Rix's bedroom.

Rix closed her eyes briefly and blew out a long breath. She knew her reaction was a conditioned response, learned from years of Hollywood movies and TV programs where the woman put on the man's shirt in the morning after sex and paraded around the house or apartment in nothing else. And the shirt would just cover the woman's ass, and she'd look incredibly cute and breathtakingly sexy all at once with her hair cascading, unkempt and wild, down her back. But it had long been one of those instant turn ons, and Rix owned it, nonetheless. And having Layla, her perfect woman, in her bedroom wearing nothing but one of her favorite shirts and looking exactly like all those leading ladies Rix had drooled over in her youth, was a dream come true.

"Looking like that, you can do anything you damn well please and get away with it." Rix patted the bed. "Come back to bed. I'll make you breakfast after."

Layla stuck out her bottom lip. "I need fuel if you want more sex before I leave to help Syd get ready for the wedding. I've dropped a dress size since we got together." She gave Rix the full puppy dog eyes. "Feed me."

Rix thought Layla was perfect exactly as she was but reluctantly got out of bed and pulled on a T-shirt. "You should know that I'm doing this under protest, and I'd much rather be showing you how much I love you by worshipping your body. But I don't want you wasting away and getting crazy skinny."

Layla grinned and squeezed her own hips. "There's no chance of that, honey, but duly noted."

When they got down to the kitchen, Rix pulled a box of ingredients from the fridge. "Eggs benedict work for you?"

Layla frowned and looked doubtful. "Really?" She pulled a chair out and hitched herself up to the breakfast bar.

Rix clasped her hand to her chest and feigned offence. "You don't think I can cook something complicated?"

"Given that every time I've stayed over, you've had the evening meal and breakfast delivered, I think my doubt is justified. Don't you?"

"Huh." Rix grinned. She lifted the lid of the box she'd gotten from the fridge and turned it to so that Layla could see inside: the container of pre-prepared Hollandaise sauce, four slices of thinly sliced salmon, two poached eggs, and two English muffins. On the inside of the lid were the instructions. "This is ordered in too. All I have to do is warm most of it up and cook the salmon. Does that give you more confidence?"

Layla laughed. "Yes. Yes, it does. I'm much happier knowing you're not going to poison me." She peered into the box. "Good to see salmon rather than bacon, or I'd have to report you to your doctor."

"Hey, I've made all sorts of changes, you know that. Doesn't that mean I get the occasional cheat meal?"

"Not until your bloodwork shows your cholesterol level is significantly reduced, no."

Rix rolled her eyes but secretly enjoyed the bossy, caretaker side of Layla that showed how much she cared for Rix. The dietary changes had been working, and the chest pain had almost entirely gone away. She poured them both coffee and set it on the counter. "I wanted to make you breakfast because it's a celebration meal."

"What are we celebrating? I thought we'd already celebrated at the wrap party. You're not one of those people who celebrates month-aversaries for every little thing, are you?"

Rix shook her head. She still couldn't quite get her head around how unromantic Layla was considering the soppy, fluffy romances she wrote, but then she also wrote kick-ass detectives and serial killers too, and Rix wouldn't be as happy if Layla were either one of those. "If I was, you'd already know, because we *didn't* celebrate the first month of our first sex, or first kiss, or the first month after you told me you loved me. Even though I have them all written down on my calendar." She unhooked a frying pan from the hanging pot rack and placed it on the stove top. "I'm reining it in just for you and your icy heart."

"Thank you, I appreciate that." Layla winked and sipped her coffee. "Just because I write the purple prose doesn't mean I live it."

Rix tried to ignore the flippant comment. This was how they'd spoken to each other from the beginning, and she loved their banter, but occasionally, the words Layla said in jest were too close to the truth. Rix told herself that it didn't matter. They loved each other, and people did that in different ways; that didn't make it any less powerful. She pushed away the part of her that considered putting the brakes on. She was all in and could visualize her future with Layla. Just because Layla hadn't talked about her own vision of the future didn't mean she didn't have one.

"So what are we celebrating?" Layla asked.

"Amazon wants us to make more than just a limited series, and they want us to start filming straight after we've finished this run before the show even goes to air. They're that confident after audience tests with the pilot episode. Layla, the show could reach millions through their streaming service, which will be epic now that they've bought out MGM." When Layla's face didn't light up or show any hint of excitement, Rix was confused. This was huge for both of them. "They want you to write all new material—they're talking about ten seasons, Layla. This is huge for your career."

Layla nodded slowly. "There's something I wanted to talk to you about too, and it kind of—well, it *does* clash with what you're talking about."

Rix rested her hands on the edge of the countertop, needing something solid to hang onto. Layla had been unusually quiet yesterday, but Rix had put it down to tiredness. They'd been working their asses off on set and falling asleep exhausted after sex. She'd thought they'd been overdoing it, but they'd finished filming now, and they could rest over Christmas. But Layla's stuttered preamble indicated there might be something more to it. "What do you mean?"

"I had a meeting with Matt yesterday—"

"I know that." Rix blinked and wanted to pull back the way she'd delivered the words. She had no idea what Layla's news was yet, but she'd already decided she didn't like it. She could call it intuition or pessimism, it didn't matter, but she didn't have to be an ass about it.

Layla raised her eyebrows. "Are you going to let me speak?"

Her question was gentler than Rix knew she deserved. She put the spatula down, let go of the pot handle, and held her hands up in apology. "I'm sorry. Go on."

Layla slid her coffee mug from her right to left hand and back again. She was stalling, which was so unlike her. What was so bad that she couldn't just get it out? They'd had no issues communicating thus far; there was nothing they couldn't handle together if they talked about it.

"What is it, Layla? You're freaking me out." Rix turned the burner to simmer and waited, trying to keep an outward impression of calm and stillness though her building anxiety had her wanting to pace around the kitchen to keep her nervous energy under control.

"Universal have offered me a three-picture deal based on my novel, *Selected*."

Layla's tight-lipped smile made it clear that wasn't the wonderful news it seemed to be on the surface. Rix picked up her mug and drank her coffee, offering Layla the time to say more. But nothing came. "Okay. Well, that sounds like a great opportunity. I'm sure we could work something out so you could do that and the Amazon deal, if Universal were open to some rescheduling. I mean, you'd be crazy busy, but you reap while you can in this business. It's better that than no offers coming in." Rix scratched a non-existent itch the side of her face to keep her hand busy. Layla wouldn't make prolonged eye contact and still didn't show any signs of excitement at the situation she was in. Any other writer Rix had ever known would've been laughing all the way to the Porsche dealership. "I don't understand your reticence, baby. This was what you wanted, wasn't it? I thought you were enjoying working in the movies—do you want to go back to writing books only? Talk to me, please." Rix pushed away from the countertop and rubbed the back of her neck, her frustration rising.

Layla sighed deeply and finally met Rix's gaze, her expression wary. "The schedule is already set, and it's pretty tight, especially since I have to write such a lot of new material. I don't know that'd it would be possible for me to do anything else for eighteen months. And they want me on the set too. We're talking about a three-to-four-year commitment, Rix."

Rix's shoulders sagged, but she offered a weak smile. The Universal offer was career gold for Layla, especially given that she hadn't been on the scene that long. Rix wasn't surprised, of course. She would've been incredulous had the offers *not* come in; Layla was a phenomenally talented writer who could turn her hand to practically anything, and it had only been a matter of time before the big studios approached her. Rix had secretly hoped she'd have Layla to herself for longer, which she supposed was professionally selfish of her, but after waiting so long to finally create TV from her books, it looked like it was over too soon. "It isn't something you've tried to do yet, baby. You don't know for sure that you can't slot both projects into your schedule."

Layla laughed. "These past few weeks have been madness, Rix. We're both exhausted. Christmas can't come soon enough. I need a break."

Rix couldn't argue with that, but the pressure had been down to squeezing the filming into the shortest window possible, which was her own doing. "I'm not saying you do them at the same time, but there'll be lulls and gaps between the production of each movie. Trust me, this is what I do. Just like I did with Rachel, if there's a way to piece it together, I'll find it."

"I know that. And you're brilliant at what you do, but scheduling isn't the biggest problem." Layla pointed to the frying pan. "I think that needs turning."

Rix hadn't seen the dark gray smoke rising from the burning oil, her focus having been entirely on Layla. "Damn it." She picked up some silicon tongs and flipped the salmon. It looked relatively salvageable, but with the way this conversation was going, she wasn't sure they'd get to breakfast before it was completely ruined. Rix turned the stove to an even lower setting and concentrated once again on Layla, whose expression was as serious as before. "So what *is* the biggest problem?" Rix took another sip of her coffee and almost spat it straight out. Coffee ruined, breakfast on its way to being ruined: what had been a promising morning had taken an unsatisfactory turn. She wanted to press reset and go back to bed. Layla closed her eyes and blew out a long breath. A tear escaped her eye and traced a lonely path down her cheek. Rix reached across the countertop and wiped it away with her thumb. "Baby, what's wrong? It can't be that bad, surely."

"Part of the deal is to make the story with straight characters."

Rix frowned. "It already had straight characters. I don't see the problem. And it's not just a hetero bad guy, is it? A few of the secondary characters on the right side are straight too."

"You don't understand." Layla shook her head slowly. "They want me to turn Kris into a guy and make the romance straight."

Layla's final sentence dropped a match on Rix's frustration, burning it away and liberating her fury. "And you've said yes? What the hell were you thinking? You're selling out for a fast buck and commercial success? What are twelve pieces of silver worth these days—a few million dollars? Turning your characters into a heterosexual couple makes a lie out of all the books you've written. It erases us, like the movies have been doing for years. And you're okay with that?" Rix turned away, unable to look at her. No wonder Layla hadn't said anything until she'd been forced to. She knew damn well how Rix was going to take it, and that's why she'd already produced the crocodile tears, to play on her soft side.

Rix clenched her fists and held them out in front of herself. She stretched out her fingers and tried to rein in her reaction. But Layla knew who Rix was when she got involved with her. How could Layla think there'd be a future for them if she was so quick to drop her community for mainstream movies?

When she turned back, Layla leaned back in her seat. "Have you finished?"

Rix shook her head. "I've barely started. I'm an activist, Layla. I make content specifically for the LGBTQ community. I raise funds for an LGBTQ charity. I'm committed to making this world a better place for people like us, though it's becoming clear that maybe you're not like me at all. I can't be with someone who prioritizes their bank balance over their moral compass."

"What do you mean? This is business; it has nothing to do with us."

"Of course it does. Where are we going with this?"

"Going? Does there have to be a destination? Aren't we okay simply enjoying the journey?"

"I don't want to just be okay, Layla, I want to be settled, married, and thinking about having kids before I get too old to run around the yard and build a treehouse for them." Her leap from business to personal had been swift, but now that it was on the table, Rix wanted all the answers.

Layla half-laughed and shook her head. "We've only been seeing each other for a couple of months, Rix—"

"So have Jack and Syd, but they're getting married tomorrow."

"And they might be divorced next month. What's the rush?"

"I'm not rushing, Layla." Rix grasped the edge of the marble counter. She was only three feet from Layla, but the chasm felt like the Grand

Canyon, and it widened with every sentence. "It's not like I'm proposing or taking you to a fertility clinic. I just want to know those things are on the table, otherwise there's just no point in carrying on."

"This is so irrational. You're mad at me because I haven't got a crystal ball, and I don't see what the future holds for us?"

And there it was. Layla was just in the here and now, whereas Rix wanted so much more. "So you *don't* see us having a future and growing old together?"

"Christ, Rix, I'm thirty-five. I don't want to be thinking about getting old period." Layla dropped her mug onto the table with a little too much force. She lifted it, as if checking to ensure it hadn't damaged the surface. "Weren't we happy? What's the obsession with happy ever after? No one can know what's around the corner for anyone."

"What's so bad with wanting to share your life with someone? With commitment? It's human nature."

Layla pressed the heel of her palm to her forehead. "I am sharing my life with you."

"No, you're just sharing moments of your life with me. I just don't get you. You're disingenuous. You're selling something you don't even believe in, and now you're dropping your responsibility to your community because Universal have flashed a fancy deal your way. You're selling all kinds of lies." Christ that was harsh, but Rix was so damn angry that she couldn't stop herself. Layla was supposed to be *the one*. The dream woman. But everything she'd imagined and hoped for was disintegrating, and the sands of their love were falling through her fingers as she tried to hold them together.

"That's not true. I'm writing what people just like you want in life. You want the two point four children and the dog running around your mansion. That's your version of suburban heaven."

"You make it sound like I want something bad."

"I'm not saying that at all," Layla said. "*You're* saying that everyone should want that and should be able to visualize it. Don't you see the pressure you're putting on me?"

Rix held up her hands. "I'm not pressuring you. I just don't want to waste my time. I want to give everything, all of me, and I need that to be reciprocated." Her voice cracked, and she paused to recalibrate. "Apparently, you can't do that because even though you write about happy ever after, you don't believe in it. Ergo, you don't believe in us."

"What does that even mean?"

Rix huffed. "I don't want happy for now, with some idea that it will all fall apart. I want happy forever, someone who will stick around no matter what. You not knowing proves my point."

"I think your point is illogical. I've never done anything that would make you doubt my love for you." Layla leaned forward and held out her hands. "Why can't we just enjoy what we have right now? You could spend your whole life looking for someone who doesn't exist. Love isn't a script you can follow. It is what it is." Layla pulled away after Rix moved her hands from the table, and her expression hardened. "Your parameters are too tight. How can anyone real fit into your neat little box of what a perfect partner is? You need a robot so you can program them to think exactly what you need them to think."

"Maybe a robot would have more emotion that you, and I never said I was looking for the perfect partner." Rix's chest tightened. The words were coming out of her mouth, but she wasn't consciously pulling them forth. She could see from Layla's expression that the barb had hit its intended target.

"Huh." Layla arched her eyebrows, but her lip quivered. "You said you were looking for perfection; it's the same thing."

"It doesn't matter now, does it? You're not the woman I thought you were. I don't think you're even the woman you think you are. You've been waylaid on the way to becoming the person you could be, and you're caught up in the Hollywood machine." Rix steeled herself against backing down, remembering how this argument had started. "Don't you see how important it is for us to tell these stories? To represent our people and give them positive, successful role models? You don't believe in real commitment and that makes it easy for you to turn your characters straight. As long as you're making money and being successful, it doesn't matter to you, does it?"

Layla got down from the bar stool. "I think I'm done with this conversation. I'm going home."

A ball of regret rose in Rix's throat. *This* was supposed to be Layla's home eventually. "You can't leave like that." She gestured toward Layla, looking as sexy as ever in just Rix's shirt buttoned at her chest. She tried to ignore the traitorous stirring between her legs. "You're half naked."

"Obviously," Layla said and left the kitchen.

If she stomped up the staircase for dramatic effect, it didn't work because her bare feet would've sunk into the plush carpet, and Rix heard nothing but an irritated harrumph. She grabbed the frying pan and tossed it, contents and all, into the sink from a distance. The salmon bounced out and slapped onto the tile splash back, leaving a greasy trail as it slid down to the sink. Rix walked toward the hallway but stopped at the door jamb, unable to go any further. She was too angry and didn't want to say anything else she might regret, because she'd already delivered a litany of insults she wasn't proud of.

What was she doing? Layla was the best thing that had happened to her for such a long time, and everything felt so... She punched the wall to stop herself saying the word Layla had thrown at her. Wasn't *perfect* a good thing? And they'd clicked in every department. This had to be the right thing to do. It wasn't about stopping things before they'd gone too far—it was way too late for that—but she couldn't keep wasting her time on women who didn't see a future with her, no matter how good it felt in the moment. And Layla's easy willingness to betray her community for mainstream success... Rix slapped her palm against the wall. Maybe *betray* was too harsh, but that's what it felt like right now.

She heard Layla's footsteps on the wooden floor of the upper hall, and her anger was evident in their heaviness. Rix didn't want to look as she came down the staircase but couldn't help herself. *Stop her.* But she remained motionless in the doorway, her jaw clenched and her hands fixed around the frame, knuckles white, stubborn and stoic. Was she really going to let the love of her life walk out of her house? Out of her life?

Layla paused at the base of the stairs and looked across at Rix. Even from this distance, Rix could see the tears streaking her cheeks and the trembling of her lips. Rix's instinct was to run to her, pull her into her arms, and kiss away her pain. Wasn't their love strong enough to get through this? Surely they could figure out a way forward that worked for both of them.

But Rix said nothing. She *did* nothing.

"I guess I'll see you at the premiere," Layla said and crossed the hallway to the front door.

And then she was gone, the act of her leaving saying more than a thousand arguments could ever hope to communicate. Rix closed her eyes and sank to her knees. She barely registered the icy chill of the stone floor until her face pressed against it and she wetted it with tears of her own. She heard Layla's engine start and waited for the crunch of gravel as she pulled away, but it didn't come.

Rix lifted her face from the floor and stared at the front door, half of her hoping and wishing Layla would come back through it. The rest of her wanted to tear her gaze away and listen to what her head was telling her. Layla wasn't the woman for her. She wasn't Rix's future. They wanted different things, and they could never align in a million lifetimes, let alone one.

Still, as the gravel finally crunched beneath Layla's car as she pulled away, Rix's heart ached with a pain so intense she thought she could pass out, something she might welcome if it delivered her into a mindless oblivion.

Chapter Twenty-Two

LAYLA PASSED JACK as she came down the ramp. He waved and she returned the gesture, glad that Syd had responded to her tearful phone call by asking him to leave. She didn't want to share her meltdown with anyone but her best friend. She drew into her allocated parking spot, where Syd was already waiting. Layla got out of the car and ran into her arms, her restrained tears easily falling into a full-blown sob.

"Come on, babe. Let's get you upstairs." Syd pulled out of the embrace, draped her arm around Layla's shoulder, and tugged her toward the elevator.

Layla allowed herself to be led, needing Syd's no-nonsense method of caretaking. She stifled her sobs into manageable sniffles when the elevator stopped at ground level, and their gay neighbors got in with their toddler and newborn. They exchanged greetings and small talk, though Syd covered for Layla's lack of words with lots of questions about their newly adopted child. Of all the people to have to share the ride to their twelfth-floor apartment, a cute little gay family was not top of her list. It was too painful a reminder of everything Rix wanted.

The hellish ride felt like eternity, and when Layla finally opened the door into the safety of their apartment, she collapsed onto the couch and unleashed the tears she'd held back so that she could see the road on the way home. Syd said nothing and simply lifted Layla's head, sat down, and let Layla rest on her lap. She gave her a tissue and stroked her hair, and Layla relaxed into a comfortable silence punctuated only with her crying.

She'd gone over what had happened on the journey back. Rix had erupted like a long-dormant volcano, throwing Layla completely. Okay, so they hadn't known each other that long, but Rix had never shown any signs of that kind of pent-up rage. And yes, Layla knew how passionate Rix was about the LGBTQ community, but she'd never given Layla a chance to explain that she hadn't signed the offer or to talk through how conflicted she was about it. Layla had needed to talk about it and to discuss it rationally and objectively so that she could work out the pros and cons before making a decision. Rix's reaction almost made her want to sign the contract out of spite, and she supposed that was also the reason she hadn't simply stopped Rix in her tracks to say that she *hadn't* signed the contract. She was already torn, and Rix's news about Amazon and MGM studios had heaped more complications onto an already complex situation.

The argument had gotten out of control, as arguments so often do, and she'd said things she regretted. She had no idea if Rix felt the same or not. The cold stare in her eyes as Layla had left suggested the latter. Layla had even waited in the courtyard, half hoping for Rix to come out and stand in front of her car, not letting her leave until they talked about it and sorted everything out.

But she hadn't come.

And maybe that was for the best. Though Layla had sometimes hoped she'd have kids one day, she never really thought it would happen, and she certainly hadn't planned anything to the nth degree, as Rix apparently had. Though they perhaps wanted the same things, the path to them couldn't be any different. Layla almost felt sorry for Rix and the pressure she put on herself, let alone the expectation she placed on her partners, on Layla.

She loved Rix, there was no doubting that. She knew herself well enough to know her own feelings in that department. And having seen how hard and fast Syd had fallen for Jack, and their instant commitment to a future together, Layla had begun to wonder about what lay ahead for Rix and her. Just as she didn't doubt her love for Rix, she couldn't deny that it felt different to the loves of her past. But she hadn't wanted to analyze it. She simply wanted to enjoy it, because who knew how long it might last, and time spent thinking about something was time lost in its pure enjoyment.

Now all she had was time to think about it, about what she'd lost—no, not lost, but had stripped from her life. Rix's dictum that she couldn't be with someone who valued money over their community was absolute, and though Layla had yet to make that decision, she didn't appreciate that Rix was unwilling to sit down and discuss it. Rix only saw in black and white, when this situation was clearly as gray as an English summer's day. It was essentially an ultimatum. If Layla took the Universal deal, she'd kiss good-bye to Rix and whatever a possible life together had to offer, though the way things had already ended seemed pretty conclusive. If

Layla refused the Universal deal, Rix would be happy because she felt it was the only morally correct choice. She apparently didn't see the doors it might open for Layla's future queer-focused work. And wasn't being an out lesbian who was also a hugely successful screenwriter in mainstream movies a positive enough role model in itself?

Layla recognized Rix's point of betrayal. She'd been fully aware of it before she told Rix, otherwise she would've already signed the contract. And perhaps that was the avenue Layla should explore with Jaimie: to see if she could write something completely new for their trilogy. Matt had said all the big studios were buzzing about her work so Universal might simply have been the first to pull together an offer. Perhaps the others would want her work as it stood or would commission new scripts. Wouldn't that make everything easy? But life wasn't easy, and people were forced to make difficult decisions in their working life all the time: ones they could get on board with and ones they couldn't; ones they hated and ones they lived with. Her decision could make her a fortune but lose her lover; it seemed too dramatic to be real.

Layla closed her eyes and dabbed the tissue under her nose. Rix was so much more than a lover, so much more than a partner. She was Layla's equal and match in every way and on the occasional mornings when Layla awoke before Rix, Layla had allowed herself to stare at Rix and wonder how easy it would be to go to bed with her every night and how wonderful it might be to wake to her face every morning. Did that count as seeing their future together? Wasn't that enough? Could she even bring herself to dare to hope for a forever love? Certainly she hadn't had an inkling of such a thing with previous lovers, even ones she'd been with for a couple of years. Syd could be right; forever was hidden behind a veil until the right person came along to tear it down.

But if Rix had torn the veil down, she'd now torn the whole building down. Rix's anger had been visible and loud, but Layla's bubbled below the surface. She wasn't one for confrontation, but nor would she back away from it or be cowed by virtue of volume. Layla was angry too, and she wouldn't be the one to go running back to Rix to beg her forgiveness for not seeing things the same way. She needed time to simmer and time to discuss it with Syd. She didn't know if there was a way back to Rix or even if that might be something Rix wanted. What Layla didn't want was for that path to be conditional on her decision on the Universal offer or on her acceptance that commitment meant forever.

"How are you doing, babe?"

Syd's timing was impeccable. She knew that Layla always needed some internal processing time before she'd be ready to talk. Warmth rose in her chest, and she was grateful for having her life graced by such a wonderful friend. "I'm pretty sure I'm single again."

"What happened?" Syd continued to play with Layla's hair.

She gave Syd a full recap of how the morning had played out, omitting the morning sex, which Layla would have recorded in more detail had she known it might be the last time she'd touch Rix that way. What a dark detour the morning had taken after such an intimate and tender beginning. She'd felt Rix truly letting go every time she allowed Layla to touch her, and the intensity of their connection almost took Layla's breath away.

"Why didn't you tell her that you hadn't signed the deal?"

"She didn't really give me a chance to talk. She just hopped up on her high horse and rode headlong into her incorruptible rainbow sunset."

Syd tapped her finger on Layla's forehead. "Since when do you need someone to give you a chance to talk? If you've got something to say, nothing and no one can stop you. Why didn't you tell her?"

Layla rolled her eyes. Having someone who knew her so well could also be a curse. "Because I was too busy lashing out when the argument became about more than just that. If I'd told Rix I hadn't signed, she would've calmed down. And if she softened, I would've capitulated and we would've ended up in bed, making up. But by then, that wasn't the point."

"What was the point?"

"The fact that she didn't give me the time and space to discuss the deal. I could see the problem with letting down my readers, but I still needed to discuss it rationally." Layla screwed the tissue up in her hand, willing herself not to shed more tears. "It's a complicated issue, and there's so much more to it. I needed some understanding; I didn't need vilifying. And I definitely didn't need it to devolve into my lack of commitment to growing old together."

"She's got strong feelings when it comes to queer issues, babe. You've always known that."

Layla turned onto her back so that she could see Syd's face. "You're saying I should've backed down and that her behavior was acceptable?"

"Not at all. But you didn't call her on it either. If you had stayed calm and talked it through, maybe she would've seen your point of view…or maybe she wouldn't, but you're not going to know unless you have that conversation with her, are you?"

"I don't know if I want to try revisiting the conversation." She sighed deeply and heaviness seeped into every fiber of her being. "You know how I hate confrontation, Syd, and this was a side of Rix I'd never seen."

"And now you have. Is it a dealbreaker?" Syd moved a strand of Layla's hair from her eyes. "That's the question you need to ask yourself. She's an alpha, Layla. Chances are that no one has ever called her on it, so how's she supposed to know she needs to change? And if you don't sort this out by tomorrow, it's going to make our wedding awkward."

"Why?"

"Because Jack asked Rix to be his best person, remember? You're my maid of honor. That's some close proximity for two people having relationship troubles. I can't have your negative energy bleeding onto our love, babe."

Yep, she could see how that would be awkward. Would Rix be able to handle attending a wedding when it was clearly something she wanted so desperately? Especially with Layla being so close. "You seem pretty solid. I don't think anyone else's crap is going to affect you."

Syd made a grumbling sound and pressed her finger to Layla's nose. "Well, you have to sort it out one way or the other. I don't want any lesbian drama overshadowing my big day."

Layla harrumphed. "You should be more understanding given how much lesbian drama you've been responsible for."

Syd gestured toward herself. "Is it my fault that some women just didn't want to let me go?"

"I guess not." Layla laughed at Syd's exaggerated arrogance, glad of the levity and light relief from the desperate ache in her heart.

"And speaking of not wanting to let go, maybe this is hurting so much because Rix is not Ms. Right Now and she's actually—"

"Don't say Ms. Right or I might vomit roses and unicorns." She hadn't wanted to hear the first part of the sentence either, but she could hardly slap her hand over Syd's mouth and stop her speaking. She hadn't been looking for either of the options Syd had almost vocalized.

But just because she hadn't been looking for something didn't mean it hadn't found her, regardless of whether or not she wanted it.

"You're happy to fall in love, Layla; why aren't you open to finding your happy ever after? What is it that scares you about the idea of true, lifelong commitment?" Syd asked after a long period of silence.

Layla averted her gaze from Syd's gentle, questioning expression. It wasn't something as trite as not believing she deserved happiness. Her therapist had warned her though, that the effects of her parents' relationship might manifest in curious ways. Had she shut herself off from the possibilities of a forever love based solely on their inability to find it with each other? No. Maybe that was the seed from which her life choice had been sown, but divorce rates were at an all-time high, and romance novels were seeing ever-increasing sales. People wanted to read what they could never seem to find. Perhaps because Cupid didn't favor everyone, the ideal became more enticing even as it became less attainable. If forever love were commonplace, it wouldn't be so special, it wouldn't *feel* so special. She hadn't been looking, but that's what she'd found with Rix, although special didn't seem a powerful enough word to describe it.

Syd tapped her on the nose. "Is the penny dropping, babe?"

Layla swatted at Syd's finger. "I hope Jack didn't see your dress."

"Massive topic change, but I'll run with it since the next couple of days should be all about me anyway. No, Jack did not see my dress because I put it in your room."

"Thanks for kicking him out before I arrived."

"He was leaving anyway, babe." Syd winked. "We were just getting some last-minute pre-wedding naughtiness in before I sent him on his way."

Syd's admission assuaged Layla's guilt somewhat. Syd had always been quick to drop whatever she was doing to support Layla, but her wedding was tomorrow, and she didn't want to impinge on those preparations. God, it was really happening. Syd, avowed bachelorette and lover of all people, was getting married. "I still can't believe this is all happening. And so fast." She hoped Syd didn't interpret any sense of judgment from her statement because there was none.

"When everything clicks into place, babe, there's no point wasting time." Syd's expression softened, and she got a faraway look in her eyes. "This life really is too short not to trust your heart. I love Jack, and he loves me, and we want to be together for the rest of our lives. We want that commitment sealed with a ceremony, and we want to wear rings that symbolize that promise." She focused back on Layla and smiled. "I never saw it coming, but I'm glad I opened my heart when it did."

Layla returned her smile and closed her eyes. Syd was still very much herself, but there was a sense of inner peace that emanated from her. Analyzing herself now, Layla felt precisely that whenever she was with Rix. There were issues that needed to be addressed, and that might be painful. But happy ever after did exist, Layla finally realized, and she'd found hers without having to search for it.

Chapter Twenty-Three

RIX SMOOTHED OUT the edges of her bow tie again, not quite satisfied that it was perfectly positioned. She tapped the pocket of her suit jacket to check her speech cue card was still there, as if some wedding party pixie might've stolen it just to mess with her. It was only a few key words to set off her thought process, but its presence was still reassuring. She checked her other inside pocket for her phone and the already weighty ball of disappointment in her stomach grew when she saw there was still no response from Layla to her numerous texts.

She deserved nothing more, of course. She'd been a stubborn ass, and she wouldn't blame Layla if she never wanted to speak to her again. In the ten hours that had passed since Layla had left Rix's house, she'd spent every minute going over the conversation and berating herself for how things had transpired. Transpired was a stretch; that inferred a certain degree of letting something takes it course, but Rix hadn't allowed that. A curtain of red had descended over her eyes, her compassion, and her common sense when Layla had given her the details of the Universal deal, and she'd launched into a viciously judgmental diatribe which left Layla with no choice but to defend herself, and the exchange had careened into the wall of self-righteousness Rix had been building for years.

She surveyed her reflection one last time and left the restroom to take her place at the table alongside Jack ready for the rehearsal dinner. When she sat down, Jack grasped her forearm and squeezed hard.

"Syd still isn't here. What if she doesn't come? What if she got cold feet?"

Rix placed her hand over Jack's. "There's no way that's going to happen. She loves you, and she'll be here." She tried not to wonder how Layla felt right now, other than hurt at Rix's behavior. Right on cue, Layla and Syd walked into the restaurant, and conversation ceased. She and Jack let out gasps, and Rix coughed into her hand in a futile attempt to disguise her admiration. She shouldn't have bothered; everyone else at the table had the same reaction. The pair were a vision of beauty in long, flowing gowns that accentuated and flattered their individual assets. Rix's inner voice continued to chew her out for the morning's events and reminded her that she could well have lost her own shot at a wedding of their own. But at least this evening had pushed them together and might allow Rix a solid opportunity to speak to Layla to make amends.

Layla and Syd walked toward the table, greeting the rest of the guests as they rushed to meet them. It was a small affair, with only ten other guests. Rix knew Jack's family wouldn't be present since they'd disowned him, but she had no idea Syd's side would also be minimal and she wondered why. It made for a gathering of mostly twenty and thirty-somethings, with Rix as the oldest guest by a decade.

Jack had pushed his chair back and was waiting at the rear of the welcome party. Rix's heart swelled at the love so obvious between Syd and him, a love so intense it had all but manifested a physical presence. When Layla's gaze settled on Rix, her heart lurched in her chest, as if in protest of their love that she'd endangered. She smiled and went to say hi, but Layla shook her head and mouthed something Rix didn't catch. Her hopes sank. Why she'd expected a second chance, she couldn't fathom. She didn't deserve it.

Syd gave her a light hug. "Well, if it isn't the Incredible Hulk. No, we don't like you when you're angry." As she pulled away, she whispered, "Make it right."

So there *was* a chance? But Syd was gone and took her place on the other side of Jack before she could get more information.

Layla walked around the table from the other side and sat beside Syd, making it impossible for Rix to make further eye contact with her. Rix sank back into her chair, confused, but her belly fluttered with the possibilities of Syd's instruction.

The army of butterflies remained resident in her stomach, making it hard to eat more than a few bites of each course, despite the delicious aromas and perfect presentation. Even when some of the guests were served rare steak and mature cheeses, Rix's nose didn't connect to her appetite, and it wasn't her doctor's orders that stopped her envying those dishes. The steak reminded her, as Layla had devised, of the boyband cows she'd taken Rix to see, followed by the most wonderful afternoon and evening of making love she'd ever experienced. The memories were as much a punch to the gut of what she'd lost as they were a reminder of what she'd had.

Jack spent the dinner engrossed in Syd, and though the guest seated next to Rix had introduced herself very briefly, she had then spent the next two hours deep in conversation with the woman to her left. The circumstances conspired to ensure that all Rix could do was cogitate her next move over and over, and mentally kick herself for getting into this situation at all. Occasionally, she slipped into justifying her actions. Turning one of Layla's pre-existing books into a straight movie was outrageous, and she wanted to know which executive idiot at Universal had thought it was a good idea. This was the twenty-first century; they were supposed to be moving forward not backward, not to taking away queer heroes but celebrating them. Why hadn't they just asked Layla to write something new for them? God knew she was more than capable of giving them whatever they wanted.

Rix wanted to believe that Layla hadn't and wouldn't sign it, but she also had to consider the implications if Layla did want to sign the deal. It would take some soul-searching for Rix to figure out how she was supposed to handle that, but what she'd come to realize since Layla had left that morning was that her politics shouldn't impact their relationship. She just hoped there might be some middle ground.

As the desserts were being served, Layla stood and walked behind Rix. She placed her hand on Rix's shoulder briefly and leaned down to her.

"If you want to talk, this is your chance," she whispered.

Rix waited for the briefest of moments for Layla to move away before she shoved her chair back and followed Layla like an eager puppy. When she turned the corner toward the restroom, Layla grabbed a handful of her shirt, pulled her into a side room, and closed the door.

"We can't be away from the table for long," Layla said and backed away a few steps to lean against the wall.

Rix wanted to take Layla in her arms and press her body against hers, to reestablish the connection she may have severed forever. But there was no way Layla would allow that, and Rix wouldn't expect it before they'd talked. She paused for too long, trying to decide where to begin.

"Tonight is about my best friend, Rix. I don't want to make it about us with people gossiping about where we might have disappeared to."

The reserved, almost cold tone of Layla's voice stopped Rix's misplaced thoughts in their tracks. "I'm sorry."

"About tonight?"

"That too, yes. I don't want to ruin Jack and Syd's night, but thank you for giving me the chance to talk to you, especially before tomorrow." She was rambling, straining for purchase in a situation where she felt completely adrift. "I'm sorry about this morning."

"Specifically, what are you sorry about?"

Rix looked deep into Layla's eyes, relieved when she saw they betrayed Layla's outward detachment. Her lip trembled, but her jaw clenched.

"Rix." Layla tapped her watch.

"All of it." She took a step forward, but Layla held her hands out in a clear instruction to keep her distance. "I didn't give you the space to talk about the Universal deal. I jumped on it and tore into you when it was the studio I was angry with." She shrugged and ran her hand through her hair. "You were reluctant to talk to me because deep down, you knew I'd react like that, even though I'd never been like that with you. Because you know me. You know me so well despite us not having been together long." Rix bit her lip and tried to keep her thoughts ordered so she didn't go off on a tangent. "I'm sorry if I scared you, and I'm sorry for reacting that way at all. My passion for the community turned into something ugly, and I had no right to direct that toward you." She paused, hoping for an interjection or response of any kind from Layla but none was forthcoming, so she pressed on. "I have this idea in my mind of the relationship I want to be in, and that includes being supportive of you, no matter what. But I failed myself, and worse, I failed you. You wanted to talk to me, and I blew up. I'm sorry, Layla. I was an asshole. Can you forgive me?"

Layla pushed an errant curl of hair away from her forehead and sighed. "You assumed I'd taken the deal and that I hadn't even considered the downside to my readership and my community. Because it *is* my community too, Rix. Sure, you do an awful lot for the center in LA, but you don't have a monopoly on caring. Some of us aren't able to show it quite as flamboyantly as you do. That doesn't mean we don't consider it any less."

Rix nodded but said nothing, wanting to allow Layla all the time she needed to speak. Layla raised her eyebrows after a few moments of silence, and Rix took that as an indication to respond. "You're absolutely right. I get carried away, and I got caught up in the magnitude of this situation because you're such an amazing writer and a wonderful role model. But it's not my place to direct you or judge how you choose to use that. I should've listened and helped you work over the problem, but I got pig-headed and went ballistic on you. I'm so sorry, Layla. I'm not making excuses for how I treated you, because there are none that would justify my behavior."

"I haven't signed the contract, but that doesn't mean I won't. I want to talk to you about it, because you've been in this business for years, and I'm only just starting out. That doesn't mean you get to dictate what I do or don't do. Partnerships don't work that way where I come from. But if we talk about it and I decide to take the deal, how are you going to handle that, Rix?" Layla clasped her hand to her chest. "I can't be around you if you're unable to get around things we don't agree on. I won't do that to myself, no matter how much I love you."

Though everything Layla said was important, Rix latched onto her final words. "You still love me?"

Layla rolled her eyes. "Don't be silly. It's been half a day, Rix. I can't fall out of love with you in that time regardless of what happened. But that doesn't mean I'll stay in this thing. I might never stop loving you, but I'd take myself away from you to keep my sanity." She pushed away from the wall and took a step closer to Rix. "Please answer my question."

"We'll get through it, and I promise to always listen to you. This is your career, and your decision, and I'll support whatever you want to do." Rix chanced moving toward Layla, and she didn't step back. "I might not *agree*, but I won't be that way again. I don't know what came over me. I've never acted like that before, and I'll happily go to therapy to see if there's a root cause. I never want you to be frightened of me."

Layla took the final few steps to bring her within touching distance, though Rix kept her hands to herself until she was given express permission. The desire to pull Layla into her arms was almost too strong to withstand, but she sensed they'd still not established solid ground and the foundations of their love might give way any second, leaving Rix to plummet into a lonely, dark future without the love of her life.

"What about the future?" Layla asked. "What about your vision of perfection?"

Rix sighed. When Layla had asked her earlier if she'd rather risk being alone in her search for perfection than simply enjoy what they had together, without certainty, Rix had baulked. But when she'd pulled herself up from her kitchen floor and truly considered her question, the answer was clear and immediate; she'd rather have two months with Layla and let her go than lose her now. "You were right. I was putting pressure on you, and I was wrong. But it's not about someone being perfect in a way that's unreal, it's about being perfect for me. And you are perfect for me, in every way." Rix lifted her hand to hold Layla's but pulled back. She couldn't make the first contact; that had to be Layla's decision. "I want you forever, and I won't apologize for that, and I'll take the heartache if you leave me whenever that might happen rather than let you go now. Even if you don't see forever, I'll take whatever I can get and hope for the best."

"As it happens," Layla cupped Rix's face and pressed herself closer, "the mist in my crystal ball cleared, and all I see is you." She pulled Rix into her and kissed her deeply.

Rix melted into the embrace and circled her arms around Layla's waist. "Does that mean we should have a double wedding tomorrow?" Rix grinned at the shocked expression on Layla's face before she realized Rix was joking. Layla arched her eyebrow and exuded her signature femme countenance that brooked no nonsense and told Rix she'd pay for that at some point.

"When we go down the aisle, it'll be in style, sweetheart," Layla said.

Her lazy, sexually loaded drawl would have been enough to explode Rix's mind, but the fact that Layla had said *when* they got married, not if, sent her dreams of forever skittering into the air. She pulled Layla closer and let her kiss communicate how much she wanted that and how she'd fulfil any and every one of Layla's demands for the rest of their lives.

Layla pulled away, breathless, and placed her hand on Rix's chest. Her heat seared through the cotton as if weren't even there, making Rix want to carry her to the car, take her home, and make love to her all night.

"Slow down, lover. Remember, this is Syd and Jack's night." She nibbled Rix's lower lip and pulled back again.

Rix followed her mouth, but Layla pushed against her chest firmly. "Come home with me when the dinner is over," Rix said.

Layla shook her head. "You know I can't do that. I have to stay with Syd to make sure Jack doesn't sneak in for pre-wedding nookie."

Rix laughed at the cheeky sexual reference then pouted and gave Layla her best attempt at sad eyes. "What about my pre-wedding nookie?"

"You'll keep, handsome. I'll reward your patience tomorrow night when the happy couple are safely on their way to Maui, which Syd is incredibly grateful to you for. That was wonderfully generous of you."

"I score points for it?"

"You do." Layla slid her hand down Rix's body, cupped her crotch, and squeezed. "And I'll reward you for that tomorrow night too."

Rix swallowed hard, and her eyes half-lidded. "I was looking forward to this wedding, but now I just want it to be over."

"Patience, Rix, patience. All good things come to those who wait."

Rix wrapped her hand around Layla's neck and kissed her one last time before they returned the table. Rix would wait—not patiently—but she'd wait. She'd waited her whole life for Layla; another night wouldn't kill her. She glanced across the table at Layla and her breath caught at her beauty. Okay, so it might not kill her, but it would be a long, torturous night.

Chapter Twenty-Four

STANDING ACROSS FROM Rix, who looked incredibly debonair in her black tuxedo and bow tie—like a butch James Bond—Layla couldn't help but imagine what their own wedding might look like. She had never been one of *those* girls who'd been thinking about their wedding since before they got to junior high and had giant folders stuffed full of color schemes, flower arrangements, and pictures of dresses snipped from bridal magazines. She hadn't even really paid much attention to the arrangements for Syd's wedding; Syd and Jack had taken care of the cake and menu choices, the venue hire, the wedding band, and so much more. Layla had nodded, agreed, and generally placated where necessary, but none of it had made her think of how she might organize her own nuptials. As maid of honor, she hadn't had to do much other than make sure she got Syd to the church on time, or rather, the beach on time, and that had been enough.

But now, after her enforced epiphany yesterday, she was looking at Syd's wedding from an entirely different perspective. Never had rose-tinted glasses been a more suitable cliché. Syd and Jack had managed to pull together a wedding in less than three weeks, an impressive feat by anyone's standards, and it was truly beautiful.

And now, Layla was thinking about which suit color would work best for Rix; what kind of style her bridal gown should be; what flavor cake she wanted (shaped like a book, of course); and where she'd like to get married. Although, Syd had nailed it there and most likely, Layla would copy her location.

Rix met her gaze, and Layla wondered if she had a folder stuffed full of wedding ideas hidden under her bed. Loving someone forever, finding that special soulmate, had been the stuff of Rix's dreams her whole life. Did she already have firm and fixed ideas on all aspects of her wedding? Had she already designed the rings?

Layla winked and smiled when Rix blushed. None of that mattered. Layla didn't care whether her dress was ivory or peach, or whether the cake was carrot or lemon. When the time came, she and Rix would figure it out together, and the result would be... yes, perfect. That word she'd always avoided in real life but used with wild abandon in her romance novels was now a word she couldn't avoid because it was the *perfect* way to describe how she and Rix fit. Everything she had thought didn't exist was within her grasp, offered in the strong hands of a beautiful butch woman who worshipped her.

And she'd almost had to lose it to recognize its existence.

"Do you have the ring?"

Crap. She should have this ready in her hand. She *should* be paying attention to her best friend marrying the love of her life instead of being off dreaming about her own life. She focused, opened her clutch, and retrieved the ring box. She looked up at Syd, popped the box open, and held it out to her. The unchecked pure joy in Syd's eyes brought a lump to Layla's throat. She tried to blink away the tears she'd promised not to shed until after the ceremony but feared her waterproof mascara was about to be tested for false advertising.

Syd took the ring and grasped Layla's hand. "Thank you."

"I love you, Syd."

Syd grinned. "I love you too, sis."

What was it parents said about their children marrying? *They weren't losing a daughter, they were gaining a son.* She gave one more attempt at pushing her tears back and convincing herself that she was gaining a brother and not losing her sister. Syd gave Jack his ring, and Layla watched intently as Rix offered Jack's ring in an identical box to hers. She didn't stop herself from drifting to a future moment when Rix might offer Layla a ring, a symbol of their commitment for everyone to see.

She tightened her grip on the bouquet, not quite believing how ridiculously gooey and romantic her thoughts were. If anyone had told her this year would end with a forever love and a burgeoning script-writing career, and that Syd would not only settle into a relationship longer than two weeks but get married within two months of meeting that person, incredulous wouldn't adequately describe Layla's response. Her life had truly mirrored her art.

She forced herself to tune back into the moment, something her life had always been about, just as Syd and Jack kissed for the first time as wife and husband. She caught a glimpse of the unadulterated adoration in

Jack's eyes before he closed them to go into the kiss. She approved; *that* was the way a person was supposed to look at their soulmate. She didn't resist a glance at her own soulmate and was rewarded with a dazzling smile and the exact same expression as Jack's.

Syd and Jack turned to face the small gathering of their friends and chosen family, and everyone burst into thunderous applause. They began to walk along the aisle between the chairs set on wooden staging to offer a vaguely flat platform, and Layla nodded slowly at Syd impressively managing not to get her four-inch heels caught in the narrow gaps between the planks as they were bombarded with a biodegradable rainbow mix of petal confetti.

Rix slid up beside Layla and offered her arm. Layla slipped her hand around Rix's bicep.

"That was a wonderful ceremony. Did you write Syd's vows?" Rix asked as they headed toward the large marquee for pre-wedding dinner drinks and to wait to be called for wedding photographs. Once again, Rix had excelled herself by commissioning world-renowned photographer Geva Doyle to capture Syd and Jack's day.

"Of course not; she wrote them herself."

Rix gave her a light tug. "She has a best-selling romance author and super successful screenwriter for a best friend, and she didn't take advantage of that?"

"I may have given her a few tips, but she didn't need much help." Layla stopped and pulled Rix to face her. "Turns out, when you're crazy in love, you can find your own words to express it."

Rix traced her fingers across Layla's lips. "I've got more than words for you."

Layla batted Rix's hand away and tutted. "It's only four in the afternoon, and their taxi to the airport doesn't leave until ten. You're going to have to dial it down if we're going to have any chance of surviving the next six hours."

The photographer's assistant called them both to the shooting area, and Layla's heels sank into the sand as she walked. Rix steadied her until they reached the rocks where Geva had Syd and Jack sitting, looking incredibly glamorous and sultry. Jack had stripped down to his wispy white linen shirt, and his tattoos and lithe frame were clearly visible as he stood astride two boulders. Syd sat at his feet, her white gown fanning out around her and the break dangerously and dramatically close. Layla already couldn't wait to see the photos.

"Isn't it tradition for the maid of honor to have dirty sex with the best person at some point during these proceedings?" Rix asked as Geva directed them to their positions on each side of the newlyweds.

Layla hadn't heard of that tradition, but boy, did she want to start it if it wasn't one. They'd had the argument and they'd made up, but they were yet to experience the best part of a blow-up: the make-up sex. If they had to wait until Syd and Jack were safely on their way to their honeymoon, she and Rix were going to explode. She looked up at the restaurant on the bluff and mentally walked around the dinner venue. The room they'd ended up in last night had a locking door, and no one had disturbed them. And it had a stack of tables she could sit on.

"You're trying to figure out where we can make the dirty sex happen, aren't you?" Rix whispered, moving into another configuration for more shots.

Layla glanced away, and heat rushed through her entire body. "Maybe. What's it to you?"

Rix almost snorted and laughed at the same time. "It's *everything* to me. I need to be inside you, Layla. I have to show you what you mean to me in ways that words can't."

Layla smiled. For a director, Rix had plenty of great lines Layla would've been happy to write in her books. "I bet you've said that to all the girls."

Rix leaned close to her ear and whispered, "I've never said that to anyone. But there aren't enough words or actions in the world for me to truly show you how much I love you."

Layla stared deep into Rix's eyes and saw the unfathomable love of which she spoke, and gravity disappeared, making her feel weightless for the quickest of milliseconds. She felt held and cherished in all the myriad ways she'd wrote about in her books but had never believed in. "I was thinking that the room we were in last night might work. Failing that, they must have a cellar given the extensive wine selection."

"I like where your head's at." Rix squeezed Layla's butt. "I'm in."

Layla gave Rix her most wicked grin. "You will be."

"Okay, thanks," the assistant said. "We'll call you back for the group photos so please don't wander off too far."

Rix helped Layla down from the rocks and twirled her around in her arms. "I feel like a kid on a school trip. 'Don't wander off.' What's that about?"

Layla kissed Rix deep and hard. "Maybe she saw the look in your eyes and figured she'd have to keep an extra watch on us."

Rix took her hand, and they strolled toward the shore. Layla could never get enough of the water; whether it was the ocean, a river, or a lake, she found it deeply nurturing, and it fueled her creative juices. She took off her heels, held up her dress, and walked into the cool water, letting it lap up around her ankles and soothe her aching feet. The sun was beginning to set, and the sky was alight with swathes of deep pink brush strokes. She looked back at Syd and Jack, who were bathed in the dropping golden haze. "Those photographs are going to be spectacular. How did you get Geva Doyle to do a wedding when she's usually gallivanting across the globe for National Geographic?"

Rix tapped her nose. "I can't reveal all my secrets just yet. I need to have some mystery to keep you interested."

Layla padded out of the water, slipped her arms beneath Rix's jacket, and pressed against her body, feeling slightly chill even though it was seventy degrees. "There's plenty about you to keep me interested for years to come, baby, you don't have to worry." She nodded toward the small marquee she and Syd had waited in until the ceremony began so that they weren't forced to troll all the way from the car park in their heels and full dress. "No one will be in there…" She extricated herself and tugged Rix in that direction. "A little reconnection in there should keep us going for a few hours."

"Seriously?" Rix asked, though she didn't resist.

"It's far enough away from the main marquee, and Syd won't be using it until after the reception. It's perfect for a quickie."

Rix pouted. "I don't want to be quick. I want to take hours with you."

Layla unfastened the opening and pulled Rix in. "And you'll get those hours once Syd and Jack are on their way to the airport. But for now, this will have to do."

Rix zipped the door closed and dug a chair into the sand in front of it. Layla hitched up on the highchair the make-up artist had used for Syd's touch-up. Rix bit her lip and stood a few feet away, staring at her.

"You are beautiful."

"I like the way you look at me," Layla said. It made her feel sexy, and wanted, and powerful, and almost like she had a magical hold over Rix.

"Good, because I really enjoy looking at you. I don't think I'll ever tire of it." Rix moved closer and pushed Layla's knees apart. She inched Layla's dress over her calves and up over her thighs. "I can't wait. Are you ready for me?"

Layla smiled. "Why don't you find out?" She opened her legs a little further, and Rix sighed deeply when she slid her fingers up to Layla's panties and found they were soaked through.

"What have *you* been thinking about?" Rix whispered. She edged Layla's panties to the side and slipped her fingers inside her.

"You." Layla moaned and pushed herself against Rix's hand. She wrapped her hands around the back of Rix's neck and pulled her in as if she couldn't get her close enough. She pressed her lips to Rix's mouth and didn't move. She lingered in that position, taking in the feel of Rix's lips on hers, the tenderness and promise so clear, the intimacy so pure and strong. Rix made love to her slowly, and Layla knew it wouldn't take her long to climax. Her desperation to reconnect in the most intimate and meaningful of ways, the joining of their bodies and becoming as close to each other as was physically possible felt more intoxicating than any tryst she'd ever had in the heat of passion. Even if she wasn't going to orgasm, the simple melding of their physical and emotional beings held a million times more significance than any time before this with anyone.

Rix was her forever, the one she'd never known she was looking for.

And as they kissed, slowly and deeply, and Layla's pleasure began to rise to an inevitable, mind-blowing crescendo, she held Rix's gaze. A wordsmith by trade, Layla couldn't find the words to fully describe the absolute peace and safety she felt, surrendering every part of her to a love so transcendent, it soared through her body, engulfing her very soul in an eternal flame. *That* would be a great line to end a book, she thought briefly, just before her orgasm shuddered through her and Rix held her shaking body tight.

When the ripples of pleasure slowed, Layla pulled away slightly. "I love you, Rix. I'll love you forever."

Rix cupped Layla's cheek and kissed her nose lightly. "Forever won't be enough time for me."

Layla pressed her hand over Rix's. "Nor for me, my love, but I promise we'll make every moment count."

Epilogue

Twelve months later

"Do you think we'll ever stop wanting each other this much? I'm pretty sure I've never been this horny, even when I was a teenager."

Layla lifted Rix's hand to her lips and kissed her fingertips. "I hope not, but that little one might get in the way of daytime sex for a while." She gestured toward Kyla, the little bundle of effervescent energy rocking out on the dance floor in an outfit she'd chosen for herself. She had quite the prodigious designing talent for a three-year-old, though how she'd decided to team up Thor's hammer with a tiara, blue camouflage cargo pants, a Captain Marvel T-shirt, and chunky-heeled lime green sneakers was anyone's guess. And the rainbow belt...well, it set the whole thing off, for sure.

Rix patted Layla's butt. "Luckily my new diet and exercise regime is giving me plenty of energy. And she's still supposed to be napping throughout the day, so we're good."

Layla was about to respond when Syd rushed across the dance floor, scooped Kyla up in her arms, and spun her around in the air. She felt Rix's hand on her forearm before she realized she was moving forward.

"Ease up on the bubble wrap, babe," Rix said.

Layla dropped her shoulders and relaxed. "Sorry. She's just so little."

Rix released Layla's arm. "I know. But she's tough, just like her mother."

Layla's heart bounced, still not used to being called that, but it had only been two months. And no amount of books that she'd read in the time preceding Kyla's adoption had reassured her that she was going to do a good job of raising a little human. Hence the bubble wrap she'd been coddling their daughter in to protect her from the big, bad, and immensely dangerous world out there.

Their daughter. Layla couldn't quite believe everything had happened so fast. After the wedding, Jack moved in with Syd, and Layla moved in with Rix. Having a pool to swim in every day had been just one of the highlights, but at the top of that list was getting to wake up in Rix's arms every morning. Their nightly pre-sleep conversations had soon turned to children, and Layla had been enthused to start a family with Rix. Conversations morphed into plans, plans into actions, and actions into adopting Kyla. And after just eight weeks of the two of them becoming the three of them, Layla couldn't imagine a life without the innocent laughter-filled squeals of their daughter echoing around their home.

Syd and Jack wandered over with Kyla swinging between them, an expression of unmitigated joy on her face.

"When do you start the *Selected* project?" Syd asked.

She lifted Kyla onto her shoulders with apparent ease, and Layla felt Rix's hand on her forearm once again. "Next month."

"And you're taking this little one with you?"

"That's the plan." Layla held out her arms, and Syd scooped Kyla from her shoulders. Layla kissed Kyla's forehead and hugged her tight. "I don't want to be away from her if I can help it."

"You're quishing me," Kyla said.

Layla softened her embrace. "I can't help it, little one. You're so darn squishable."

"Quishable!" Kyla giggled the kind of laugh that should be bottled to pull out on a bad day for immediate happiness.

"Have Amazon-MGM come through on everything you wanted?" Syd asked.

"They have, thanks to this one." Layla slipped her arm through Rix's and pulled her close. "They offered me a really good contract for a standalone movie with no major changes. And Universal came through on a three-picture deal with totally new material." Layla handed Kyla over reluctantly when she reached for Rix. She straightened Kyla's tiara then focused on Syd. "Enough about me. I can't believe I haven't seen you for four months. Tell me everything about your new job campaigning for equality all over the world."

"I will but first, this." Syd pulled Layla into a long hug. "I've missed you."

"I've missed you too," Layla whispered. "It's so good to see you." They parted, and Layla pointed to the display of Rix's chainsaw carvings. "This little lot should pay for at least another four months of your campaigning."

As if he'd magically appeared when there was talk of the LGBTQ center's money being spent, George came to Layla's side and took her hand.

"We're going to raise enough to do so much more than that, Layla," George said. "We've got the big whales of LA here tonight, and I'm going to strip them of as much blubber as possible." He looked pointedly at Rix. "Isn't it about time for you to get up on stage?"

Rix pushed the sleeve of her tux up and checked her watch. "Tempus fugit."

She popped Kyla back on the ground, and she rushed to Layla and flung her arms around her legs, almost knocking Layla off balance. She was still getting used to how easily Kyla had opened up to them being her parents and how loving she was.

Rix leaned in and kissed her. "Wish me luck."

Layla pressed her hand to Rix's chest. "You don't need luck, handsome. Your work is amazing, and anyone would be lucky to have it in their homes and yards. But that eagle is coming home with us."

"You better be prepared to bid high."

"I think I'll be okay. If the artist ever wants to…" Layla wiggled her eyebrows, "you know, *enjoy* Mummy again, she'll make sure I win it."

Rix smirked and kissed her again. "Consider it removed from the auction."

She walked away, and Layla smiled widely as her amazingly talented, handsome forever love took to the stage and warmed the crowd up with consummate ease. Kyla tugged on Layla's dress and stretched her arms out. Layla scooped her up and settled her on her hip.

"What's Da doing?" Kyla asked as she played with Layla's curls.

"She's raising money to help people, sweetheart."

"Okay." She rested her head against Layla's chest and continued to fiddle with her hair.

Layla sighed, a deep resounding peacefulness settling within her. Rix and Kyla had filled in holes she'd never known she had, as if they were three parts of a puzzle destined to come together and form the most beautiful picture of a family anyone could ever imagine, a most perfect happy ever after.

Thank You!

Thanks for reading Scripted Love. If you enjoyed Rix and Layla's love story, I'd really appreciate it if you'd pop a review on Goodreads and Amazon and help other readers love them too. And do you want exclusive news and content? Early release previews and competitions to win free books? Free stories? Feel free to sign up to my Hartesome Heroes newsletter (bit.ly/HartesomeHeroesFreebie) and come talk to me!

What's Your Story?

Global Wordsmiths, CIC, provides an all-encompassing service for all writers, ranging from basic proofreading and cover design to development editing, typesetting, and eBook services. A major part of our work is charity and community focused, delivering writing projects to under-served and under-represented groups across Nottinghamshire, giving voice to the voiceless and visibility to the unseen.

To learn more about what we offer, visit: www.globalwords.co.uk

A selection of books by Global Words Press:
Desire, Love, Identity: with the National Justice Museum
Times Past: with The Workhouse, National Trust
World At War: Farmilo Primary School
Times Past: Young at Heart with AGE UK
In Different Shoes: Stories of Trans Lives

Self-published authors working with Global Wordsmiths:
E.V. Bancroft
Valden Bush
Addison M Conley
Emma Nichols
Dee Griffiths and Ali Holah
Helena Harte
Dani Lovelady Ryan
Karen Klyne
AJ Mason
John Parsons
Ray Martin
Robyn Nyx
Sam Rawlings
Simon Smalley

Other Great Books
by Independent Authors

Music City Dreamers by Robyn Nyx
Will their love song remain unfinished?
Available on Amazon (ASIN B08WR5ZMN6)

Call to Me by Helena Harte
Sometimes the call you need the most is the one you least expect.
Available from Amazon (ASIN B08D9SR15H)

Come Dream with Me by Karen Klyne
When your past and your future collide, who do you become in the present?
Available from Amazon (ASIN B096PB3HMF)

Elodie by Emma Nichols
There's such a thing as a perfect life so why won't she let herself live it?
Available from Amazon (ASIN B08WRFXGRG)

Nero by Valden Bush
Banished. Abandoned. Lost. Will her destiny reunite her with the love of her life?
Coming September 2021(ISBN 9781915009012)

Warm Pearls and Paper Cranes by E.V. Bancroft
A family torn apart. Love is the only way forward.
Coming October 2021 (ISBN 9781915009029)

Addie Mae by Addison M. Conley
Maddy and Jessie bond over scuba diving, and as their friendship grows, so does the attraction.
Available from Amazon (ISBN 9780998029641)

The Women and The Storm by Kitty McIntosh
Being the only witch in a small Scottish town is not easy.
Available from Amazon (ISBN 9798654945983)

The Proud Weed by Sam Rawlings
Children's picture book about discovering your place in the world.
Available from Amazon (ISBN 9798728860617)

Lightning Source UK Ltd.
Milton Keynes UK
UKHW020615270822
407756UK00007B/203